Danger Zone

By

John Tommasi

Dedicated to Blue Lives Matter
and
all the fallen heroes.

Table of Contents

Prologue
Renegades, Rebels & Rogues

1939

Curt Scott couldn't wait to get home. It was his last Friday night in the states. He was going in the service next week and his girl had promised him an extra special night that he wouldn't forget. He was looking forward to fighting the Germans. He knew he'd be coming home a war hero and with enough battlefield promotions to be a major. His parents were upset that he had enlisted when he didn't have to, but he had always rebelled against their authority. All he had left to do was a magna flux test on this last cylinder. He checked his watch again. The magna flux test would take a good hour and one-half. He had already put in two hours overtime, and this test would make him late for his date.

Scott thought about it. He had tested forty-eight cylinders today and they were all perfect. This cylinder was from the same lot and it had to be just as good. Ordinarily, he would have stayed, but tonight was special. Instead of running the test, he ran his hand over the interior and made a visual scan. Smooth as a baby's ass he thought, nothing wrong with this one. Scott signed it off, said good-bye to his co-workers and was off without a second thought.

What Scott didn't know, was this cylinder was flawed. The microscopic crack was in the casting and not only would it have been impossible to detect by any human eye, it would have been extremely difficult to have been picked up by the magna flux test. In fact the crack was so minute, that it wouldn't manifest itself for many years to come, and only after the cylinder had been reamed a number of times, but it was there, and it would eventually make its presence felt.

****

Three Years Ago

The DC-3, or Dakota as the English called it, first made its appearance in 1935 and even now many pilots felt it was the best all-around plane ever built.

The plane was originally built as the Douglas Sleeper Transport, DST, for American Airlines, and was an enlarged version of the DC-2. After entering service in 1936, it soon proved itself, and orders for the plane increased. Every airline wanted the DC-3/DST.

It's two twelve-hundred horsepower radial engines propelled the craft through the air at one-hundred-ninety MPH and had a useful load of five-thousand pounds. It had large wide wings, which gave it excellent short field performance, and since the fuel tanks were in the wings, they were also oversized which gave the plane a range of over one-thousand miles. It was a tail dragger which gave the props more ground clearance and better control, which in turn allowed it to land on rough fields. As a result, the military realized the potential of the plane, and ordered large quantities. As a transport, it had the designation, C-47.

C-47's made such an impact during the war, that General Eisenhower considered them to be one of the four most significant weapons during WW II.

All in all, more than 10,000 of the civilian and military variants were produced.

The same qualities that made it the premier cargo plane of the forties made it the premier drug smuggling plane of the day, and no one knew this better than Tim Campbell.

He had Knight Moves written below the pilot's window and this was his third run in what he now considered his DC-3, and it was going to be his last. He was now a millionaire, and he was going to retire. Hell, he was even thinking of starting a charter service with his new DC-3 and going straight, but first he would have to get rid of his special modifications.

Campbell had installed extra gas tanks in the fuselage. He thought that he had really outdone himself on this one. The fuel tanks were waterbed mattresses filled with gasoline with an auxiliary fuel pump. It added some weight to the plane, but he was able to make the Bolivia to Texas run non-stop which more than made up for the disadvantage of the extra weight. Another advantage was that the mattresses could fit around bulkheads in the fuselage and he was able to put the cargo of cocaine on top of the "tanks".

Campbell had been smuggling for three years and had an ongoing romance with lady luck. He had never been spotted by any of custom or DEA interdiction planes, and the DC-3 he was flying was a step up from the midsize twin Piper's and Beachcraft, he use to fly, which were always overloaded and underpowered. They never really performed well until about three hours into the flight when a significant amount of fuel was burned off thereby reducing the weight of the plane.

Campbell was flying out of a jungle airfield in Bolivia's Llamos region, one hundred miles east of Santa Cruz. Since this was going to be his last trip, he was taking on a little more cargo than he normally would. In addition to his regular cargo of cocaine, he was running a cache of guns he was sure he could sell to any one of the local Texas militia's in his home state. He especially liked the grenade launches he was able to procure. Those Texas rednecks would have a sexual experience over them. If his estimates were correct, the combined weight of the gas, guns and coke was over 7000 pounds. This was two thousand pounds more than the maximum useful load specified by the manual, but Campbell felt that if he lived by the book, he wouldn't be the millionaire he is now.

After the last sacks of cocaine were loaded, he latched the cargo door and made his way to the cockpit to start his pre-flight run-up.

As usual, he carried a more than ample quantity of water and freeze dried food behind the pilot's seat, a carryover from his hiking days along the Colorado River. And of course, a bottle of Jack Daniels his girlfriend gave him from his favorite bar in Austin, Texas called Renegades, Rebels & Rogues.

Campbell strapped himself in, turned on the master switch, and turned over the starboard engine. Ever so slowly the propeller started turning and with a puff of black smoke the large radial engine caught and its twelve-hundred horses roared into life. Campbell started the sequence on the port engine with the same results.

With both engines engaged, he stepped on the brakes and pushed the throttles forward increasing the engine RPM's. He tested the two mag's on each engine and noticed with satisfaction that both operated within limitations. One of the magneto's on the right engine caused the engine to run a little rough, but after leaning out the engine and increasing the RPM's to the red line, it had finally begun to run smooth. Campbell wasn't concerned, that was normal on a lot of planes, particularly in the steam bath atmosphere of lower Bolivia.

After checking the gauges, Campbell noticed the same engine was running a bit hot, but he attributed this to the run-up. After checking the controls and setting the compass and altimeter, he was ready to go.

Once again he ran the engines to the stops and pass the red line. The roar filled the cockpit and assaulted Campbell's ears. He could have worn his headset to dull the noise, but this was the part of the flight that he felt the most invigorated. Campbell viewed himself as the rogue pilot that women dreamed about.

He took his feet off the brakes. Instead of leaping forward as the plane usually did, it slowly pick up speed and was three-quarter's down the runway before the tail section lifted into the air. At the runway's end, the plane was barely above stall speed when Campbell put in ten degrees of flaps, which had the effect of decreasing the stall speed and increasing lift, and hauled back on the yoke. Even with the trim set to the full up position, Campbell had to maintain a good deal of pressure to keep the nose in the air.

The plane shuttered and begrudgingly began to fly with an occasional pre-stall buffet.

Campbell raised the landing gear which gave him a few extra knots of airspeed. But for all this, he couldn't get the plane to climb more than two-hundred feet per minute, and this while maintaining full power, a far cry from the planes normal rate of climb of over two-thousand feet per minute.

Both engines were revving past the red line, and the starboard engine was running increasingly hot. At five hundred feet above ground level, AGL, Campbell would have generally throttled back on the engines, but he was concerned about clearing the mountainous plateau ahead and kept the throttles nailed to the stops.

At fifteen hundred feet AGL, the starboard engines heat gauge was in the yellow and still climbing. He throttled back on the engine and increased the pressure on the left rudder to compensate for the difference in torque produced by one engine running at less power than the other.

This reduced his rate of climb to just over one hundred feet per minute, the temperature gauge of the right engine still remained in the yellow but stopped its upward climb. Campbell still wasn't worried, he figured that once he got to his planned altitude of fifteen thousand feet, he'd reduce power and the engine would operate back in the green.

As Campbell continued his climb through three thousand feet above ground level with his port engine at full power, it too began to get creep into the yellow. Not wanting to chance both engines running hot, he reduced power even though he was confident the plane could take whatever he threw at it.

Campbell wondered briefly why the starboard engine hadn't cooled as quickly as the port after reducing power, but at the moment, he had more pressing problems to worry about. The reduced power on the port engine had an almost immediate effect of returning the temperature gauge to the green. The rate of climb dropped to eighty feet per minute, but after doing a quick calculation at his current rate of climb, he felt that he was out of the woods, or more appropriately, the jungle.

Thirty minutes into the flight, his rate of climb had increased to a comfortable five hundred feet per minute due to the decreased weight of the plane from the used gasoline, more than enough to reach the altitude needed to clear the thirteen thousand foot Andes mountains he would be flying over.

At five thousand feet, Campbell once again turned his attention to the starboard engine. To his dismay, the needle had not stopped in the yellow, but had climbed ever so slowly into the red. He reduced the power even more which had the effect of reducing his rate of climb, but with no effect on the needle's inexorable climb into the red. He reduced it even further to the point that it was barely producing any thrust.

Campbell finally got the desired effect of not only halting the needles climb, but reversing it back into the yellow range. The downside was that not only was his rate of climb reduced to zero, but he had all he could do to maintain his airspeed so as not to stall the plane.

For the first time, Campbell realized what pilots meant by the pucker factor. He was barely able to keep his plane in the air, let alone generate the rate of climb needed to clear the mountains in front of him.

He had to make a decision. Either abort the run and land at a local airfield and chance discovery by the Umopar, Bolivia's version of a cross between the drug enforcement agency and military police, or increase power and take the chance that the engine was alright and the temperature gauge was off.

Campbell thought this over briefly and remembered the pilot's adage "that there are old pilots and there are bold pilots, but there are no old, bold pilots".

He knew the prudent move was to land and eliminate all doubt about the temperature gauge, but as he increased power to the starboard engine, he told himself that he didn't get this far by being prudent.

When he was learning to fly, his instructor once told him, always listen to the engines, this will tell you what the plane is doing and its condition.

Campbell listened as the needle climbed well into the red and increased his rate of climb. He continued to listen for a full five minutes while his rate of climbed went to one-thousand feet per minute and the temperature gauge pegged itself all the way into the red.

After ten minutes Campbell relaxed and reached the conclusion the temperature gauge was off since he knew of no engine made that could remain in the red for ten minutes without seizing or catching fire.

Campbell was right in one respect, none of the engines on any of the planes he had previously flown would be able to take the punishment that the DC-3's Pratt & Whitney's could take, but Campbell had no way of knowing this.

Twelve minutes after he increased to full power, one of the starboard engines pistons flew through the weakened cylinder head wall.

The effect was the loss of all engine oil within thirty seconds and a condition occurred that pilots referred to as catastrophic engine failure, or in more simple terms, the engine stopped working, forever.

Ordinarily, the DC-3 would have been able to hold altitude with just one engine, but with the combination of the added weight and stifling atmosphere, Campbell's rate of climb became a rate of descent.

Campbell didn't get as far as he did in life by giving in to panic. He immediately assessed his situation and realized he was VSF, very seriously fucked.

The only thing he had going for him was there wasn't any fire when the engine exploded or part of the wing wasn't ripped away.

Campbell increased the power to the port engine and trimmed the rudder. The best he could do was hold the plane to a descent rate of five hundred feet per minute with full power.

If the port engine held, he would have about twenty minutes of flying time and at his speed of ninety miles per hour at an altitude of ten thousand feet, Campbell would have to find a landing strip in thirty minutes.

Campbell was approaching Santa Cruz and would have no problem landing at that airport, but since it was a provincial capital, it was sure to be manned by the police or military, and he didn't want to lose his DC-3 or his cargo, not to mention being thrown in jail. He looked at the map and turned to the Northwest. Cochabamba was about two hundred miles west of Santa Cruz. To the east and north of Cochabamba was jungle, but in this jungle there were a number of airstrips used by smugglers like himself. He had flown out of one a few years ago and remembered seeing other strips on his trek to the states.

His mind was made up. He'd fly towards Cochabamba, find a strip, put the DC-3 down and then see what he could do about salvaging the plane and cargo. Campbell didn't doubt for a minute that his luck would hold.

Twenty minutes later, his descent rate hadn't decreased and he hadn't found anything that remotely looked like a break in the jungle, let alone a landing strip.

Five minutes later and just two thousand feet AGL (above ground level), Campbell resigned himself to faith, and started making plans in order to land the plane in the jungle. He figured he was about one-hundred miles east of Cochabamba and after ditching the plane, he would make his way to one of the outlying villages. Looking at the map, he decided he would head towards either Buena Vista or Pojo.

At five hundred feet AGL, he increased engine power to the left engine and slowed his rate of descent for the jungle landing. The overburdened engine jumped into the red, but Campbell was no longer concerned with saving the engine, at present, his ass had priority.

It was odd that Campbell was still thinking in terms of landing as opposed to crashing. Campbell knew that a triple canopy jungle was very dense in leaves and that many pilots would prefer to land in a triple canopy instead of water.

At one hundred feet, he pulled on his shoulder strap and lowered the flaps to full while pulling the control yoke into his stomach. This had the effect of further slowing the plane while giving it a nose high attitude.

Campbell had long since stopped brooding and was thinking very cooly and logically. The Dakota hit the jungle belly first and lurched forward. Campbell's luck was holding. The top canopy was nothing but leaves and slowed the plane as it descended into the second canopy.

Leaves and limbs flew past the windshield and one limb impaled itself into the port wing. All this appeared in slow motion to Campbell who felt he was on the ride of his life.

As the planed slewed into the final and densest layer, Campbell became aware of the screeching metal as thicker and heavier limbs pierced the plane's fuselage as easily as a knife through tissue paper.

Campbell knew that if one of those limbs came through the cockpit, it would be all she wrote.

As quickly as it happened, it was over. The forward motion stopped and Campbell was aware of only a slight swaying motion of the plane. He looked around him and saw that the plane was still one hundred feet in the air and was being supported by its massive wings that were imbedded in the trees.

His luck was still intact. He had come through without a scratch even though there was a massive four-foot diameter tree trunk not two yards away from the pilot's window.

Campbell smiled to himself thinking how he would recount this story at the local watering hole to his renegade friends and admiring ladies, especially Darcy. He was sure it would be good for one or two dates.

Campbell unbuckled his seat belt and stripped his jacket off as the sweat poured down his face from the near one hundred percent humidity and ninety degree heat.

Even though he was one hundred feet in the air, he still wasn't worried. He always carried a survival kit which had more than enough rope to reach the ground and plenty of food and water to get him through the jungle and to some form of civilization. As for any jungle creatures foolish enough to cross his path, he had his Smith & Wesson nine millimeter not to mention the stash of guns he was running.

Ordinarily, Tim would have noticed the impending danger, but he was on a high after once again beating the Grim Reaper at his game. What he should have noticed was how delicately balanced the plane was on its wings. He mistakenly thought that the plane was solidly embedded into the jungle canopy, but as he began to walk aft from the cockpit, his one hundred eighty pounds disturbed that balance.

He didn't realize what was happening until it was much too late.

The plane teetered momentarily and then fell backwards onto its rear stabilizer immediately crushing it and the attached fuselage. Campbell was thrown about the cabin like a rag doll. His shoulder dislocated as he hit a support and he came to rest on one of the pallets of cocaine. He was on the verge of blacking out from the pain in his shoulder, but he felt he had to hang on to consciousness. The plane stayed in a vertical position for five seconds until both wings snapped.

Newton's first law of motion worked against Campbell that day. As he lay on his precious load of cocaine, the pain in his shoulder was numbing. The DC-3 pitched forward and the equal and opposite reaction of the combined weight of the gasoline and cocaine pinned Campbell against the forward crash bulkhead. His last thought before the blackness engulfed him was how strange it was that he could no longer feel the pain in his shoulder, or feel anything else for that matter.

Mere flesh and bone was no match for the kinetic energy of three thousand pounds of dead weight intensified by inertia. Tim Campbell's marriage to lady luck had ended in an abrupt and permanent divorce.

Present Day

Chapter 1
For A Few Dollars More

Ricky Richards wiped the sweat from his forehead as he unloaded the last bale of marijuana from his van. It was ten of the best bales of pot that Mexico could produce. Ricky had been dealing with the same people for eight years and both the products and profits kept getting better and better.

With only some of the profits, he had bought a fifty-acre farm in a small southeastern New Hampshire town. The location was perfect. In order to get to the house, one had to travel ½ mile down a dead end road and then travel another five hundred feet up a meandering driveway. In addition to a fifteen room farmhouse, he had a four thousand square foot barn that he used to store his product and experiment in growing his own special brand of marijuana.

The money was staggering. Ten bales weighed about five hundred pounds which he could turn around in a month. At an average of three hundred dollars a pound profit, he made nearly two million dollars per year. With all the money that Ricky was making, his biggest problem was where to keep it and how to hide it from the IRS. A friend of his had come up with the idea of opening a restaurant to launder his money. This was not only a convenient way to wash his money, but it also gave his wife something to do with her spare time since kids were never in Ricky's equation. She had been on her "when are you going to get out of the business" kicks, and by having her manage the restaurant, it had taken a lot of heat off of Ricky.

Ricky had thought about retiring, but the money and the excitement were just too good to pass up. He wasn't a big person and was never very physical. But what Ricky didn't have in physical stature, he more than made up for in brains. His wife had always worried about him being in a violent business, but he was very careful. Ricky had always dealt with the same people. Not only the people he bought from, but the people who were his clients too. All of his people knew that if they were ever arrested, Ricky would beat them back to the station and have their bail money and lawyers ready even before they were booked. His people would never "rat" on him and he was one of the few people in the business who could claim that he had never been ripped off.

At this point in his life, Ricky felt invincible. The town that he lived in had a population of three thousand and a police force consisting of six part time officers and a full time police chief. They were tasked with forty square miles to patrol. The dumb ass cops were the least of Ricky's worries.

He smiled inwardly to himself. Things were going very well for Ricky Richards.

****

Chief Nolan sat back in his chair and gazed out his office window. He was completely frustrated. He didn't have the manpower to do half the things that he wanted to do; especially conduct a full-scale drug operation that demanded around the clock surveillance.

He knew that Ricky Richards was a major dealer. He fit the profile to a tee and his restaurant/lounge was such an obvious front, a blind man could see through it. If only he had half the resources he had when he was a detective sergeant in charge of narcotics in New York City. After his retirement from NYPD, Nolan figured the Chief's job in a small New Hampshire town would be a cakewalk without the stress or pressure he went through in the big apple. However Nolan was learning very quickly that rural New Hampshire was becoming a haven for upper level and major drug dealers in the northeast.

The area was perfect. It was close enough to major urban areas so as not to be inconvenient, but also offered the privacy and seclusion desired by drug dealers. In addition, dealers were becoming increasingly aware that with so many small towns, and even smaller police departments, it would be difficult if not impossible for the police to conduct a well-coordinated drug investigation.

Things were not going very well for the chief.

He continued to stare out of his office window. The white church steeple in the town square was the typical picture you would associate with a homespun New England community. It was a cold gray day in December and the weatherman was predicting snow. It looked like it would be a white Christmas after all, something that wasn't all that common in Manhattan. Nolan hated the thought of being defeated. After a few more minutes of deliberation, he reached for the phone and dialed a number in the state's capitol of Concord that was recently given to him.

****

The twin engine Piper Aztec F knifed through the air at 200 MPH. The Aztec was one of the workhorses of the Piper line. It was a six-passenger plane that could carry payloads of over 1200 pounds. With wing tip tanks, its range could exceed 1600 miles. Its fuselage sat high off the ground which gave it sufficient clearance to operate safely out of rough cut grass airstrips. To many of its pilots, it was affectionately known as the Az-truck.

Reputed drug dealer and pilot John MacCloud, the name that he was going by this month, and Mac to his friends, sat at the controls of the twin engine Piper listening to the

Automatic Terminal Information Service, ATIS, for the Manchester, New Hampshire airport. He listened to the recording one more time, making sure he had all the information prior to contacting approach control.

"Manchester Airport, information Hotel, 2015 Zulu. Visibility forty miles, ceiling eight thousand, scattered, fourteen thousand broken, altimeter, three-zero-zero-one, landing and departing runway three-five. Advise the controller on initial contact you have information hotel".

MacCloud changed the frequency to approach control of 124.9 and spoke into his headset.

"Manchester Approach, this is Aztec five-four-four-papa-x-ray. We're ten miles to the south at three thousand feet with information hotel, inbound for landing."

Aztec five-four-four-papa-x-ray, this is Manchester Approach, squawk zero-two-five-one and ident."

MacCloud leaned over and turned the dials of the Aztec's transponder to the appropriate numbers so as to give the Piper its unique radar blip to the air traffic controllers.

After a moments delay, MacCloud once again heard the disembodied voice of the controller.

"Aztec five-four-four-papa-x-ray, radar contact established, nine miles to the southeast, report a two mile right base, runway three-five."

"OK Ray, let's go through the pre-landing checklist."

Ray Marino, MacCloud's partner and friend of one year, sat in the co-pilots seat of the Aztec. Ray and John were a contrast in style and appearance. Where Ray was five-eight and looked like two hundred pound of bad news bone and muscle, MacCloud was six feet, 180 pounds and looked as if he would be at home attending a celebrity ball. Ray had Latin features typical of his Mediterranean background. MacCloud was a little lighter skinned with dark hair and mustached, but he had some distinctively Latin features despite his Scottish surname. MacCloud loved flying. Ray couldn't care if he ever saw a plane again.

"The pre-landing checklist," Ray parroted.

"Thank God. That means we're landing soon."

"Come on Ray," John answered. "We've been doing this for a year now and you have about 200 hours of flying time. This is great. Aren't you use to this yet?"

"Not no Mac, but fuck no. Like the man said, if we were meant to fly we'd have wings. I don't know why I do this shit?"

"Yes you do," Mac answered.

Both partners looked at each other and laughed.

MacCloud eased the throttle back on the Aztec and began the task of slowing the plane and getting it into landing configuration. As the Aztec slowed to below one hundred forty five MPH, MacCloud pushed the landing gear into the down position. After about five seconds he heard the gear snap down. MacCloud checked the gear position lights that were in the center of the Aztec's console. The three green lights indicated that the gear was in fact down and locked into place. This was always comforting MacCloud thought, particularly prior to a landing.

The additional drag of the gear helped slow the plane down even more. As the Aztec slowed to one hundred twenty MPH, MacCloud added ten degrees of flaps and started a slow descent to Manchester Airport's pattern altitude of fourteen hundred feet.

"Manchester Approach, Aztec five-four-four-papa-x-ray, reporting two mile right base, runway three five."

"Roger five-four-four-papa-x-ray. Number one cleared to land, contact tower upon turning final. You have a Cessna 150 in a right closed traffic doing touch and goes.

MacCloud silently went over the acronym GUMPS for the landing checklist: Gas on fullest tank, Undercarriage, down and locked, Mixture, full rich, Pumps, auxiliary fuel pumps on and Seatbelts fastened.

As MacCloud turned the Aztec onto final approach to runway three-five, he changed to the tower frequency.

"Don't worry Ray, I'll take care of the radio. Wouldn't want you to overwork yourself," John said while laughing.

Ray was in his usual land position. Eyes screwed shut and hands griping the arms of the seat as if the wings remaining attached to the plane depended on it.

"Manchester tower, Aztec five-four-four-papa-x-ray is with you, turning base to final."

"Aztec five-four-four-papa-x-ray, cleared to land," answered the controller.

"Roger tower. OK Ray, ready to land?"

"No," Ray answered, "but go ahead anyway."

As MacCloud was on short final he went to full flaps and heard the tower talking to the other plane in the pattern.

"Cessna six-three-three-eight-seven, Aztec on quarter mile final, clear touch and go."

MacCloud briefly remembered his days as a student pilot and the endless practice landings and takeoffs, referred to as touch and goes. He was glad those days were over. Most of the time the touch and goes ended up being bounces and jounces. Everyone had to learn sometime.

As the Aztec crossed the runway threshold, MacCloud cut the engines, flared the plane and touched with barely a jolt.

"Damn I'm good," MacCloud said with a grin.

"Give me a break, but just keep getting me down in one piece and you'll be my hero forever."

"Aztec five-four-four-papa-x-ray, next left, contact ground control on one-two-one point niner once clear the runway."

"Roger tower."

MacCloud taxied off the runway and contacted ground control.

"Manchester Ground, Aztec five-four-four-papa-x-ray, we'd like to taxi to general aviation parking."

"Aztec five-four-four-papa-x-ray, taxi to Stead Aviation north of the tower via delta taxiway.

Stead Aviation is what pilots refer to as a Fixed Based Operator or FBO. They're the oasis for pilots at strange airports. Stead was one of the better one's that offered fuel, maintenance, refreshments and even a bunk room where pilots could sack out in between legs of their trips.

As MacCloud taxied to a halt at one of the tie downs, one of the line boys in an Exxon fuel truck was approaching the Aztec.

MacCloud went through the post-landing checklist, shut the engines down and turned the master switch off. As Ray and John were getting off the plane they were approached by the line boy. MacCloud told him to top off the tanks and make sure the oil had ten quarts in each engine. As the partners started walking towards the exit gate, Ray was nearly stopped in his tracks.

"I don't believe my eyes. That little shit is on time for a change."

"Yea I know," John answered equally amazed, "truly fucking amazing. I guess he knows what's in it for him."

"He thinks he knows," Ray answered while grinning under his breath.

MacCloud nodded in agreement.

The object of their conversation was Joey Schultz who was standing behind a chain link fence that surrounded Stead Aviation.

Joey was a twenty-year old thief that John and Ray met about a month ago in a Manchester bar. As MacCloud approached Joey, his thoughts flashed back to the chance meeting three weeks ago that led to today's flight....

****

20

Manchester is New Hampshire's largest city with a population of over one hundred thousand. It's known as the Queen city. Contrary to what people think, it wasn't because of a gay population but because it was named after its counterpart in England, which at the time happened to be the home of the reigning monarch.

Ray and John were seated at the bar of one of the local establishments they frequented when they were in Manchester. The name of the lounge was the Zoo. The name did the place no justice. To call the place a zoo would be an understatement. The place was currently a favorite of one of the local biker gangs, and they were the better clientele. The only dress code was you had to have them and if you weren't carrying a gun, knife or some blunt instrument on your person, you were either very brave or very stupid, not to mention under dressed. If someone wasn't taken out on a stretcher, it was a slow night, and it was still one of John and Ray's favorite places. They did their best business here.

"Another round you guys?"

"Yea, if you really forced me, I think I could get another beer down."

"Me too Bob."

Bob Fudala, the bartender, had gotten to know the two partners over the months they had been coming to the Zoo. Bob suspected the type of business they were in, but never asked questions. It was usually a lot healthier. Besides, they were good tippers.

"Ya know Ray," MacCloud said, "it's so you can't get any good weed anymore."

"I know," Ray answered. "That's if you're lucky to get any smoke. Shit, it's easier to buy an Oh Zee of coke these days than to buy a joint."

As Bob came over to them with the beers, Ray said, "Hey Bob, you don't know where we can get some smoke do ya?"

"Hey guys, give me a break, I'm just the bartender, but I'll keep my eyes and ears open."

"Oh well, it was a nice try anyway," Ray said as he began sipping his beer.

John and Ray finished their beer and told them they'd be back.

It wasn't a week until they returned, but when they did, Bob had some news for them.

"Hey, where you guys been?"

"You know us," John answered. "We jungle fighter are always on the move. Makes us harder to hit."

"So I hear. Listen, you two hot shots still interested in scoring some weed?"

"Hey is a bear Catholic, does the Pope shit in the woods?" Ray answered.

"Funny. Well you're in luck. There's a kid over at the other end of the bar who may be able to do something for you."

"Who is he?" John asked.

"His name is Joey Schultz," Bob said while pointing him out to Ray and John.

"He's primarily a car and stereo thief, but every now and then he'll come in here to get rid of his goods and throw me a sawbuck for looking the other way. He's a real big mouth. Says he's got some connections, but only for people who can do quantity.

"Bob, the last thing I need in my life is a big mouth."

"Hey guys, like I always say, I'm just the bartender. You wanna meet or not?"

Ray and John looked at each other for a moment.

"What the hell, what've got to lose," John said.

"Ok Mac, but if he's a pain in the ass, he's history."

"No problemo."

With that, Bob went over to where Joey was sitting at and whispered something in his ear.

Joey grabbed his drink and started walking towards John and Ray. Joey was about five foot seven, had short spiked hair that was dyed blonde on top and looked all of fifteen even though they knew he had to be at least 21. If there was one law that Bob enforced it was the drinking age. Joey's clothes looked like something out of a bad MTV video. He was wearing black leather driving gloves, black nylon parachute pants, a lime green collarless shirt and a three-quarters length black leather coat.

"How you dudes doin', Bob here tells me you're looking for something that old Joey can put you onto."

Ray and John looked at each other. Ray shook his head and took another swallow of his beer. John took an instant dislike to anyone who referred to themselves in the third person, not to mention his snappy dress and equally snappy use of the word dude.

"That could be," John answered. "But we got better things to do than to listen to bullshit. Bob said you could deliver quantity."

"Listen man," Joey said. At least he didn't call him dude John thought.

"Joey Schultz does what he says. I'm not the one who delivers, but I set you up with someone who does, and of course, as a middleman, I get my commission."

John wondered if Joey knew the meaning of words longer than two syllables.

"So far so good Joey, what do you have?" John said.

"Bob tells me you're looking for some weed. I've got this dude who does weed in quantity but he don't like dealing with people he doesn't know. I wouldn't give you guys a second look, but Bob says you're cool."

"Well thank you ever so much," Ray said looking up from his beer for the first time. "And by the way it's doesn't like."

Joey continued, failing to note Ray's sarcasm or the fact that he corrected his grammar. "What're you guys looking to do for weight?"

"MacCloud looked at Ray and then shrugged his shoulders.

"Why not Mac, like you said, what have we lose?"

John turned to Joey and said, "We're looking to do about 20 pounds a week. But before we do anything big we'd want to get a sample."

"Yea, that's cool. I'll tell you what, I'll talk to my man and I'll meet you dudes back here next Monday," Joey said.

"Ok, we'll see you at eight."

Joey then walked back to the end of the bar and started talking to the groups of people who came with him.

"Mac, you're not really serious about coming back here next Monday. Are you? That shit head couldn't deliver even if he worked for Domino's Pizza."

"Ray, stranger things have happened, besides,"

"Yea I know, what do we have to lose? I need another beer."

****

Next Monday night saw John and Ray back at their usual spot at the Zoo. Eight o'clock came and went and it was getting nearer to nine and still no Joey.

"I told you that asshole wouldn't show Mac." Ray said.

"I didn't really expect it either, but at least it was an excuse to go out for a beer."

"Who says we need an excuse for that," Ray said as he lifted his draft to his mouth and nearly choked as he started to sip it.

"I don't believe it, that little shit showed."

Much to the surprise of Ray and John, Joey cane sauntering in and started walking towards them.

"Where the fuck you been? You get lost" Ray said.

"Hey dude take it easy, there were business meetings and arrangements to be made."

"Joey, be serious, what's the story? Do we have a meet or not?" John said.

"No problem. Didn't I tell you that Joey can deliver. My man Pat says he'll see you tonight to talk. He wasn't too crazy about making any new contacts, but I told him you were my cousin from out of state. By the way, where you guys from?"

"Out of state," John said.

"All right Joey, let's do this," Ray said. "You and John here are cousins on your mother's side. That'll explain for the difference in last names. Also, John and I are partners and we're from Rhode Island. You got that?"

"No problem. Why don't you two jump in my car and we'll go see Pat."

"No thanks, we'll follow in our car," John said.

"Sure, suit yourself."

All three left the Zoo and followed Joey to his car, a red two seat Miata.

"Joey, tell me something. How were the three of us going to fit in your car?" John said.

"Oh yea," Joey answered

As Ray and John were walking towards John's car, Ray turned to John and said, "Why do we get all the Rhodes Scholars."

"I know," answered John. "Just the nature of the business."

The partners got into John's blue Camaro, which was this month's car, and began to follow Joey.

"Ya know Mac, I still doubt if this is going to amount to anything, but if it does, let's give Joey a C note and cut that shithead out of this as soon as possible."

"No argument from me there, and by calling him just a shithead, you're giving all the other shitheads of the world a bad name."

Joey, as John suspected, also drove like a shithead, and it was only through divine intervention that he didn't get into an accident or get stopped by a cop. They drove down Elm Street from the Zoo's parking lot, through a red light while taking a left onto Lake Street, and heaven forbid, Joey should slow down at a stop sign before turning onto Union Street.

"Mac, I think I prefer flying then following this guy in a car. I'm going to kill him when we stop."

"Stand in Line."

When Joey finally came to a stop, it was in front of a blue three decker on Union Street. The building was in desperate need of a paint job and replacement windows.

"Well here we are," Joey said as he was getting out of his car while wearing his perpetual shit-eaten grin.

"Hey Joey, this hole is where your man lives who does quantity?" asked Ray. "If you're screwing with us."

"No, no man," Joey stammered. "He just lives this way. Over there, look," Joey pointed to a new BMW. "That's his car over there, every things cool."

"What the hell Ray," John said. "I'll go up and check this guy out. You wanna stay here?"

"Yea, watch yourself."

"Always do partner."

John followed Joey up to the top floor of the three decker, and went over the cover story with Joey one more time.

"OK you got it Joey, I'm your cousin from Rhode Island and we get together every now and then to party."

"No problem. Ole Joey got you covered."

They reached the top floor and were able to hear voices and a stereo through the door as if a small party was going on. Joey knocked on the door.

"Who is it?"

"It's me Joey, and ah, my cousin John."

McCloud looked down and just shook his head.

"OK. Hold on one."

John heard footsteps walking towards the door and a lock click open.

"Hey Pat. What's happening dude."

"Joey, what's up? And you gotta get another word besides dude."

Pat immediately gained a couple of points in John's book.

"Hey Pat, this is my cousin John from Rhode Island, John, Pat."

Pat and John shook hands and gave each other the once over. Pat was about 5 foot 10, medium build and looked to be in his late twenties with prematurely graying hair. He was wearing jeans and a blue UNH t-shirt.

John broke the ice.

"Don't worry, I won't call you dude.

Pat laughed and Joey started to turn red.

"Lighten up Joey, we love you like a fifth cousin," Pat said.

The other four people in the room laughed, and for once, Joey kept his mouth shut and sulked over to a chair on the other side of the room.

MacCloud walked through the door into the living room and was introduced to the other four guys in the room.

The only one who caught MacCloud's attention was a blonde haired muscle builder who looked to be in his mid-twenties whose name was Jeff. He was Joey's height, but just as wide without an ounce of fat.

"What do you do in the spare time," MacCloud asked, bench press Volkswagen's?"

Jeff chuckled at that. Like any muscle head thought MacCloud, he liked to be noticed.

"Nah, I'm up to Chevy's now," again, more laughter.

MacCloud then realized that everyone in the room was stoned and noticed the sicky sweet smell of marijuana smoke. This would also account for the ease of laughter and three open bags of potato chips. MacCloud didn't feel threatened and took the time to view his surroundings as he sat in an armchair besides the couch.

To the right of the living room was a small corridor that led to a kitchen. In the kitchen was another guy in his late twenties or early thirties with long brown hair and a beard. He was sitting at the table eating a happy meal with about a five-year-old boy. On the other side of the kitchen was another hallway that led to the rear of the apartment.

Pat noticed MacCloud looking into the kitchen and said, "Don't worry, he's cool. That's my roommate and his kid. He gets him a couple of days a week from his ex."

"Sure. No problem," MacCloud answered. "Seems like everyone has an ex these days."

"Yea, that's the best kind," Pat said, which elicited another round of laughter.

Pat's roommate seemed to take no heed of what was going on in the living room. Pat didn't offer his name and MacCloud didn't ask.

Turning his attention back to the living room, MacCloud thought that it was a typical bachelor's apartment. There was a bar and stereo equipment, with the obligatory oversized speakers, and clothes strewn about the room. On one of the coffee tables was a picture of Pat with his arm around a girl. Next to this was a vase of flowers. Nothing like a women's touch.

As MacCloud was taking in the surroundings, someone had lit another joint and began passing it around. Pat took a tote and passed it to MacCloud.

"No thanks, not tonight, I have to fly back to Rhode Island and that fucks me up," MacCloud said.

Pat nodded his head and passed the joint to Joey. After Pat exhaled he turned towards MacCloud.

"Yea, that's what Joey tells me. You're a pilot and you want to do some business. I didn't know you guys were cousins.

"Yea, well you know what they say, you can pick your friends but you can't pick your relatives." MacCloud said in reference to Joey. Everyone thought this was funny except Joey who was trying to figure out what MacCloud meant.

"I'm looking to do some business," MacCloud said, "but I wasn't looking to make this many new friends."

"Don't worry, they're cool," Pat said sensing MacCloud's concern. "I'm just finishing up with them. As a matter of fact, they were worried that you may be a cop."

MacCloud just shook his head, "Yea and I thought you guys were virgins."

"Ya can never be too careful," Jeff the bodybuilder said. "But ol' Joey has never led us astray."

Pat then turned to the other three, "Listen, I should have the shit next week. It's real primo, you'll like it."

"OK, we'll wait for your call."

Goodbyes were said and the three left leaving John, Pat and Jeff in the room. Joey went into the kitchen and started talking to Pat's roommate.

Pat settled back into the sofa, took a sip of beer and began talking to MacCloud.

"I can get the shit from one of two places. One guy has some real primo Afghani. He's kind of hard to get hold of. He's opening a new business, all legit, and that's taking up a shitload of his time. What kind of weight can you do?"

MacCloud leaned back in his chair and scratched his head.

"Well, he said pensively, if the dope is good, as well as the price, I can do twenty plus pounds a week."

Pat arched his eyebrows and whistled. "If you can do that much, why the hell are you up from Rhode Island? Joey tells me you do major shit down there, make a few trips to

Florida in your plane. What gives?" Pat was seeing dollar signs, but one or two alarm bells were also going off.

John looked at Joey who was still in the kitchen and shook his head.

"Ya know, he talks way too much. He's not a bad kid, but he's a few French fries shot of a happy meal," John paused before he continued.

"There's this city in Rhode Island, Central Falls, it's only four square miles in area and has a population of twenty thousand."

"So what's the big deal?" Pat asked as he popped a can of Coors.

"What the big deal is, is that sixteen of those twenty thousand residents are Columbians, and as you can probably guess, Central Falls is known as the cocaine capital of the east coast."

"Sounds like a dream come true," Pat said. "Are you one of the lucky minority of four thousand?"

"No, I live in Warner Rhode Island. It's about twenty miles north of Central Falls on the Mass, Rhode Island border. I keep my Aztec at the airport at Fall River. It's right over the line and convenient as hell with no control tower to keep track of my comings and goings."

"You keep your what, where?"

"My Aztec, it's one of the twin engine Piper series of planes. Piper named all of plane models after Indian tribes. It does about two-hundred miles an hour, and if the winds are right, I can make Florida in about 6 hours."

"No shit, last time I flew down on United, it took me twelve hours with all the delays," Pat said.

"Only twelve hours on a United flight to Florida, you did well. Anyway, Central Falls is where I get all my connections and I make about two ta three flights a month down to F L A." MacCloud pronounced the states initials separately.

"So what's the problem, and back to my initial question, what are you doing up here?"

"The problem is those fucking Columbians are crazy and all they do is coke. The money's good, but at times it's not worth it. I'm lucky they need me and my plane. Those fuckers have more guns than brains and would just as soon shoot you than look at you. I don't need the aggravation and figure it's time for a new product line to market."

Pat looked at John trying to figure out whether to believe him or not. "Shit man, why do you do it?"

John leaned back in his chair for a moment before saying anything.

"You can't beat the money man. For every load of coke that I haul back from Florida, I get thirty-grand, and I can haul about eight hundred ponds no problem. If I do two trips a month, well you add it up."

Pat arched his eyebrows after he did the math. "Shit, you make over a half mill a year. What are ya nuts giving that up?"

MacCloud leaned forward and pointed a finger at Pat for emphasis. "I'm not greedy and life's too short. I've made enough money to keep me comfortable but not to retire, and short of marrying someone who has enough money to support me in the manner I want to be accustomed too, I've got a little more work to do. I can move enough weed to keep me happy and take care of my people. I also plan on moving up here, the climates a lot healthier without all those Columbians."

As John was talking, Pat kept nodding his head in understanding. "Yea, I know what you're saying, I've got my people too and it sure beats working for a living."

Pat leaned back in the couch and gave some thought to what MacCloud had said. He didn't really like dealing with someone that he just met, but he was Joey's cousin and his story made a lot of sense. Pat made a decision.

"OK John, what do you have in mind?"

"Well depending on price, and if this shit is as good as you say it is, I'd like to buy a pound later this week, and then ten pounds next week. If everything works out ok, I'm looking to move twenty pounds a week thereafter. Can you do what Joey says or am I getting stroked?"

"No, no problem," Pat said with an edge of excitement in his voice.

John sensed that Pat was getting interested and for the first time thought that something might come out of this,

Pat continued. "Like I said before, I got two people I get weed from. It's good stuff. Nothing home grown."

"That's fine," John answered. "I don't care who you get it from, as long as it's good, and as the man says, the price is right."

Pat paused for a moment before he answered. The quality is no problem, but good pot is scarce these days, the price is eighteen hundred."

"Wait a second, am I buying pot or coke. That's way too much," John snapped back. When Pat didn't say anything, he went on.

"I don't mind paying a little extra for quality, if it is in fact quality. I'll tell you what. I'll give you fifteen hundred for the first pound, and if we do twenty, twelve hundred per pound," and as an afterthought, "What about Joey?"

"The lowest I can go for an elbow is sixteen hundred." Pat used the slang term elbow for a pound.

"If we end up doing twenty, I'll get you a better price, but it ain't gonna be any twelve hundred. I'll take care of Joey on the pound deal and you can take care of him on the first delivery of ten, then he's out of it."

John didn't say anything for a while as he did some adding and multiplying of his own. The price was high, but not too bad considering it was the first time Pat was doing business with him, a sort of risk premium.

"Alright, I can live with that for now, but if we're going to continue to do business, I want to realize some economies of scale."

"What?"

"A better price as we do more business and quantity."

"Got you covered," Pat said after John explained basic economics. "I should have the weed by the end of next week. Can you get your end together by then?" Pat asked in reference to John having the money ready.

"Piece of cake," John answered. "I can get the sixteen hundred anytime and I don't have anything planned for later this week. How do you want to get in touch, and don't say Joey?"

"Don't worry, how 'bout I give you my phone number, and how do I get in touch with you?"

"I've got a beeper."

"Beeper? No one uses beepers." Pat said.

"I do, and then I call you on a burner phone." John said referring to a phone with prepaid minutes that you can buy at Wal-Mart."

"It's a lot safer that way."

John then gave Pat a card with an 800 number on it and a winged messenger that was superimposed over the word, "Mercury Aviation".

"Mercury Aviation is the cover I use and the 800 number is good from anywhere in New England."

Pat was nodding his head as he was writing his number down for Mac Cloud.

"OK Pat, I'll give you a call in a couple of days and we'll try to do this at the end of the week. If anything comes up, beep me."

"Gotcha," Pat said.

"Hey Joey," John yelled. "Get your ass in here."

"Don't you guys forget to take care of ol' Joey now. How'd it go?"

John got up from his chair and zipped his leather flight jacket.

"We worked a few things out. I'll be getting a sample later this week or next and some quantity if all goes well, and that's when we take care of ol' Joey."

"Yea, that's cool, as long as I get mine."

"Joey," John said beginning to lose his patience, "that's the least of your worries."

John and Joey said their good byes and left through the same door they entered. As they were walking down the stairs John asked Joey, "Who was the guy you were talking to in the kitchen.

"The guy with the beard? That's Pat's roommate Jim, and the little rug rat is his kid. He gets him once a week from his ex."

"What's his act?"

"He's a heavy dude man. He makes Pat look like small potatoes."

That so," John said.

"Why didn't you set me up with him?"

Joey shrugged his shoulders. "He won't deal with anyone he don't know."

"Doesn't know," John said correcting Joey's English.

"Huh," Joey said.

"Forget it, go on."

"Well yea, Pat's roommate Jim has a set number of people he deals with. He says he gets his dope from some people on some way out fucking island in the Caribbean. .""

"What's the name of the island?"

"I forgot, but it sounds like you want to make her."

"It wouldn't be Jamaica by any chance, would it?"

"That's it. How did you know?"

"Well besides passing fourth grade geography, I've been there once or twice on business."

"No shit dude, wait 'til Jim hears that. He just may do some business with you if things go good with Pat."

John was thinking about correcting Joey's English again but figured it would be wasted.

As they went out the front door of the three decker, Joey was thinking how he could make some more money setting John up with Jim.

"Ya know, if I was to set you up with Jim, we can all get a pretty good piece of action."

Hey Joey," John answered, "Let's get settled with Pat first. I'm not too crazy dealing with people I don't know either."

"Ok cool, but you won't regret dealing with ol' Joey."

John already regretted dealing with ol' Joey.

"We'll see Joey, we'll see."

As they rounded the corner they approached John's car. Ray rolled down the window and asked how it went.

"How do you think it went?" Joey blurted out not giving John a chance to answer. "Great dude."

Ray looked to the heavens and rolled his eyes.

"It went better than expected," John said, "in spite of Joey."

John then turned to Joey as he opened the driver's side door, "Listen Joey, I'll be in touch with Pat by next week and I'll let you know how it goes."

"Don't worry," Joey answered. "It'll go fine."

Joey then got into his own car and did his usual peel out fishtailing his Miata as he drove down the street.

"Partner," Ray said, "It's only a matter of time with people like Joey."

"And the way it went upstairs, sooner than you might think."

"Really."

John then recounted to Ray the events that had taken place including what Joey had said about Jim.

"That would be an added bonus if we could link up with him," Ray said.

"Absolutely," John answered. "Anyway, I'm thirsty, let's go get us a beer."

"Show me the way home."

****

It was Sunday morning the following week when John's beeper went off waking him out of a sound sleep. The constant beeping didn't help his hangover. MacCloud shook his head thinking that he had never gotten hangovers in college. He gently extricated his arm from the blonde next to him in bed. MacCloud had been going out with Darcy for about three months and was finding himself uncharacteristically attracted to her. One of the differences between her and other girls that he dated was that Darcy didn't put demands on him or ask a lot of questions about his work. She seemed to be a rare find, but it was only three months and MacCloud never did anything hastily, especially with women.

John rolled over and looked at his beeper muttering to himself that someday he would take great pleasure doing a Mexican hat dance on it. He wondered if all people who carried pagers felt the same way.

"What time is it?" Darcy asked softly. She too was feeling the effects including pleasant memories of the previous night.

"It's still early Darcy. I have some business to attend to and then I'll be back."

Darcy then did a feline stretch causing a significant amount of flesh to pop free of the covers.

MacCloud noticing this began to have second thoughts about business and was beginning to tolerate the beeper for waking him.

Darcy saw John and looking at her and smiled coyly. She then ran a hand through his hairy chest. John made an immediate decision that business could wait. After all, there were priorities in life.

John woke up for the second time that day feeling much better, and happier, than the first. He glanced at the clock and saw that there was only fifteen minutes left in the morning and it was time to get his sorry ass out of bed. He also noticed that Darcy was no longer beside him in bed at the same time smelling the aroma of bacon and eggs coming from the kitchen.

"That woman has a good attitude," he said to no one in particular.

As he was getting out of bed, MacCloud remembered the pager, grabbed it and looked at the number on the display screen.

"Son of a bitch," he said to the same no one in particular somewhat surprised at the number he saw.

As he walked into the kitchen, Darcy smiled and threw back her long hair prior to getting a kiss from him. As John kissed her he gave her backside a soft pinch.

"You're incorrigible," she said kiddingly. "Haven't you had enough?"

"Not of you."

"Good reply. The coffee's done and the bacon and eggs should be ready in about five."

"Thanks sweets," John answered as he grabbed the phone and walked into the adjacent room.

"I've got a call to make anyway."

"Oh, another one of those calls I can't hear," Darcy said with a mischievous look on her face. Darcy knew the type of business John was in, and though she wasn't crazy about it, she thought it was exciting and loved hearing some of the stories he would sometimes tell her.

John looked at her and smiled back. He was very happy with the relationship. As he dialed the number, he leaned back on a chair and peered out the double glass doors of the living room that overlooked the lake where the house was located. The view was fantastic. MacCloud was proud of his house. It was a contemporary that he had bought unfinished from the previous owner for a song after he ran into financial troubles. John, with the help of a couple of friends, had then finished it to his liking. The bathroom had Italian marble, the Jacuzzi was in California redwood and his office had imported mahogany from Belize. The house was spacious at thirty five hundred square feet, but MacCloud liked open spaces.

Things were going very well for John MacCloud.

His thoughts were interrupted by a voice at the other end of the line.

"Hello."

"Pat, it's me John. How ya doing."

"Pretty good," Pat answered. "I was beginning to think that your beeper wasn't working."

"It's working, but I wasn't. Mornings and me don't always agree."

"I hear ya," Pat answered. "What we talked about last week, I got my end together. Are you still interested?"

"Bet your ass I am," MacCloud said without hesitation. "All I have to do is give Ray a call and we'll be all set. How's Tuesday sound?"

"Tuesday's good," Pat said. "I got nothing planned all day."

"Tough life," John said jokingly.

"Hey, someone's got to do it."

"I'll tell you what Pat, I got a car I keep at the airport in Manchester. Ray and I should be there by mid-afternoon. Why don't I give you a call when we get there?"

"Sound's good. Did you say you keep a car at the airport? Aren't you afraid of it getting ripped?"

"Not really. It's in a pretty secure area at Stead Aviation and it's one of a couple that I have."

"Must be nice," Pat said. "Just don't tell Joey about it."

John started to laugh. "You're right on that. If there are any problems, I'll call ya. If not, speak to you Tuesday when I get in."

"Good," then as an afterthought Pat said, "Hey John, you'll have your end together right?"

"Absolutely. That's the way I do business. I don't believe in fronting."

"Great, see you then."

John hung up and began to dial Ray's number as Darcy told him that breakfast was ready.

John looked in at her and smiled.

Things were going very well indeed.

****

For the second time in as many weeks, Ray and John pulled up to the dilapidated blue three-decker on Union Street in Manchester.

After John and Pat had spoken Sunday morning, events progressed rapidly. The call to Ray, getting the money together on Monday, and for Ray, the white knuckle plane ride into Manchester.

John turned up the collar of his leather flight jacket as he got out of his Camaro. It was a clear sunny day in early March, but there was a typical biting wind which brought the wind chill factor to well below freezing.

Ray stayed in the car with the money.

"Holy shit, it's cold out," John said.

"Then get the fuck in the house Mac. Even my dog knows enough to come in from the cold."

MacCloud went bounding up the steps and into the house. It was too cold to stay outside and trade wisecracks with Ray.

As MacCloud walked up the stairs he looked around to see if there was anything unusual. He had done his usual counter surveillance routine coming from the airport, and he was sure he wasn't followed. It never hurt to be too careful. No matter how many times he did it, he always got butterflies before a deal, especially when doing business with someone new. There was always a chance of a rip, or something worse.

MacCloud didn't think so in this case. The deal was going down in Pat's house, and unless the house was a cover, which he didn't think it was, it would be too easy to get back at Pat. MacCloud was still being careful. That's why the money was with Ray. It was a general rule of thumb in the drug trade to always keep the money and the drugs separated.

As MacCloud reached the top of the stairs, he heard a stereo blaring from the apartment. He knocked on the door, and in a couple of moments, Pat opened the door.

"Hey John, come on in."

Pat was barefoot and only wearing jeans. As John entered the apartment, he noticed the temperature inside was in sharp contrast to the cold outside and MacCloud quickly took off his jacket. He was only wearing a shirt underneath the jacket and he noticed Pat giving him the once over, possible looking for a gun or hidden wire. Guns weren't all that uncommon for drug dealers. It came with the trade and some even had portable radios, but a wire was a sure give away that the person you were dealing with was a cop.

MacCloud wasn't worried. Most wires police used were in a shoulder harness, and he wasn't wearing one. His 8 shot .380 caliber automatic was safely nestled in his back pocket, virtually undetectable. It wasn't much of a gun, but it was a good belly gun, and if anything went wrong today, he felt that's all he would need.

"Pat, how's it going? Cold as a witches tit outside with that wind blowing, but you more than make up for it with the heat in here."

"Yea, the heats included with the cost of the rent so I don't mind cranking it up. Makes me think that I'm in Florida. I'll be going there in a couple of weeks with my girlfriend."

"Where are you going?" John asked.

"We're going down to Miami and spend about two weeks."

John smiled while digging in his front pocket and threw a pack of matches at Pat.
On the cover was a colorful display of an outdoor lounge in Miami, *Monty Trainors*.

"I make it a point to get there every time I fly down. It's in Miami just outside the Coconut Grove section. I was there about three weeks ago mixing some business with pleasure. It's a good time."

"Really, I remember you saying you fly down there a lot."

"Not as much as I used too. Now I'm making them to New Hampshire."

"Yea, I remember you telling me it's a lot safer. By the way, where's your partner?"

"He's down in the car with our end. How's yours?"
"Wait one."

John saw Pat go into the bedroom that was off the living room, go to a floor safe by the bed, spin the combination and take out a brown paper bag. Pat then walked out of the bedroom and handed it to John.

"Here it is."

John took the bag from Pat and was immediately assailed by the pungent marijuana odor. MacCloud reached in and rolled some of the greenish brown vegetative matter between his fingers.

"Lots of buds and nice and sticky."

"That'll put you on cloud nine," Pat said. "Do you want to weigh it?"

"Na, this looks good. I'm gonna go down and get the cash."

"Sounds good to me." "Why don't you have Ray come on up, I'd like to meet him."

"Sure."

John left the bag of pot with pat and went down to the Camaro. Ray had the car running and was listening to the local rock station WGIR.

"How'd it go Mac?" Ray asked through the open window.

"Smooth as silk. He says for you to come on up and meet."

"No shit!" Ray said arching his eyebrows. "Trusting sort isn't he. Anyone else with him up in the apartment?"

"Not as far as I can tell. If there is someone he didn't show himself. But I wouldn't sell him short."

Ray grabbed the money, which was also in a brown paper bag, buttoned up his jacket, shut off the engine and followed MacCloud into the house. Ray was a little more cautious than John. He carried a Smith & Wesson nine mm in the pocket of his bulky army jacket. It was easily concealable and easy to get.

As John and Ray entered Pat's apartment, John made the introductions. Ray also felt the heat of the apartment and unbuttoned his jacket but left it on.

"Give the man the money Ray," John said as he noticed the bag of pot on the couch where he left it.

Ray handed the bag to Pat who went over to the bar, sat on a stool and started counting the hundred dollar bills.

John took the bag of pot and gave it to Ray who opened the bag and began nodding his head up and down approvingly.

"All here", Pat said. "You guys still interested in doing some quantity?"

Ray looked at MacCloud who nodded.

"Yea, I think so depending on price. This looks like good shit. Will the rest be as good?"

"It could be even better," Pat answered. "What you got there is some real good Jamaican ganja. If I can get in touch with my other source, he's got some Afghani weed that will curl your toes."

"What are we talking for price?"

"I'm not sure, but if you're going to do quantity, it'll be better than what you got this pound for."

Ray thought about this for a moment and then looked at John.

"What do you think Mac?"

MacCloud paused and then turned to Pat. "I'll tell you what, let's see how this sells and you get me a price for ten of the Jamaican and ten of the Afghani, and then we'll decide. I'll give you a call at the end of the week.

Pat though this over for a minute and answered, "Why don't you call me at the end of the weekend instead. I may not be able to get to my sources by then."

"No problem," John said. "It'll take a day or two to get our part together anyway. How 'bout you?"

"With either source only a couple of hours. I don't keep that much on hand and I'll have to go run for it. We've been doing business for quite a while and both will front me the shit."

Ray and John looked at each other. They were both amazed at how open Pat was with them and how much information he had volunteered.

Ray then said, "All right, Mac can give you a call and we can work the details out later."

"Fine by me," Pat said.

John and Ray then said their goodbyes, took the bag of pot and left the house. Neither of them said a word to each other until they were in the Camaro. Ray still the cautious one was looking around for any type of surveillance or something out of the ordinary.

"You gotta be shittin' me. That was just too easy," Ray said.

"Hey Ray, what can I tell you, I have a trusting face."

Ray began shaking his head. "Could he be that trusting Mac?" People like that usually don't stay in business long, but as far as we know, he's never been busted and he's been dealing for quite a while. Mac you have a unique talent for making chicken salad out of chicken shit."

MacCloud just smiled and said, "I think it's time to tell the boss."

****

It was the following Monday and Pat had just gotten out of bed and was making coffee. He was surprised that neither Ray nor John had called him since their dealings last week. He had called both his sources over the weekend and both assured him that they could supply him up to ten pounds on a days' notice for the next week without a problem.

Pat felt pretty good about doing business with MacCloud. In his business he had to be careful. There were threats from two sides. Not only did he have to worry about the cops, but also other dealers who specialized in rip offs.

Narcs tended to be pushy when they tried to make a buy and would agree to any price. This was usually a sure tip off that the buyer was a cop and Pat would always pass on the deal. Hold up artists would often be paranoid and would always carry guns. Pat was pretty much a nonviolent person and even though he owned a gun, he had always kept it in his safe. The moment Pat suspected a rip off, he would get hold of Jeff and a couple of his other muscle head buddies and they would always give anyone second thoughts of doing anything foolish.

Pat had been dealing since his days at Manchester Central High School and was proud of the fact that he had never been busted or ripped. He walked to the counter and poured himself a cup of coffee, went to the living room, leaned back in his chair and thought how good his lifestyle was. He'll be in sunny Florida with his girlfriend this time next week with plenty of money in his pocket. Damn, she looked good in a thong.

If the deal went through with John and Ray, he would have that much more money in his pocket. If not, he still had a six-figure bank account to draw from that he had accumulated over the years. The drug trade had been very good to him.

Pat's thoughts were interrupted by the phone.

"Your dime"

"These days it's a quarter. Pat. It's me John."

"What's up? I was just thinking of you and beginning to think I wasn't going to hear from you. How'd you like the product?"

"Real good. It's been a long week for me."

"I know what you mean. You and Ray still interested?"

"Yea we are, depending. What can you do ten for?"

"I spoke to both of my people over the week and I can get you the same stuff as last time for twelve each, or I can get you this real primo shit."

When John didn't say anything Pat went on. "The primo stuff is great and it's just a few dollars more at fourteen.

"I was expecting better," John said. "Hang on one."

"I'll tell you what," John said after a pause, "we'll do ten if you can do the primo for thirteen."

Pat did some quick adding and subtracting. He liked to make four hundred a pound when he did this quantity. At thirteen he would be making three thousand as opposed to four thousand. Pat thought for another second.

"I'll tell you what. I'll do it for 1350 and I'll take care of Joey, then he's out of it."

"You hit a weak spot there Pat, Joey's all yours and it's a deal. When can you do it?"

"Pick a time, all I need is a days' notice."

"How's Wednesday sound? The forecast is for good flying weather for the next couple of days and it's a lot more enjoyable flying if you're not in the clouds"

"Sounds good to me. I'm going to have to run for the product. Where do you want to do it?" Pat asked.

"How 'bout we do it at the airport. Ray and I will fly in about eleven and give you and Joey a call from there."

"Be waiting for your call."

Pat hung up and took another sip of his coffee. He liked doing business with John. He was good to deal with and he had picked a nice public place to do the deal. Pat wouldn't have to worry about a rip and the last thing he suspected John for was a cop. A cop would never have let all that money walk after the first pound deal.

A little extra spending money would be a great way to start his vacation.

****

John's thoughts were now back to the present. The events of the past few weeks had flashed through his mind in a matter of seconds. As he and Ray walked past Stead Aviation to the perimeter fence, he was able to take a better look at Joey.

Joey wore his perpetual shit-eaten grin, black racing gloves and long black leather coat with jeans and sneakers. Some things never change.

"Hey dudes, what's happening?"

"Hello Joey," Ray answered. "For once in your life you're on time."

"Hey, its payday for ol' Joey. So if you want, you can pay me and I'm outta here.

"Not quite Joey," Ray said. "The deals not done yet and ol' Joey doesn't get his until we get ours. Besides, Pat's paying you. Dig dude?" Ray said mimicking Joey.

"We're going to call Pat and have him come here, and then you'll get your money," John said as he was walking through the gate.

Joey just shrugged his shoulders and said, "Oh well, I've waited this long."

"Yea you have," John said. "Now let's go to the terminal building and call Pat.

"Hey Mac, don't they have a restaurant in there?" Ray asked.

"Yea, I think it's called the flight deck or something. We can wait there."

The walk from Stead Aviation to the terminal building took under ten minutes across a crowded airport. As John walked through the lot, he marveled at how quickly Manchester Airport had grown in the past five years. It had become the primary feeder airport for Boston's Logan International and was already supporting six major airlines and a number of puddle jumpers and charter services. It had come a long way since the Grenier Field days of WWII

The parking lot they were walking through was one of five and was just south of the terminal building. There were two rows of rental cars from Hertz and AVIS. John remembered when it was only a public parking lot and generally just half full. He made a mental note that this would be a good place to have the deal go down.

As the three entered the terminal building, John went to the bank of payphones to the left of the entrance. "Why don't you guys go up to the restaurant and I'll join you after I give Pat a call."

Joey needed no prodding and went bounding up the stairs ahead of Ray.

"Mac, if you leave me alone with him for more than five minutes, I won't be responsible for my actions," Ray said.

"Don't worry, I'll be done before you can say hey dude," and then as an afterthought, "Trust me."

Ray looked at John over his shoulder and said, "Yea, the checks in the mail and I love you."

As he dialed Pat's number, he looked around the lobby of the terminal. There was one of the airport police officers sipping the inevitable cup of coffee while talking to the pretty receptionist at the AVIS counter. There were worse jobs. John figured it must be a fairly boring assignment but it beat standing over a hole in the road freezing your ass off. John heard Pat answer the phone after the sixth ring.

"Pat, it's me John. Ray and I are at the airport."

"Great. How 'bout Joey?"

"He's here too."

"Can't win 'em all," Pat said. "But when there's a buck, he's there."

"Yea," John agreed and then got down to business. "We're all set with our part. How you doing?"

"Real good. I was waiting for your call and all I have to do is go run for it.

"Ok. We'll be in the restaurant in the terminal building. How long will you be?"

"I should be there in about sixty to seventy minutes."

"Right. That'll give us time to grab a bite. See you then."

As Pat hung up the phone he was elated. This would be a good chunk of change that he would be getting every week or every other week from John and Ray, time for another new car.

Pat grabbed his keys and jacket as he went out the front door. It was another cold day and he was wondering

48

when they were going to get some warm weather. He then thought to himself that he should be thinking more about the deal and not take things for granted. In this business, people got hurt, ripped or busted when things were taken for granted. He would go get Jim who was working out at the athletic club by the airport. This way he would have some back up if something went wrong.

As Pat pulled into traffic at Union Street, he didn't notice the blonde girl driving the blue SUV two cars behind him. As he pulled onto Willow Street, he didn't notice any one of the four cars that were following his every move. As he turned onto 101 eastbound, Pat certainly didn't notice the green and white Cessna 182, two thousand feet above him tracking his progress as he drove to Ricky Richards's house.

Pat turned onto route 107 from 101, he did notice the two people changing a flat tire and as he took a right onto the dead end road where Richard's lived, he also noticed the two-telephone lineman working on the side of the road. Poor bastards Pat thought to himself, working for a living sure sucks. He was going to make more money in two hours than these guys were going to make in two weeks; great country America!

****

"Air one to ground, we have an eyeball. He's leaving the car and going into the house." State trooper Scott Nelson radioed to the other cops of the New Hampshire Drug Task Force who were keeping tabs on drug dealers Pat Mason and Ricky Richards.

"Roger that, keep circling over the house until we advise otherwise."

"Air two, this is ground one, do you have a visual?"

Air two was the designation kiddingly given to Manchester detective Rick Kilman who was one of the telephone lineman Pat had saw while pulling onto Richard's street. Kilman was perched atop of the telephone pole that gave him an unobstructed view of Ricky Richard's house and barn.

"Yea Jim, I got 'em," Kilman answered.

Good radio reception, Kilman thought. Then again, it should be, Jim Morris, the team leader, was only forty feet below him in the telephone repair van.

Jim Morris, a sergeant with the state police, was the head of the NH Drug Task Force that was comprised of state and local police and answered to the Attorney General. Jim was seated in the back of the specially designed surveillance van. Today, the van was painted the colors of Fair Point. Seated next to Jim was Chief Nolan.

Nolan had started the ball rolling three months ago when he had called the task force and asked for some assistance with a drug dealer in his town. Since then, through a series of informants, surveillance, and plain luck of a couple of task force cops, they were not only on the verge of getting Richards, but a couple of his other dealers as well.

"Ground one to ground units, stand by."

Kathy Morse of the task force parked her SUV at McDonalds and was soon joined by Mike Bird of the task force. Kathy was from Laconia and Mike from Derry, both medium sized towns from opposite ends of the state. Tim O'Conner, also from Laconia, went through the drive up at Dunkin' Donuts, bought a cup of coffee and positioned himself in the parking lot and radioed Jim that he was standing by to stand by.

Jim laughed to himself. One of these days Tim was going to take life seriously. Tim's favorite toast was to his patron saint, Peter Pan. He may grow old, but he wasn't going to grow up.

Both Nolan and Morris sat in the van in silence. A lot of "ifs" had to happen if this was going to go down, but a lot of "ifs" had already happened to get them this far.

In about ten minutes the silence was interrupted by Scot Nelson's voice over the radio with the drone of the Cessna engine in the background.

"Air one to units, he's coming out and it looks as if he's carrying a box."

"Rick, do you have him?" Jim asked.

Rick put a three inch pocket telescope to his eye and squinted.

"Yea, got 'em. He's carrying a cardboard box and going to the trunk. Now he's getting in and here he comes."

Both Jim and Chief Nolan looked at each other. The ifs were happening.

As Pat came out of Ricky's driveway, the units of the Drug Task Force fell in line behind him.

"Alright people," Jim said over the radio, "let's give him a real loose tail, we don't want to spook him. Scott, do you have him?"

"I've got a clear view of his Beemer and traffic's light. I've already contacted Manchester approach and they're giving us priority and vectoring other planes around us."

"If he starts doing some counter surveillance tricks, everyone back off and Scott will keep him in sight," Jim said over the radio.

"Have no fear boss," Tim said, which was his usual answer.

As Pat pulled onto route 107, he began retracing his way back to Manchester. As he turned onto route 101, Pat saw a car in the breakdown lane with a State Police cruiser behind it. The trooper was behind the wheel of his car with his head bent down.

Probably writing a ticket Pat thought. Pat instinctively took his foot off the accelerator and slowed to 60. The last thing he needed was to get stopped with ten pounds of pot in his trunk.

As he passed the trooper, Pat looked in his rearview mirror and saw for the second time a blue SUV behind him.

Pat thought it was probably nothing, but he didn't come this far in life believing in coincidences. Ordinarily, he would have pulled over to the side of the road and let the SUV drive by, but it had passed him before he began to slow down.

Another mile further and Pat saw the SUV take the exit three off ramp.

"Ground three to air one, I'm pulling off Scott, he may have made me," Kathy radioed to Scott.

"It's ok Kath, I still have him. Mike do you have him?"

"I'm about a quarter of a mile back, but I still have him. Jim you getting this?"

"I got it. Everyone's doing fine." Jim was staying behind in the van with Chief Nolan and Kilman who had come down from the telephone pole and was warming up inside the van. If all went as planned, they would be hitting Richardson's house and barn later in the day with a search warrant.

Pat continued down route 101 while occasionally looking in his rear view mirror. Satisfied that no one was following him, he started thinking of upcoming events. He hoped that Jim, his roommate, would already be at the airport. He really didn't like hanging around the airport with a trunk full of pot.

From 101, Pat turned onto route 293 and then took the Brown street exit towards the airport. As he turned onto the airport and approached the terminal building, Pat was relieved to see Jim waiting for him on the sidewalk.

"Been waiting long?" Pat asked as he pulled up next to his roommate.

"Nah, just got here about ten minutes ago."

"Ok, I'll go park the car and I'll be with you in a minute."

Pat drove to one of the newly paved lots west of the terminal building and pulled into the first open space. He made sure the doors and trunk were locked and joined Jim at the terminal building.

As Pat and Jim walked into the lobby of the terminal building, Pat noticed a janitor sweeping the floor and thought how much better his life was then that poor stiff. Selling dope beat shoveling shit any day of the week.

What Pat didn't know was that poor stiff was one of the task force's surveillance team.

As Pat and Jim took the escalator to the second floor restaurant, the other members of the task force surveillance team were positioning themselves around the terminal building.

"Air one to Ground one."

"Go ahead Scott, Jim here." Both Jim Morris and Chief Nolan remained in the van coordinating the members of the task force surveillance team after arriving at the airport.

I've received clearance from the control tower to remain in the pattern at two thousand feet.

"Good," Jim answered, "If they start moving, we'll keep you advised, but hopefully everything will go down here."

"Roger," Scott said. "If it's more than an hour, the tower may start vectoring me around, they have a 737 coming in."

"Keep your fingers crossed that it's over by then."

After Jim checked to make sure all the units were in place, he settled down and waited.

If it's one thing cops hated, it was sitting, waiting and doing nothing, but not as much as paperwork. One author of police texts described police work as seven hours and fifty-nine minutes of boredom followed by one minute of sheer terror.

Pat and Jim entered the restaurant and saw John and Ray sitting at a table in the far corner. They were next to a large bay window overlooking the main runway and taxi area. It was two o'clock and there was a sparse crowd in the restaurant. It was after the noon rush and before the late day commuter traffic that started at three.

Pat looked around as he walked towards John and Ray. He noticed two apparent businessmen at the bar sipping their afternoon drinks. What Pat didn't notice was the slight bulge in their jackets or the hidden microphones that enabled them to communicate with Jim Morris.

When Ray and John saw Pat and Jim walk in, they breathe a collective sigh of relief. It was a combination of waiting for two hours wondering whether or not the deal was going to happen, and as could be expected, Joey was wearing very thin on their nerves.

"Hey guys, good to see ya," John said as he got up.

"We were beginning to wonder if you were going to show or not."

"All set," Pat answered as he and Jim sat down. "Just had to go and run for the stuff. By the way, where's Joey?"

"If we're real lucky, he got sucked into a jet engine," Ray said.

John leaned back in his chair and laughed. "We gave him a roll of quarters and he's busy in the arcade."

"He can be trying after a while," Pat answered as he picked up a menu. "I just remembered, I haven't eaten yet."

Within a couple of minutes a waitress came to the table and took Pat's order for a hamburger and a beer. Jim just ordered a beer and John and Ray had their coffee refilled.

"Aren't you guys going to have a beer?" Jim asked.

"Naw, we have to fly back as soon as we take care of business. There's some weather coming in tonight and I want to beat it back to Rhode Island," John said. "By the way, everything all set on your end?"

"Everything's fine. It's out in the car," Pat said. "How 'bout you?"

John paused a minute as the waitress arrived with Pat and Jim's drinks.

"We got our shit together," John said as Ray reached under the table and reached for John's flight bag. Ray then placed the leather flight bag on his lap and unzipped the top. Jim looked into the flight bag, saw the stack of bills, and smiled.

"Looks like you do have your shit together."

"Hey dudes, what's happening?" Joey said as he made his presence known at the table.

"I knew it was too good to be true," Ray said

"You guys got everything all set?"

"Don't worry Joey, try as we may, we won't forget you."

"Ok, just checking in, well you dudes carry on and I'll be downstairs."

"Thank God," Ray said.

There was another pause in the conversation as the waitress arrived with Pat's food.

"How do you want to do it?" Pat asked John in between bites of his burger?"

"Why don't you and I go down to your car, you count the money, I check out the product, and if we're both happy, we go our separate ways."

Pat chewed on his burger for a while, swallowed and then said, "I'd like to keep the drugs and money separated first time we're doing something this size."

John nodded his head in agreement. "I know what you mean. It'll be nice after we do this a couple of times and build up a trust."

"It's not that I don't trust you guys," Pat said. "But like the man said, nothing personal, just business."

Ray then spoke up. "I'll tell you what, why don't Jim and me go in the plane, it's right over there," Ray pointed to where the Aztec was parked on the tarmac. "We'll be in the plane and Jim can count the money. Pat and John can go to

Pat's car where John can check out the shit. Pat drive's the car to the parking lot by the plane where we can see each other. If everyone's happy, Jim leaves with the money and John leaves with the dope."

Pat and Jim looked at each other for a moment.

Pat began nodding his head and said, "Sounds good to me, what do you think Jim?"

"Yea, not bad. The money and the dopes apart and we're out in the public."

"How bout Joey?" John asked.

"I'll take care of him," Pat said. "He can stay in the arcade out of harm's way and I'll give him his cut later.

"Great."

Pat finished his sandwich, threw a twenty on the table and asked if everyone was ready

"Let's do it," Ray said.

John and Ray got up and followed Pat and Jim out of the restaurant. As they walked out the door, one of the undercover cops who was sitting at the bar spoke softly into his hidden microphone.

Sitting in the van, Jim Morris felt the butterflies in his stomach, even after fifteen years of drug work.

"Alright everybody," Jim said over the radio. "It's show time. Kathy why don't you and Tim drive over to the corner by Stead Aviation and look couple-ish."

"Roger that," Kathy said.

"Thank you God," Tim said. "I can give couple-ish new meaning."

Kathy looked over at Tim and said good-naturedly, "Enjoy it Tim, because it'll be only in your dreams."

Tim still kept smiling and began to say something but remained quiet as Jim Morris kept giving instructions over the radio.

"Kathy, you two will be joined by BJ and Bob when they leave the restaurant. When it goes down, you guys will be taking down Pat Mason and John in the car. Make sure the car is boxed in so it can't go anywhere."

After a moments pause, Jim continued, "Dick, Are you there?"

Dick Curry picked up the microphone from the Exxon Av-gas truck he was sitting in and answered. "Yea Jim, we copied."

Dick was dressed as an airplane fueler along with Mike Bird. For all intents and purposes, they were just two employees just passing time.

Jim continued. "Dick, you and Mike along with the Chief and Kilman will be taking down Ray and Jim in the plane."

"Ok, we got it."

"Heads up everyone, the final act is about to begin. Scott, are you copying all of this?"

"Air one has it."

As Ray, John, Jim and Pat walked into the parking lot, they split into two groups. Ray and Jim went through the general Aviation security gate and headed towards the twin engine Aztec while Pat and John walked towards Pat's car.

As John got into Pat's car he was rubbing his hands. "I hope your car warms up fast."

"It should still be warm, I wasn't away that long," Pat said.

Pat started the car, turned the heater on and drove to the far corner of the parking lot where they could see Ray and Jim in the Aztec.

"Actually, this is a pretty good idea Ray thought of," Pat said.

"Yea, there's no one in this section of the lot and we can see each other fine. Where do you have the dope?"

"It's in the trunk," Pat answered. Pat put the car in park and kept the car running. As Pat left the car and walked towards the trunk, he looked around the lot and tarmac. He saw a fuel truck with a couple of the line guys fueling a

Cessna two tie downs from John's Aztec that Ray and Jim were in, and he also saw a couple of businessmen get into a rental car at the far end of the lot. There was also a telephone repair van in the lot, but nothing out of the ordinary that would alarm him.

Pat opened the trunk and took out a box that he had loaded at Ricky Richard's house. He got back in the car and slid the box so that it was resting between him and John.

"Here it is. This Afghani shit will blow you away."

As Pat was saying this to John, Jim was counting the money with Ray in the plane. John opened the box that Pat had slid next to him and saw a green trash bag secured with duct tape. As he ripped open the top of the bag, John smiled as he inhaled the sicky sweet odor of the marijuana. He then reached in and felt the stickiness of the buds. John then looked at Pat intently, particularly where his hands were and smiled.

"Pat, this looks like marvelous shit."

"I told you, it doesn't get any better," Pat said.

John kept on smiling and said, "You're right Pat, it doesn't get any better."

Pat thought John was beginning to act a little strange. He was startled by his door being yanked open and having a gun stuck in his face.

****

"Put your hands on your head and come out of the car. Get on the ground"

To the controllers in the tower it seemed that all hell had broken loose. There were five people with guns surrounding a car in one of the commuter parking lots with one person spread-eagled on the ground.

58

In the general aviation tie down area, the same scene was occurring, only around a twin engine Aztec, again with one person spread-eagled on the ground. The wail of sirens could be heard as marked cruisers were coming down the airport perimeter road and a uniformed sheriff was escorting a handcuffed blonde teenager who was wearing an ankle length black coat.

"Manchester tower, this is Cessna three yankee zulu."

"Cessna three yankee zulu, Manchester Tower. What the hell is going on?"

"Tower, this is Corporal Scott Nelson of the New Hampshire Drug Task Force. What you see down there is the arrest of three drug dealers.

"Roger three yankee zulu, nice job."

****

Pat couldn't believe what was happening. He was face down on the ground with his hands handcuffed behind his back. He was being arrested. Cops! What happened? Where was his partner Jim, and MacCloud. He looked up. He saw Jim who was being marched towards him also handcuffed. Joey was handcuffed too. Pat looked up again and saw Ray and John standing over him. Neither was handcuffed.

Ray walked up besides John and said, "Nice job partner."

Pats mind was racing. He couldn't believe it. Ray and John were fucking cops, narcs.

"I knew it, I knew it," Pat blurted out. "I knew you were fucking cops."

Ray looked at John and said, "Once, just once Mac, I wish they'd say something different after we arrest them."

John laughed and looked down at Pat and said sarcastically, "Yea, you knew we were cops, that's why you sold us ten pounds of pot. Another Rhodes scholar."

Pat realized the foolishness of what he had just said. He just couldn't believe it.

****

Ricky walked into his spacious living room, plopped himself on the couch, and turned on his big screen TV with the remote. He was rolling a joint and beginning to settle down for the evening. Ricky was wondering what was keeping Pat so long. They had been doing business for five years and Pat always paid on the same day whenever Ricky fronted him the dope. It wasn't like Pat to be late with the cash. He wasn't worried. Pat had always came through and there could be any number of reasons as to why he was late.

Ricky leaned back on the couch and took a long drag from the joint. This load of Afghani was particularly good. He would be stoned on two hits. The days were getting longer and he was able to see the setting sun outside his living room window.

What Ricky didn't see was the uniformed police in the woods adjacent to his house, or the two cruisers at the end of his driveway. It took Ricky a few moments to realize what was taking place. The pot was having its effect and Ricky saw events in slow motion. Police had knocked and then broken down the front and back doors. He saw cruisers coming down the driveway with flashing strobes. He was taken off the couch, handcuffed and put face down on the floor.

What was happening?

It couldn't be. He couldn't be getting busted. He was too good and he had more than 200 pounds of Afghani in his barn. As he was marched outside and placed in the back seat

60

of a screened cruiser, he still couldn't believe what was happening to him.

It must be the weed. He was hallucinating. That was it. He knew the pot was good, but not that good.

****

Pat, Jim and Joey shared the same cell at the county jail on Valley Street. As the door to the cellblock opened, they looked and saw Ricky Richards being walked towards their cell by a guard. The guard opened the cell door and brusquely pushed Ricky into the cell. All four stood in a circle and looked at each other.

The effects of the pot had worn off long ago on Ricky. He looked at Pat and asked, "What the fuck happened?"

Before Pat said anything Joey spoke up. "We wouldn't be in this mess if Pat didn't sell some cop dude some dope."

"Joey," Pat said getting up, "if you were a light bulb, you'd be about twenty watts," and with that, Pat punched Joey square in the nose.

Chap 2
N17 H21 NO4

Two months later

Jim Morris leaned back in his chair, put his feet on his desk and looked at the sun setting out his window. It was an unusually warm day in early April, and Jim was enjoying the moment. Everyone else in the office had gone home, and he was alone with his thoughts.

Jim had been a State Trooper for fifteen years, and the past year had been the best. A little over a year ago, he was transferred from the Narcotics Investigative Unit of State Police to head up the newly formed Drug Task Force under the auspices of the State Attorney General's office.

The idea of the task force arose as a result of a need to combat the increased drug activity in the state, and to further the political interests of the attorney general. It was rumored that he had his sights on the governor's job and this was an impetus to that ambition. It appeared that in a lot of states, AG stood for aspiring governor.

The task force was comprised of cops from local and state agencies who would be on temporary assignment to the agency ranging from six months to two years. At first, the going was tough. The task force had no equipment and there were inherent problems with the inception of any new agency. However, Jim was an excellent organizer, and though he had no aspirations to political office, an excellent politician.

As a result, within six months, he was able to procure all the latest equipment needed to conduct an effective drug operation. These ranged from high tech night scopes to hidden microphones that could be concealed in a pen. After a year in operation, the agency was a huge success. The cars the agents drove, anything from Camaro's to Cadillac's, were from seizures, and the assets that were confiscated as a result of drug arrests, twice covered their yearly operational budget.

The latest arrest and seizure of assets was by far the best. Wason's bank account was in the six-figure range, and by the time the assistant attorney generals finished with Ricky Richards, they estimated total cash and assets approaching 10 million. All the lawyers had to prove was that an asset was used in the commission of a drug related crime or had been procured by funds gleaned from drug transactions, and it became the property of the state.

Bob Lions and Dirk Garrigan were the two assistant attorney generals assigned to the task force, and by the sixth month of operation, it had become a full time job for both. Jim was happy with them. They were both hardworking and had a good sense of humor. They had to, especially to put up with the agents on the task force.

Jim's thought's then turned to the people of the task force. By the very nature of drug work, most of them were young. Ten of the fifteen agents were under thirty and had less than six years' experience of police work. Jim was the oldest at thirty-nine. What they sometime lacked in experience, they more than more made up for in talent, diligence and dedication to duty.

By far his two most successful were L. John MacLennan and Ray Melena. They had been with the task force from the start. Their recent case, posing as MacCloud and Marino, the two Rhode Island drug dealers, was just another feather in their caps. However, if there were any two people in this world who would give him gray hair, it was these two. In addition to being excellent cops with unbelievable luck, some of their antics bordered on the sophomoric.

The Vaseline on the ladies restroom toilet seat was a big laugh to everyone but Kathy Morse, a cop from Laconia who sat on it. However, she didn't stay mad long, and like most others, had become endeared to them.

MacLennan was a Sergeant from Salem, NH, whose father was a retired Chicago cop. Their careers had a strange parallel. In the sixties, the elder MacLennan was assigned to a special federal task force on organized crime and his feats and methods were somewhat legendary. He had a quote from Al Capone on his wall that read, "You get more accomplished with a kind word and a gun, than just a kind word alone." It was rumored his actions were consistent with the quote, particularly in the years prior to the Miranda decision.

After he retired, he moved his Italian wife and only son to New Hampshire where he had once visited, and fallen in love with the area during one of his cases.

The younger MacLennan was a mystery to Morris. MacLennan had been a cop for eight years and a Detective Sergeant for five of those. Even though he had finished first in the last three tests for lieutenant in his department, he had refused promotion. When asked why, he just shrugged his shoulders and stated that he still liked being a cop on the street with the guys. If he took the promotion, he would have been confined to a desk on the God forsaken midnight shift.

He had his Master's Degree in Business Administration and undergraduate degrees in computer science and behavioral psychology. When asked why he had so many degrees, he would say he wasn't sure what he wanted to be when he grew up. At age thirty-four he still said this.

Prior to becoming a cop, he had been a financial analyst at a well-known company that specialized in making surface to air missiles for the government. He had soon become disenchanted working for a corporate entity, and quit. He then bought a bankrupt flight school and charter business with the money he had made from the stock market. After one year, the bottom line was in the black, and halfway through the next, he sold the business for a one hundred thousand dollar profit. With that money, he re-invested in the stock market and doubled it within a year.

At age twenty-six, relatively financially independent, he joined the police department. The Salem Police Department considered him quite a catch. In addition to his education, he spoke Spanish fluently, partly from four years of college Spanish and partly from dating a Puerto Rican co-ed, held his commercial flight license and was able to fly anything up to and including a DC-3. He was also an accomplished scuba diver and had a second-degree black belt in karate.

When asked why he was a cop, he would give a lopsided smile and just say it was fun and his favorite hobby. Naturally, this drove his Chief bat shit. But as aggravated as his chief would get at MacLennan for his cavalier attitude and usual resentment towards authority, he couldn't help but admire him for his prowess as an investigator.

When the opportunity at joining the task force was presented to MacLennan, he jumped at it, just another adventure for the Tom Sawyer in him. A mystery that Morris had to solve was what MacLennan's first name was. He went by his middle name and the only thing people knew about his first name was that it started with L, one of these days Jim had to find out what the L stood for. Melena was a cop with ten years' experience from Hudson, the last three of those as a detective. He had been in the military, a marine, and after his discharge, married and had two little girls who referred to MacLennan as Uncle Johnny. During his early married years, he had earned his bachelor's degree, and was thinking about law school.

Melena was built like a bull elephant. He was only five foot eight, but was as wide as he was tall with very little fat. He would often get ribbed by the lean MacLennan, but ate his words one day when Melena picked him up and held him against the ceiling.

The two had hit it off from the beginning. The biggest problem that Jim had with Melena and MacLennan was that they would free-lance cases without letting him or their group leader, Scott Nelson, know about it. Jim had constantly stressed to both of them that the essence of drug work was control. If Melena knew MacLennan's first name, he wasn't talking.

During the Wason case, they didn't let him know what they were during until they had already made the pound buy. Jim had chewed them out like he had never done before. However, it was difficult to stay mad for long. A couple of other agents had been working the Ricky Richards case for two months, ever since Jim received a call from Chief Dolan for assistance, and had gotten nowhere. Wason was an immediate in to Richards, and the long shot had paid off.

Jim was now faced with assigning both cowboys to a case that gave them total autonomy. Pat Wason's roommate, whose full name was Jim Apley, was not only willing to turn States evidence on the Wason/Richard's case, but for a suspended jail sentence and entry into the witness protection program, he would give details of his own cocaine operation and set up a five hundred pound buy of cocaine out of the Island of Jamaica destined for New England via Miami.

After checking with the Boston office of the Drug Enforcement Agency, it was learned they had some information on Apley's operation, but not enough to start an active investigation. With Apley about to turn informant, they jumped at it. Instead of handing the entire case over to DEA, it was agreed that it would be a joint operation with MacLennan and Melena doing the undercover, and DEA supplying the support.

The first meeting with DEA was tomorrow in their Boston office.

Knowing MacLennan, he'd probably want to spend half the day at Faneuil Hall watching the girls.

Come to think of it, that wasn't such a bad idea after all.

****

MacLennan went to the refrigerator of his house and grabbed another Bud Light before joining Darcy on the living room couch. It was still relatively early in the evening and they were just settling down to watch a Star Trek re-run where Jean Luc Picard was about to do battle with the Borg.

His relationship with Darcy had progressed further than he had ever anticipated. It had gotten to the point that she was moving in with him next month. This was a first for MacLennan. He had never lived with a girlfriend before and he looked forward to it with an eager trepidation. He had become very attached to Darcy and as he had often said before, why ruin a good relationship by living together, much less marriage. MacLennan figured it had to happen sometime, and seeing they were spending about four or five nights together each week, this seemed like the thing to do.

Tonight was just another fun night of sitting together on the couch and hugging. He could think of worse ways to spend an evening.

MacLennan's thoughts then turned to the next days scheduled events. If all went well with the meeting with DEA, both he and Ray would be on their way to sunny Jamaica. He chuckled at the thought of Ray flying over fifteen hundred miles. He'd probably have to tranquilize him hourly.

"Anything the matter hon? You seem preoccupied," Darcy said.

"No, not at all. Just thinking about an upcoming case."

"Oh, ok." Darcy never pried into his work. She felt that if John wanted to tell her about it he would. But it still didn't stop her from worrying.

"If everything works out, I may be away for a few days to a week."

"I won't say be careful, but you know I'm going to miss you."

"I'm going to miss you too, and don't worry, I'll give careful new meaning."

"Yea right." Darcy said and then good-naturedly jabbed him in the stomach.

John gave her another hug and then let his mind drift off once again. In this operation, he and Ray would be totally on their own without any backup. If the shit hit the fan, it was just them. They had been in tight spots before, but this presented an element of danger not previously encountered.

John had doubts as to whether Jim was going to let them work on this. Both of them had gotten new assholes on the Wason case for not telling Jim what they were doing. If there was one thing Jim hated, it was a case without close control, and buying a pound of pot without any backup was not Jim's idea of control. However, the very next day Jim wrote commendations to their departments on their excellent work in apprehending Wason and Richards. Without a doubt, Jim was the best boss he ever worked for. John's thoughts were interrupted by Darcy tickling him in a couple of his sensitive spots.

"What do you think you're doing?" he asked.

"Oh I'm sorry, my hands slipped," Darcy said in a not so convincing voice.

"You're asking for it." John said.

"I thought you'd never notice."

****

The next day saw Ray and John traveling southbound on route 93 into Boston. They were in John's personal car that he had just put on the road after restoring it over the winter. It was a 1961 red MGA roadster that John had picked up the previous year while vacationing in Fort Lauderdale. He had found it while out jogging one morning. It was nestled under a Cyprus tree without any top, floorboards or paint to speak of.

John had always like British Leyland products, and after buying the car for one thousand dollars drove it the seventeen hundred miles back to New Hampshire, four days and three breakdowns later.

The car was now in showroom condition and John was determined to drive it at every opportunity.

It was a brisk spring morning in New England with the temperature hovering slightly over fifty, but that didn't deter MacLennan from driving with the top down.

"We would have been a lot more comfortable in your task force Camaro," Ray said as he hunched down and pulled his collar up from the MG's passenger's seat.

"Ray, this car's a classic. Have you noticed all the looks we've been getting?"

"Yea, I have, and they're probably saying look at the two classic jerks with the top down freezing their asses off."

"It's supposed to get warmer," John said. "The weatherman said it should get up into the low seventies."

"Oh yea, when, next month."

It was nine-thirty and they were supposed to meet Jim and Scott at DEA headquarters in the JFK building located in Government Square at ten. Rush hour traffic had pretty much abated as they cruised past the Sullivan square exit and John figured they would be on time for a change. After the last ass chewing, he didn't want to take any chances. If you're walking on eggs, it's best not to hop.

John turned onto Storrow drive, took the Government square exit onto Cambridge Street and pulled into the forty dollar a day public parking garage two blocks away from the JFK building.

As John and Ray walked into the fourth floor reception area for DEA, they were greeted by Jim and Scott.

"On time? This is a first." Jim said kiddingly.

"That's not true Jim, we were on time for lunch two months ago," Ray said.

"Actually, I think it was three months ago," John added.

"Will you guys please be serious for once," Scott said.

Ray and John looked at each other. Scott was their group leader who was on loan to the task force from NH State Police. At six foot three, he was very regimented, and a perfectionist who paid close attention to every detail. John and Ray, like most cops, hated paperwork and attention to minutiae. MacLennan felt that was why God invented secretaries. However, Scott kept them honest.

Any further discussion was cut short by the entry into the room by Bill Waite, the special agent in charge of the Boston office.

"Hi Jim. Good to see you again," Bill said.

Introductions were made by Jim to the other task force members before the agent in charge ushered them into his office.

In Waite's office were two other DEA agents, Kevin Finn and Steve Novel who were introduced.

As Bill sat behind his desk, his admin came in with a tray of coffee, placed it on the table and left the room.

Once everyone was settled, Bill began the meeting.

"Jim the information that you passed on to us from Jim Apley is good. If we follow through on this, and it works, we're going to put some people away. Apley wants to work off his charge. He's told us everything about his operation and he's willing to arrange a delivery to New Hampshire. He's currently on bail with house arrest and a bracelet."

Bill paused before continuing and took a sip of his coffee.

"Apley first went to Jim, and when Jim realized the scope of the operation, he passed it on to us. The operation involves boats, planes and knowledge of the island of Jamaica. Jim tells me that MacLennan fits the bill.

John, having been to Jamaica once on a scuba diving vacation, nodded his head and said nothing as Bill continued.

"Apley gets the cocaine from Jamaica by boat in two thousand pound lots. As the boat makes it way up the Atlantic, about fifty miles offshore, he arranges to have planes fly over the boats and run interference looking for Coast Guard cutters. If the pilot sees any coasties, he contacts the boat captain and vectors him away from the cutter."

"If Apley does that much weight, what was he doing living with Wason in that shit hole?" Nelson asked.

"It's not really his cocaine," Jim said. "He's the middle man who arranges the meet with his people in Jamaica, hires the boat and plane, and arranges the drop offs up the coast. For his troubles, he gets a cut from everyone. For making all the arrangements on a trip up the coast, he clears about thirty thousand easily."

"Not bad," Ray said. "He never touches the dope, makes a few telephone calls and bang."

"Not only that, but it would be difficult to arrest him, let alone prosecute him."

"What we hope will happen is that Apley will introduce Ray and John to his Jamaican connection as the pilots who will do the flyovers," Bill said.

Ray sat up in his seat and interrupted Bill.

Flyovers? As in over the water?"

"I think that's what he means Ray," John said with a smirk. "But not to worry Ray, we'll be flying a plane with two engines."

"Great, twice the chance of something going wrong."

Ray then settled in his seat and started to brood.

"After the meet, you get half your cut, and the rest after the last delivery, which we hope will be in the Piscataqua River either in Portsmouth, or across the way in Kittery Maine. In between Jamaica and New Hampshire, after every flyover, the Coast Guard and custom agents will be following the boats that meet the mother ship back to their docks where DEA will be waiting to make the arrests. If all goes according to plan, we'll be able to hit some pretty major drug dealers all the way from Florida to Maine."

"Why do they make their primary delivery in Maine," Ray asked.

"Outside of Florida," Bill answered, "there are more drugs smuggled in through the Maine coast than anywhere else on the Atlantic seaboard."

"The Maine coastline is nothing but nooks, crannies, outlets and islands. If you were to stretch the coast into a straight line, it would be more than two thousand miles long. The smugglers will travel forty to fifty miles off the coast, as if they're fishing, and once they reach Maine, in they come. The coast Guard gets a few, but that's about it. Impossible for a total interdiction effort. If we interdict 5 to 15 percent, we're happy."

Ray shook his head and then asked, "What about the Piscataqua?"

"The Piscataqua River is a pretty deep water port that separates Kittery, Maine and Portsmouth, New Hampshire. Out by the Portsmouth Navy Yard, which incidentally is in Maine not New Hampshire, it gets as deep as 90 feet. That's why they're able to work on so many nuclear powered subs, and given that, they have pretty good security. Between the Navy yard and the Coast Guard station, which is the old revolutionary war Fort Constitution, the coasties have constant patrols. Hell, even Portsmouth and Kittery Police departments have launches that patrol the river. While I'm sure there's some smuggling going on, I don't think it's to any great degree."

"At this stage, we think that the big delivery will be in the Saco River, about twenty miles north of the Piscataqua," Bill said.

"If Apley is the go between, and he does all the organizing, why do the people in Jamaica want to meet a pilot?" John asked.

"I'm going to let Steve answer that," Bill said. "He's the one who's been to Jamaica and is more or less the expert."

Steve Novel was a lean six foot two blond haired agent with a deep tan. He would have looked more at home with a surfboard on Malibu beach than in DEA where he had been for the past five years. He had come to DEA from the army where he was a Captain in the Army Rangers.

Steve sat back in his chair and began to speak. "I've spent the better part of the past year in Jamaica. You'll be dealing with Rastafarians who are members of the Jamaican posses, and these guys are fucking nuts. They don't like to lose their dope and they want to meet everyone who's going to be involved in the operation. A lot of people don't like dealing with them and as a result, Apley hires pretty much the same people every trip."

"What happens if they don't like you or they think you're a cop?" Ray asked.

Steve paused for a moment and looked at the people in the room.

"We don't know. We just don't hear from them again. On top of that, we don't know how they make their decisions or whether they're going to deal with you or not. Sometime last summer, we lost two informants who we thought were in to them."

"Explain lost," Ray said.

"Probably dead. Sacrificed at one of their rituals. We don't know for sure. But the wife, errr widow of one, received some blood stained chicken feathers on her doorstep two days later. That's one of the voodoo signs that signifies death to non-believers."

"Mac, I think I prefer flying," Ray said.

"Aren't Jamaican posses just into pot? What are they doing with coke?" MacLennan asked.

"You're right," Steve answered. "That is until just recently. Someone has put together an operation where the cocaine paste is flown to Jamaica from Bolivia. There's a lab somewhere in the mountainous region by Kingston where it's processed into cocaine. From there, it's shipped to the states. We're pretty sure that someone is one Dr Julian Katanga, a local government official, and Major Manuel Estaben, one of ex-General Noriega's henchmen."

"General Norriega? As in Panamanian General Norriega?" Ray asked.

"The one and same. It seems that after the US of A invaded Panama and put the not so good general out of business, there was a void in the cocaine highway that had to be filled. We're not quite sure how the alliance came about between the two, but suffice to say it happened, and compared to the Rasta's, Noriega's a Boy Scout. The Rasta's are still potheads, especially in their voodoo ceremonies, and though they deal big time in cocaine, they don't touch the stuff. That's usually the difference between a successful dealer and an easy arrest.

"How'd Apley get involved with these guys?"

"It seems that our boy Apley has been involved since a vacation he took in Jamaica about five years ago. He went down there to get some pot. After he bought three pounds, he taped then to his legs with plumber's tape, the stupid bastard, he didn't know it was metallic. He set off the metal detector at the airport and got arrested. After he spent two weeks in prison, Wason bailed him out, but not before Apley was able to make a couple of friends and contacts in jail. He started off in marijuana and then graduated to cocaine. His bank account was bigger than Wason's, and like Wason's, it now belongs to the state."

"What's Apley getting out of this and how's he going to set it up?" Jim asked.

"Apley agreed to one year in jail and a nine year suspended sentence. He still forfeits his bank account, but gets to keep his personal assets which aren't that much. As for how he's going to organize everything, it'll all be done from this office where we'll be taping it. That's not unusual for Apley because that's how he usually conducts business. This way, we're able to control all the facets of the operation. The only sticky area is setting up the initial meet between John, Ray and the Rasta's. That is, if you guys are going to do it."

"Go ahead, I'm all ears," Ray said.

Steve continued. "The first meet for you guys will be down here in Boston. Apley will be with you and he'll introduce you to his connection. The connections usually a local guy and rarely the same person twice. Apley says these meets are generally quick. Price is discussed and the connection gives you the name of an airport to fly to in Jamaica and a contact. You fly down there and convince the Rasta's you're a smuggler."

"And if we don't?" John asked.

"Hopefully, we'll be able to cover you and get you out. It's a loose operation and we're working in a foreign country. There's a lot of risk and we're not sure who we can or can't trust in the Jamaican government. But the moment it gets too hairy, it's your asses, pull out at any time."

"I don't like it," Scott said.

Jim spoke up also. "Neither do I. You weren't able to protect your two informants that got whacked, what makes you think you can protect John and Ray any better?"

All three DEA agents looked at each other and said nothing.

Bill then spoke up. "You're right. No question there's a good element of danger, and I wouldn't blame anyone for not taking the assignment. But it was your case initially and you guys would be involved one way or the other. Besides, MacLennan with his flying ability and knowledge of Jamaica fits the bill, not to mention that we wouldn't be here to begin with if it wasn't for him and Ray."

"Bill, I don't know," Jim said. "There's too much risk and not enough control and coverage for these guys if the shit hits the fan. I can't authorize it."

"Wait a minute," MacLennan said. "Isn't anyone going to bother to ask Ray or me? It's our asses."

"There's no discussion here," Scott said. "We don't operate in that fashion and there's too much risk."

"Scott, if I was afraid of taking risks, I'd quit being a cop and get a job as a librarian. The moment we stop taking assignments because there's too much risk, we might as well become drug dealers ourselves and the bad guys win. If I don't get the OK on this, I'll quit the task force and get the green light from my department."

"Don't threaten me, you can do that any time you want," Scott said.

"That's enough you two," Jim intervened. "We're here to talk and work out a plan." Jim paused for a moment while looking at Scott and John. When nothing was said, Jim turned towards Bill and continued.

"Let's do this if you don't mind. Have Apley start making the phone calls and start the ball in motion. If it looks pretty good, we'll do the meet with the Rastafarians and then we'll re-evaluate. In particular, I want to go over the different scenarios that could happen in Jamaica, and if we can't provide the coverage, it's a no go," Jim said the last sentence while looking straight at MacLennan. MacLennan knew enough to keep his mouth shut. He had won a minor victory by getting this far over Nelson's objections and didn't want to push it.

"Alright Bill, what do you have in mind for coverage?" Jim asked.

"We have an office with eight people in Kingston, the capital of Jamaica, that'll be augmented by Novel and Finn once this gets in motion. As far as coverage goes, we can't say for certain, that'll depend on how everything develops. Both Katanga and Estaben are exceptionally careful. They go everywhere with bodyguards and they always carry Radio Frequency detectors. Those nifty little gadgets will detect a body wire pronto, so that's out. The best that we can give you is a loose ground surveillance and we have a pilot in the office who can also give you aerial surveillance. If you go into the mountains, both will be tough.

Jim shook his head. "I don't like it. How about going to and from Jamaica, and when MacLennan, if MacLennan, does the fly overs for the bad guys?"

"That's the easy part," Steve answered. "We'll have one of the Custom department's jets in the air. They use Cessna Citations and they're literally a flying control tower."

"I've heard about those," MacLennan said nodding his head in approval.

"We'll give MacLennan and Ray a certain squawk code on the plane transponder and we'll know where he is at all times. We'll have to clear it with the FAA approach control in whatever area he may be in; but it's nothing we haven't done before. Hell, if your Aztec is quiet enough, Customs has a wire they can put in it that will pick up all cockpit voices with 50 miles."

"That doesn't sound too bad," Jim said. "How about the mother ship that's going to be carrying the dope?"

"That's Kevin's department," Steve said.

Kevin Finn, relatively quiet until now, spoke up. "This is the nice part of the operation. We should have some indication from Apley as to where the pick-ups are going to be and the general location of where the dopers are going to go after the pickup, but he's never really sure. He's dealt with some pretty smart characters, and they constantly change their routine. Sometime before the first pick up, we're going to board the boat and take over."

Who's we?" Jim asked.

"We are going to be an assault group comprised of DEA and customs on one of the Coasties 210 foot cutters. We've all worked together before so it's nothing new. After that, we continue up the coast. We'll know which course to take and where the drop-offs are going to be from Apley. Once the bad guys get their load of coke, they'll also get something added as a nice little bonus."

Finn paused for a second to take a sip of his coffee before he continued.

"Each load will have two homing devices in it. Two, just in case one fails. It's happened before. We'll then follow the bad guys back to their dock where we'll do the take down. That's it in a nutshell. It's a big operation that's a lot more complicated than it sounds.

"I agree. The logistics of coordinating all the different agencies are difficult, but it can be done," Bill said.

"What do you think Jim?"

Jim didn't hesitate. "I like it. Except for the lack of coverage in Jamaica, I like it. The only commitment I can give you now is right up to the meet with the Rasta's. After that, it depends."

"I have no problem with that," Bill said. "In light of the circumstances, I can't say I blame you. John, Ray, do either of you have any questions or anything to add. After all, it's your butts."

John and Ray looked at each other.

"Just one question," John said.

"Where are we having lunch?"

****

"Lunch wasn't such a bad idea after all John," Jim said as he settled back to admire the afternoon lunch crowd at Faneuil Hall. The day had turned pleasantly warm and they had decided to eat at Dick's Last Resort, which was one of the outdoor cafes that dotted that particular area of Boston.

"Ya know," MacLennan said to no one in particular as two girls walked past their table, "miniskirts were a wonderful invention."

"Yea." Ray agreed. "Not to mention yoga pants."

All four task force members plus Steve Novel and Kevin Finn were enjoying the view. Bill was unable to join them due to a working lunch meeting he was already committed too.

"Excuse me, would anyone like dessert?" a waitress asked as she was cleaning up the dishes from the table.

"Please," John said. "I'd like a piece of German chocolate cake and a cup of cappuccino please."

"Anyone else?"

Jim Scott and Steve ordered coffees while Ray and Kevin passed.

"Cappuccino and German Chocolate cake," Ray said questioningly to John.

"Aren't we the internationally acclaimed epicurean?"

"Epicurean, good word Ray. Next week we'll teach you what it means," John answered trading barb for barb with Ray.

"This is one of the few places where you can get homemade German chocolate cake and the cappuccino is almost as good as in the North End."

By the way Mac," Ray said changing the conversation.

"What's that on your t-shirt?"

John was wearing a blue t-shirt with white lettering that read $C_{17}H_{21}NO_4$.

"Some drug guy, it's the chemical formula for cocaine."

"Do you guys think you could be serious for two hours in a row?" Scott said.

"Why?" John said.

Scott just shook his head.

"From what I've heard and seen from your last case," Steve said, "both Ray and John have their share of serious moments."

"Don't tell too many people that," Ray said. "We have our bad reputations to uphold."

The banter paused momentarily as the waitress, delivered the coffees and cake.

"They're not too bad," Jim said in response to Steve's statement. "They just have to learn the meaning of control and maturity."

"Oh no, the M word," Ray said.

"Steve I'd like to re-iterate what I said back in the office," Jim said to the DEA agent. "The scenario sounds good, but I've got to have a long talk with these guys," John said in reference to Ray, John and Scott.

"Not a problem," Steve answered. "I wouldn't be too crazy about doing it myself, but we'll try to work things out and we'll see if Apley can deliver.

"Hey Steve," John said with a smile. "Do you like history?"

"It's Ok, why?"

"Because if we take this case, we'll make it"

Everyone but Scott laughed.

"MacLennan, you have an awfully high opinion of yourself."

"Thanks Scott, I've always felt it was a prerequisite for being a cop."

Once again Scott just shook his head.

The coffees were soon finished and Steve paid for the bill.

"Well Mac, at least it'll be a lot warmer in your MG than it was coming down."

"What I'd tell ya, trust me."

"Yea right."

****

Ray was right. The ride back to Concord NH was a lot warmer, but John seemed to get an occasional chill as he thought about the case and going to Jamaica. Both partners were surprisingly quiet for most of the trip.

"As John took the exit off of route 93 in Concord he said to Ray, "You know, we really don't need two people on this case."

"What're saying Mac?"

"What I'm saying is one way or the other, I'm on this case and it'll probably be the most dangerous undercover we'll be on. "I don't have a wife and two kids to worry about Ray. Your commitment to them is a hell of a lot greater than to me or the task force."

"Sorry Mac, but someone needs to look after your bony ass."

Chap 3
Be Good to Me

"Tracy, it's me Steve. Is Dennis there?"

"Yea, he's right here what's the matter with your voice?"

"Give me the fucking phone," Dennis said, as he grabbed the phone from Tracy's hand.

"This better be fucking good to call me at three in the morning."

"Dennis it is. I'm in the Charles Street jail."

"They got me with an eight-ball of coke and my bail is a grand"

"How the Christ did that happen? No wait don't tell me now. Tell me when I get you, right before I wring your God dam neck, and what the fuck is with your voice. "

Before the voice at the other end could form a reply, Dennis Green slammed the phone back on its cradle.

"What's the matter Dennis"?

"Don't you have fucking ears? That stupid bastard Morency got himself arrested and I have to travel all the way from Hampton, New Hampshire to Boston, Mass to get him out."

Tracy curled up in a little ball on the bed. "Dennis why can't you be good to me."

"Be good to you, look at this fucking house, the Porsche in the garage and the fucking boat, not to mention your dress of the week club. I don't want to hear it. Go down and make me some coffee while I get dressed."

Tracy looked down at her hands as if there would be some condolence. But none came. However the tears did.

"Dennis, I think I want to leave you." Tracy said still looking down at her hands.

She never knew what hit her. She never saw the look of anger on Dennis' face or the punch to the eye that knocked her off the bed. Before Tracy realized what was happening he was on her and had her by the throat, lifted her off the floor and slammed her against the bedroom wall.

"No one, but no one ever leaves Dennis Green. When you leave, it'll be when I throw you the fuck out. You ever think that again and I'll cut off a fucking finger."

Tracy looked at Dennis, too terrified to speak.

"You know I'll damn well do it. Forget the coffee, it sucks anyway."

Dennis finished tucking in his shirt, and went to the closet to get a jacket. He looked at his blue jacket and decided there was no need for it. It was bulletproof and he hardly ever wore it. But when he did, the peace of mind it gave him was well worth the amount of money he paid for it. It would stop a .44 magnum at close distance and was better than most of the vests the cops wore. And unlike their vests, his kevlar jacket protected his whole upper body.

Instead he opted for a LL Bean light spring jacket.

As he went out the front door he decided that he would take the Cadillac instead of the Porsche or the Chevy Blazer.

As he pulled out of the driveway, he admired the twelve-foot high fence he had just built around his ten-room house. He couldn't believe that fucking Tracy. She was living like a queen and she gave him that "I want to leave you shit." She'd leave all right, in a pine-fucking box.

Dennis turned right onto Route 101 and accelerated Eastbound towards 95. At this time of night he figured he could make Boston in about one-half hour. He'd be breaking some speed limits, but fuck the cops. He never met one he couldn't buy and sell.

As he went south on ninety-five, he turned off at the route 110 exit in Salisbury and went through the drive-up at the Dunkin Donuts.

As expected, he saw a couple of cops at the counter screwing off and sipping their coffee.

When Dennis pulled out of the lot he was thinking about squealing the tires and having some fun with the cops, but at this hour of the morning, he wasn't quite up to it. Besides, he still had Morency's neck to wring after he bailed the dumb shit out of jail.

****

Dennis made pretty good time getting to Boston. He kept the Cady at a steady ninety and there wasn't a cop on the road. "If they're not at the coffee shop, then probably cooped up somewhere sleeping," Dennis thought.

As he crossed the Tobin Bridge, there was no traffic. At this hour, there shouldn't be. Dawn was just beginning to show her tell-tale signs at the far end of Boston Harbor.

After the toll at the end of the Bridge, Green went through the Callahan Tunnel and turned onto the Southeast Expressway. At the end of the Expressway, he took the Storrow Drive Exit and then got off at the Beacon St exit.

Like everyone else, it took Dennis awhile to learn his way around Bean town. Unlike the streets of most cities that were laid out in a coherent grid pattern, Boston streets had no rhyme or reason to them. It was if someone was playing a game of pick-up sticks, and designed the city streets after the sticks were randomly thrown on the ground.

At the end of the exit, Green took a right onto Beacon Street and then took his third left onto Charles St. Halfway up the street on his right was the Charles Street Jail. At this hour of the morning, Green had no problem finding a parking space and parked half-a-block away. He was tempted to double-park behind one of the cruisers in front of the station, but figured some asshole would probably tow his car.

Even though it was May, it was still chilly in Boston at this hour of the morning and Green buttoned his coat as he walked the distance to the police station. Maybe it was the cold, or the hour of the morning, but the usually observant Green failed to notice the two men watching him from the red pickup truck across the street.

He opened the front door of the jail and spoke to the dispatcher behind the bulletproof window. Long gone were the days of the precent Sergeant sitting behind his oak desk.

"Can I help you?" The pretty female dispatcher asked as she got up from her chair.

"Yea," Green answered impatiently. "I'm here to bail out Steve Morency."

The dispatcher picked up a clipboard from her desk and scanned the names.

"I'm sorry, we don't have any Steve Morency locked up."

"What do ya mean you don't have any God Dam Steve Morency locked up? He just called me to bail him the fuck out." Green yelled at the dispatcher.

There were two cops in the back room that walked into the dispatch center when they heard the tone of Green's voice.

"You got a problem buddy. You don't watch your language and you're gonna find yourself on the wrong side of a jail cell door." The larger of the two said.

Green felt that he could take both of them and the girl to boot, but wasn't in the mood. He went on as if the cops weren't there, but in a different tone of voice.

Both cops remained in the room as if daring Green to say anything out of line.

"He called me and said he was arrested in Boston, could he be anywhere else?"

"Let me check." The dispatcher said as she went to the computer terminal behind her desk.

After a few minutes, she looked up and said to Green, "no Steve Morency anywhere, not tonight or anytime this week."

"Thanks for nothing." Green said and as he walked out of the station as he slammed the door behind him.

Green was fuming as he walked back to his car. If this was Morency's idea of a joke he was going to beat him within an inch of his life.

The red pickup that was parked down the street was still there, but the two men who were sitting in it weren't. As Green was walking to his car, they walked towards Green from the opposite direction.

Green noticed them walking in his direction but paid them no heed.

"Hello Dennis, hope you got a good night's sleep?" The larger of the two asked.

"What the fuck!" Dennis was taken by surprise, and only then took a good look at the two men who confronted him.

Green was beginning to think more clearly. He recognized the voice of the man who spoke to him. It was the same voice that had called him claiming to be Morency. No wonder why it had sounded strange to him. Green then looked at the other man and was beginning to realize the seriousness of his situation. Though he wasn't as large as the other, Green was able to clearly see the two-and-a-half inch .357 pointed at his midsection.

Green then looked at the man behind the rock steady hand. He was a small man, almost slight. He was balding and in his late fifties. The raincoat he wore would be something given to him by the Salvation Army. He was anything but imposing, even while holding a gun in his hand.

"What's the matter Dennis?" The small man with the gun said. His voice matched his statute. Very soft and high. Don't you recognize me? That really hurts not recognizing an old friend Dennis."

It took Green a couple of seconds before he was able to recognize Vinnie Muzo, the most feared hit man of the Boston Mob. It was rumored that Muzo got paid fifty thousand dollars per contract and over the years had killed more than twenty people. His appearance worked much to his advantage. Muzo was more likely to be mistaken for a diminutive accountant than the most feared man in the Boston underworld.

"I remember you Muzo. It hasn't been that long. What the fuck is going on?" Much to Green's credit, he was still the tough guy, when most other men would have been begging for their lives.

"You should have made your peace and payments to Raymond," Muzo said. Muzo never used last names. Raymond was the local Mafia Godfather of the Boston and New England area.

"You used Raymond's docks and his airfields and you didn't give him his share." Muzo went on, "Very poor business Dennis. As to what's going on, we're going for a little ride." Muzo then motioned to Green's car with his hand that wasn't holding the gun.

"Get in." He said.

Green began to walk over to the driver's side door.

"No Dennis." Muzo said. Get in through the passenger's side door and slide over."

Green did as he was ordered, and once he was settled behind the steering wheel, Muzo got in behind him and cradled the gun in his right hand, still pointed at Green, but far enough away that he would be able to shoot him three times over if he should be dumb enough to try anything.

"Ok Dennis, get back onto the expressway and go through the Callahan tunnel back onto route 1."

"How 'bout after that?" Dennis asked.

Muzo just smiled and said nothing.

Dennis' mind was racing a-mile-a-minute as he pulled onto the street. Instead of getting back onto Storrow Drive, Dennis drove cross-town through the financial district and picked up the Callahan Tunnel outbound to the Tobin Bridge and route 95. During this time, Green noticed the red pickup following his car.

As Green went passed the Bridge and onto route 95, he glanced in his mirror and began to accelerate.

For the first time since they got into the car, Muzo spoke.

"Slow down Dennis. Keep it pegged right at fifty-five. You won't lose our friend behind us and I know you certainly wouldn't want any cop to stop us."

Dennis slowed to fifty-five without saying anything. He knew this was going to be a hit, but he wasn't going easy. Muzo liked to dispose of his victims in the water after shooting them. That was his trademark. A bloated, floating corpse with one bullet hole between the eyes.

Route 95 paralleled seacoast communities and they could be getting off the highway at any time. He had to do something soon and his best bet was to try something on the highway. He regretted rushing and not wearing his bulletproof jacket, that fucking Tracy. If she didn't get him so worked up he would have worn it. She was going to get a beating when he got home.

"Pull off onto route 1 northbound." Muzo said interrupting his thoughts.

As Dennis turned right onto the exit, he glanced into his rear view mirror and noticed the pickup still behind him on the exit. That was going to be another worry.

Time was running out for Dennis. He weighed his options and decided that he would drive off the road and go for Muzo. Probably his eyes, his gun was too well protected in his right hand. Muzo was no fool.

Another couple of miles and Green saw the sign welcoming you to Ipswich. Green then saw his opening. He couldn't believe his good luck.

With one swift move he accelerated and drove off the road into the side of the parked police cruiser. Green heard a shot ring out as he braced himself before smashing into the Ipswich Mass Police Cruiser.

****

Sergeant Marchand was on his fourth cup of coffee for the night and at five AM, his shift was only half over. He hated the graveyard shift, but it came with the stripes he had just got. If he was lucky, he'd only be on the shift for a year or two before some other poor schmuck got his stripes and would take his place. Besides, not a damn thing ever happened on the shift. He was bored to tears when he heard the horn and saw the brown Cady coming right at his cruiser.

****

Muzo was taken by surprise and instinctively threw up his hands as Green's car struck the Ipswich cruiser. The impact caused Muzo to hit the windshield with his head, stunning him and causing him to drop his gun on the floor by his feet. Green, who was expecting the crash, braced himself before hitting the Ipswich cruiser. Green hit the cruiser at an angle so the air bags wouldn't go off. He noticed that Muzo wasn't wearing his seatbelt and when he hit his head on the windshield, it was the effect Green was hoping. Green picked up Muzo's gun and pressed it against his neck. As Muzo came around he felt the cold, hard steel of the gun and heard Green's voice, the last voice he would ever hear. "Fuck you Muzo."

Green fired twice and was splattered by blood as Muzo slumped over on the dashboard, blood pumping out from his fatal wound.

Green then pointed the gun at Sergeant Marchand thinking he would have to shoot him and then report his car stolen. He then saw Marchand face down on the ground by the cruiser and thought of another plan.

Green took his pocketknife and stabbed himself superficially in his leg. He then placed the knife in Muzo's

hand. In a few moments, Green saw Marchand start to get up.
Green then slumped over Muzo and waited.

****

Marchand didn't have time to think, just react. He opened
his door and dove out just as Green's Cady struck his cruiser.
On impact, Marchand was in mid-air and was struck in the
forehead by the doorjamb. He fell to the ground in a state of
semi-consciousness.

Marchand didn't go out totally, but for a period of time he
saw everything through a gray haze. He heard two pops and
thought that it was too early for the Fourth of July celebration.
The haze started to clear, but it was still gray. Of course it
would be gray, you dumb shit Marchand thought to himself, it
was dawn. Marchand then saw his cruiser and the Cadillac
that hit him.

"Forty-five to headquarters, start two units and an
ambulance to just north of exit 54, northbound on route 1,
someone went off the road and hit my cruiser.

"Roger sarge, unit's enroute."

As Marchand walked towards the Cadillac, he began to
think of the paperwork ahead of him. He'd be lucky if he
were done by noontime.

As he approached the car, he saw two slumped forms.
Thinking that they would be suffering from possible
concussions and a broken bone or two, he called for a second
ambulance.

When he got closer, Green started to stir.

"Help. I've been stabbed."

Marchand then saw Muzo with his neck half blown away
and blood pouring down Green's leg.

"Headquarters, holy shit, there's been a shooting, contact detectives, the chief and State Police."

Not waiting for a reply, Marchand grabbed the gun he saw on the car floor and threw it away from the car. He then began putting pressure on Green's wound. It was obvious that Muzo was beyond help.

"I hate this fucking shift." Marchand said aloud to no one in particular.

****

Sergeant Marchand was just beginning his paperwork at eight that morning when Dennis Green was on his way home after his attorney satisfied one of the assistant district attorney's that Green killed Muzo in self-defense.

Green had called the real Steve Morency who had picked him up at the Ipswich police station and was now driving him home. During the first part of the trip, Green told Morency what had happened.

"Dennis, I swear to you I had nothing to do with this," Steve said as they were driving northbound on route 95 back to Dennis' house.

"I believe you, because if I didn't, you'd be dead already Steve."

Morency was relieved and said nothing for a few minutes while he kept driving to Green's house. He knew that Dennis was bad, but killing one of mob's best hit man was going to give Green a reputation that would make no one want to screw with him.

"What are you gonna do Dennis? Do you think they'll try again?"

"I don't think so, but if they do I'm going to fuck with them. I'm going to make a phone call with the message 'to live and let live'. If they go for it fine, if not, I think another phone call to our friends the Rasta's will straighten things out."

"Yea those guys are crazy motherfuckers."

Dennis just sat back and smiled. He knew the mob had enough problems and one of the last things they wanted was to play fuck-fuck with his Jamaican friends. He knew the Jamaicans would just as soon slit your throat then look at you, but as long as he kept his end of the deal, which was setting up the initial deal for the Rasta' and watching the New England end, the money kept flowing.

To date everything went smoothly with them. If they came after him, it might be a little different than with the mob, but he knew he could handle himself.

"Dennis, what do you think of this upcoming deal that Apley has goin'?" Steve asked as he interrupted Green's thoughts.

"I don't like it. I don't like dealing with people I don't know and that fucking Apley can be a weasel."

"Yea but this new guy he's got is supposed to be a real high roller."

"Morency, for once in your life, use your fucking head, that's just it, a new guy. We haven't dealt with this fucker before and I don't like dealing with people I don't know. I don't know why I even agreed to meet with him in the first place."

Dennis knew why, the money. From what Apley had told him, this promised to be his biggest deal, and this new guy was supposed to have a couple of hooks into the Coast Guard. But that remained to be seen. Anyway, he wasn't going to tell Morency anything more than he needed to know.

Morency wanted to remind Green that Apley had dealt with him before and everything went fine, but he knew when not to press his luck with Dennis, and this was one of those times. The meet was scheduled for next week and he would know by then. In the meantime, it was healthier to shut his mouth and let Dennis call the shots.

Chap 4
Oh God

John grabbed a can of Bud as he settled down on the couch to watch an old James Bond re-run. Darcy was out shopping with some friends and John decided to stay home with the new husky puppy he had given Darcy for her birthday. John was never really fond of animals, but he had taken an immediate liking to the brown and white husky.

He turned on the tube and switched to a channel that was playing a Bond film just as James Bond was preparing to do battle with Spectre. He felt that watching James Bond was a mandatory training film for a cop. John's thoughts then wandered to the meeting earlier in the day with DEA.

He wasn't sure whether the case would materialize or not, but if it did, he was looking forward to going back to Jamaica. He had been there three years ago on vacation with an old girlfriend, and ever since they left, he wanted to return.

His thoughts then turned to Jamaica.

Jamaica was the largest English speaking country in the Caribbean. It was discovered by Columbus on his second trip to the new world in 1494, while on a mission to find gold and a shorter route to the West Indies. John remembered reading that the name was derived from the aboriginal Indian word 'Xaymaca' meaning 'land of wood and water'. With all the forests, streams, springs and beaches, the country was aptly named.

The French plundered Jamaica in the early sixteenth century prior to English colonization in 1661. The country soon became a haven for pirates and English privateers. Port Royal in Jamaica was billed as the wickedest city on earth before it was swallowed by the ocean during the earthquake of 1692. John remembered diving on some old wrecks outside the harbor from that era.

During the eighteenth century, over 600,000 slaves were brought to Jamaica from Africa. This enhanced the slave trade to America in addition to the island sugar trade. A band of fierce runaway slaves known as the Maroons, started communities in the mountains and fought the British until the slaves were emancipated in 1838. These were the first Rastafarians. Soon afterwards, they began practicing voodoo, which had its roots in the neighboring island of Haiti, and quickly spread to other Caribbean islands.

When John had been to Jamaica, he and his old girlfriend had attended some voodoo ceremonies put on as entertainment for the guests at the hotel he was staying. Along with the ceremony, the master of ceremonies had given a brief history and explanation of voodooism on Jamaica.

The voodoo cults worship a high god, Bon Dieu, who is considered to be the ancestor of all the worlds dead. Voodoo ceremonies invoke these living dead by the high priest called a Hungan or a high priestess called a mambo.

The spirit then inhabits a body that engages in a ritualistic dance that behaves in a manner characteristic of the possessing spirit. This was shown in the James Bond film, Live and Let Die.

On occasions, the ceremony may end in the sacrifice of the victim from the bite of the poisonous mambo snake. If the victim dies it is a sign that he or she was not a true believer and this was Bon Dieu's way of purging the cult.

John's curiosity had been aroused and during that week he had looked into the legend on the island.

He had gone into one shop, in which the Rastafarian owner was putting dry soap into his hair to hold the telltale dreadnoughts in place, and asked for some souvenirs. The old shopkeeper had shown him everything ranging from voodoo dolls to tarot cards. As John thought of that, he had regretted not buying the doll, he could have used it on one or two people he knew; maybe next time.

****

Jim and Scott were having Pizza and beer that night at a local Pizza Hut in Concord, discussing what had taken place during the day.

"Scott, you still don't know MacLennan do you?" Jim said. The quickest way to get him to do something, is to tell him he can't do it, and he does have a point when he said we have to take some risks."

"I know Jim, but Jamaica is a little out of our realm."

"Ordinarily, I'd say yes, but this is a good continuation of the Richards case, and whether you like to admit it or not, MacLennan is a good person for the job."

Scott said nothing, and finished off a slice of pizza.

"Put your personal feelings aside for a minute," Jim said, "and give me your unbiased decision."

"Jim, even if it wasn't John, I see your point, but it's still too dangerous."

"I'm not disputing there's an element of danger that we haven't seen before. But MacLennan has a point, we're cops not librarians. It comes with the territory." Jim went on. "In addition, after we called Apley this afternoon, we found out that there contact is going to be Dennis Green. Every law enforcement agency in New England has been trying to nail that bastard for the past ten years."

"Yea, I know." Scott said. "MacLennan's luck is amazing. DEA had a tap on his phone three years ago and they still couldn't get him. Word is, he's moving sixty to a hundred pounds of coke per month."

"I know," Jim said. "I read the intelligence report on him and that's probably on the low side. The problem we have is no informant will try and get near him. He's reported to have killed three people."

"What's almost a good idea, is after the meet with Green, we try to nail him for conspiracy."

Jim thought about that for a moment before answering. "We'll at least go through with the meet. You know as well as I do that conspiracy is a bitch to prove, and I doubt that Green will commit himself anyway."

"Jim, for the first time, we're going to be dealing with a Jamaican posse. Those guys are crazy."

Jamaican posses were gangs of Jamaicans who were active in the drug trade. There were about thirty different posses operating in the United States. These posses were named after specific neighborhoods in Jamaica were the members originated, and were scattered throughout the major cities in the United States.

Key members formed the posses based on geographical and political ties in Jamaica. The primary motivation behind their actions is the accumulation of vast amounts of wealth.

Most of the posse members were convicted or illegal aliens fleeing prosecution in Jamaica, and viewed coming to the United States as a way of bettering themselves by joining a criminal enterprise.

The posses thrive on terror, they would kill anyone who crossed them, whether they were rivals in the drug trade or other Jamaicans. It was a successful way of insuring loyalty and silence.

The posse's cocaine distribution is in a continuous piecemeal manner rather than in bulk quantity like their marijuana operation.

This was a result of the higher profit in cocaine and the lowered likelihood of federal drug interdiction.

"What posse did you say Green's tied too?" Jim asked.

"He's with the Spandler posse. That's the posse that was originally from Miami and now has members in five major cities on the Eastern seaboard."

"That's probably why they're making deliveries all the way up the coast." Jim said.

"Exactly, it's consistent with their practice of small deliveries of under a ton, and they're also taking care of all their gang members."

"Any posse members going to be in on this meet with Green?"

"Not sure." Scott answered.

"All we know for sure is Green will be there and Apley will be making the intro to John and Ray."

Jim paused and took a sip of his beer while Scott asked for the check.

After Scott paid the check Jim said, "The meetings slated for next Thursday at a place in Newburyport, place called Jacob Marley's. Do you know anything about that?"

"Yea, it's right by the water front. Nice place. I've eaten there a couple of times. Dress is pretty casual, and surveillance shouldn't be a problem. They have a lounge inside, a big parking lot, and there's a Municipal Lot right by there also."

"That makes life a little easier." Jim said. "If I remember the intelligence report correctly, Green's originally from Newburyport, and Jacob Marley's one of his hang out's. Let's get together with DEA and scope out the place within the next couple of days."

"Sounds good Jim, but I hope I don't have to say I told you so."

"Scott, neither do I, because if you do, it may be at someone's funeral."

****

It was close to midnight and John was driving home after dropping Ray off in Londonderry. The meet with Green had gone surprisingly well not to mention surprisingly short, a total of ten minutes. Green seemed to care less about checking out Ray and himself and appeared more interested in the girl sitting next to him at the bar even though she was with her husband.

That was fine with John; Green had given the term asshole new meaning. He was cocky, loud and obnoxious, and those were his good points. His "checking out" of them consisted of running a RF scanner by them to see if they were wearing a wire. His line of thought being that no police agency would have the balls to have some undercover come up to him without a wire and a crew of plainclothes cops providing cover. After that he told them the name of a landing strip in Jamaica to be at in three days. Greene was getting careless and he was going down. It would only be a matter of time and MacLennan was looking forward to taking him down. He was long overdue.

After the meeting with Green, Ray and John met with Jim at the 99's in Hookset, and after a quick briefing were given the go ahead. So far the going was easy, but the best was yet to come.

Chap 5
Fly By Night

MacLennan was just finishing his inspection as he bent under the port wing of the twin engine Aztec and drained some gasoline from the sump. He was checking it for water or other contaminants. His pre-flight had taken longer than usual. For a two-thousand mile flight this was only one of his preparations. If there was anything wrong or unusual, he wanted to find it now, not over the water, two hundred miles from land. The Aztec had just come out of its annual inspection last week and was running like a top. It should, for the amount of money he spent on the inspection.

MacLennan had previously called flight service. They advised him of good weather with the chance of a weak low causing some rain showers over Virginia, but no serious disturbances. Ray would be happy.

At nine o'clock in the morning, there was still a chill in the air and the sun was burning off the last traces of fog. John decided that he would start the flight under visual flight rules, and if the weather deteriorated, he could always file an instrument flight plan while in the air. It was much simpler flying under visual rules, there was less direction from air traffic controllers, and the flights were usually quicker as a result of being able to take a more direct route.

John saw Ray coming out of the terminal building and walk towards him. He was only carrying a duffel bag and his jacket. Like John, he was traveling light.

"Ya know Ray it's still not too late to cancel."

"John, enough," Ray answered. "We've been through this.

"In that case, let's go."

Without anything else said, Ray loaded his gear in the back seat of the plane, climbed into the right hand seat, strapped himself in, and once again grabbed the arms of the chair as if the wings staying on the plane depended on it.

John was getting use to Ray's pre-takeoff ritual. Takeoffs and landings were the worst for him. Once the plane leveled out, his heartbeat usually dropped to a mere one-hundred beats per minute.

He was getting better.

John began taxiing to runway two-three after receiving clearance from ground control.

"Flight service says we're in for some pretty good weather Ray, it shouldn't be too bad."

Ray cast a quick sidelong glance at John. "Don't you mean flight circus? The last time they told us we were in for good weather, we flew through a blizzard, I can hardly wait this time."

John chuckled to himself as he reached the run-up area of runway two-three.

As he ran up the engines of the Aztec and cycled the props, he eyes glanced over the gauges.

Everything was in the green and sounded good.

"Lawrence Tower, this is Aztec five-four-four-papa-x-ray, ready for takeoff, request straight out departure."

After a brief pause, the control tower answered, "Aztec five-four-four-papa-x-ray, clear for takeoff, straight out departure approved."

As John advanced the throttles to full, the Aztec surged ahead quickly gathering speed. At 90 MPH, John eased back on the yoke and eased the Aztec in the air. This was the point that Ray screwed his eyes shut. A quick look at Ray confirmed this. As John flipped the lever to raise the landing gear, the Aztec gained even more speed. By the time they were five hundred feet above the ground, the Aztec had settled into a fifteen hundred foot a minute, 140 MPH climb.

John continued his climb to the VFR altitude of nine-thousand-five hundred feet after contacting Boston approach and receiving permission to fly through their airspace.

Ray open his eyes as they were passing through five-thousand feet just as John was turning on the Aztec heater.

"Why's it so cold up here?" Ray asked.

"Look who's back amongst the living." John said

Ray ignored the remark as John went on. "The temperature drops about three degrees every thousand feet we climb. At the altitude we'll be leveling off at, it'll be around freezing."

By the time John leveled off at ninety-five hundred feet, Ray had relaxed his death grip on the arm rests of the chair and even began to look out the window.

"Are we there yet?" Ray asked, and as an afterthought, "Where's there?"

John adjusted the air to fuel mixture and eased the throttles back before answering. "Well Ray, we're almost to Worcester, our first stop is going to be Kitty Hawk North Carolina."

"Kitty hawk? Isn't that where..."

"Yup, where flying all began with the Wright brothers." John said with a laugh.

"Why Kitty Hawk?"

"Couple of reasons." John answered.

"It's about halfway to Boca Raton where we're going to spend the night before leaving for Jamaica tomorrow. On top of that, both Kitty hawk and Boca Raton are uncontrolled, no control tower, so it's a lot easier getting in and out, and I've got friends in both places."

"We're crusin' at about 200 MPH, plus we've got a slight tail wind," John was saying as he glanced at his GPS," which gives us a ground speed off about 220. We should be there in about three hours."

"I have to go to the bathroom, can we land now?"

"Nice try Ray, but you'll just have to hold it."

"Hold this," Ray answered and then went back to his brooding.

John dialed in the Hyannis VOR, turned on the autopilot, and settled back to enjoy the flight. They were flying above a very scattered layer of clouds, and at that altitude, visibility was about sixty miles. There was no turbulence, and they were making good time.

John's flight plan would take them across Long Island, over JFK airport, to the Jersey coast.
At ninety-five-hundred feet they would be flying over JFK's airspace and John wouldn't have to worry about putting up with air traffic control.

As they crossed over JFK, John was able to get a good view of Manhattan and the Hudson River. John remembered talking to a New York cop who was also a scuba diver for NYPD. He was telling John about diving in the Hudson river for stolen cars and how it was a requirement that he get both a tetanus and gamma goblin shot to prevent against hepatitis and other associated diseases. New York was only starting to clean up the river and harbor. Visibility was up to a foot, and there were now only about three locations now where raw sewage was dumped into the Hudson.

The trip down the Jersey and Delaware coasts were uneventful. Ray had long since fallen asleep and John was double checking his charts in order to give Dulles and Washington international airports wide berths when they started to encounter some light turbulence. The weather was starting to get more overcast when John decided to contact flight service. He tuned the dial to 122.2 and asked for a weather update.

As he was doing this, Ray started to stir and woke up with start. "For a second there, I didn't know where I was." Ray said as he shook the cobwebs out.

"So what else is new?" John answered and then started laughing to himself.

"What's so funny?" Ray asked.

"You just brought back a memory. I remember one winter night when I was on patrol, it was a real quiet slow night when I pulled off the road to relax."

"You relax? Amazing!"

It was John's turn to ignore Ray. "It started to snow and I must have been more tired than I thought, I dozed off. When I woke up, the snow had completely covered the windows and I woke up in total darkness thinking I was dead and buried. Holy shit"

Ray started to laugh softly at first and then more and more loudly.

"It wasn't that funny Ray."

"I know, but it reminded me of the time I had just got on and I was working the midnight shift. It was my first night back and I hadn't gotten much sleep before the shift. I was stopped at a red light when I looked at my watch, it was three AM. The next thing I knew, I was still at the same red light, but it was three-thirty."

"You're telling me, you fell asleep at a red light, with your foot on the brake, for thirty minutes?"

"Yup. Bet you don't know many people who did, or can do, that."

"Only, you Ray, only you."

****

John and Ray were in the Cockpit Cafe at Kitty Hawk airport. Ray had just ordered seconds and John a cup of coffee. They had decided to have lunch at Kitty Hawk after having the Aztec's fuel tank's topped off.

While the partners were waiting for their orders, John was looking out the window at the line of clouds that were approaching from the west.

"Ya know Ray, I think Flight Service was wrong. That front's approaching a lot faster than they expected. Just to be

104

on the safe side, I'm going to file an instrument flight plan to get us to Boca Raton."

"Great, listen Mac, why don't we wait until tomorrow, Jamaica will still be there."

"Ray, where's your sense of adventure?"

"On the ground Mac, on the ground."

John and Ray were twenty minutes into their flight and had leveled off at their assigned altitude of seven thousand feet when they received their first warning of the type of weather they were about to encounter.

"Aztec five-four-four-papa-x-ray, this is Cherry Hill approach, we have a weather update for you."

"Go ahead Cherry Hill." John answered.

"We have a squall line that is materializing in front of you, at your present course and speed, you should be hitting it in about five minutes. Are you experiencing any turbulence?

"Cherry Hill, that's a negative." John answered. "We're currently IMC, but it's as smooth as glass. Can you vector us around it?"

"Negative four-papa-x-ray. It's a forty mile line and right in front of you."

"Roger, Cherry Hill. Request Block altitude."

"You're cleared for block altitude of two-thousand-feet above and below your current altitude"

"Roger Cherry Hill."

As John was talking to approach control he was tightening his seat belt and shoulder harness.

Ray had not quite fallen asleep and was taking in what was happening, but not quite understanding all of the jargon.

"Mac, would you please mind telling me what the fuck is going on? And what's this squall line and block altitude shit? And why are you tightening you're seat belt?"

"Well Ray, the good news is, the Aztec is rated to take what we're about to encounter. The bad news is, hold on to your cookies, we're going for a ride."

"Mac, what's going on?" Ray asked slowly and loudly while annunciating every word.

"Well Ray, you were right about flight service. They were wrong. We have a squall line in front of us. That's a line of thunder storms forty miles long by forty thousand feet high. As the song says, we can't go around it and we can't go over it. We're about to encounter extreme turbulence and air traffic control has approved us for an altitude ranging from five thousand feet to nine thousand feet."

"Mac, you're not kidding are you?"

"Nope."

"What's extreme turbulence?"

"Well Ray, let me put it to you like this. There is mild, moderate and severe turbulence and you hardly ever hear of extreme turbulence. Hardly. The FAA defines extreme turbulence as weather conditions in which the pilot's control of the plane is in question. We should be through it in about five to ten minutes."

"Oh Shiiieeeeeeet!"

Just at that moment, the Aztec climbed eight hundred feet within a matter of seconds. The thunderstorm was in its beginning stages of formation. At this stage, severe updrafts were common. John knew that as he penetrated deeper into the storm, the updrafts would also be accompanied by down drafts. He had been in thunderstorms before and it wasn't pleasant. It took about five to ten minutes to get through the storm, but it was the longest ten minutes of a pilot's life.

The rain then began its statacco machine gun beat on the wings of the Aztec. All view through the forward windows was obliterated by the intensity of the rain. As a result of the static electricity produced by the storm, St Elmo's fire was illuminating the wing tips conjuring eerie images of Dante's inferno.

Another wind gust caught the starboard wing and tipped the Aztec into a momentary sixty-five degree bank before

John was able to right the plane. John was in a continuous struggle against the elements.

He had long ago given up any hope of maintaining a constant altitude. He had throttled the engines back to just above idle and had the Aztec in a nose down attitude. In spite of all this, the Aztec was still climbing as a result of the updrafts.

Just as quickly and unexpectedly as the updrafts began, the Aztec was caught in a down draft.

Within seconds, it felt like a giant hand pushed down and dropped the Aztec from ten-thousand feet to eight-thousand-five-hundred. The force of the down draft caused both John and Ray to hit the roof of the Aztec with their heads.

All hell was breaking loose in the cockpit. Communications were impossible due to the static electricity of the storm and John could only hope that there wasn't another line of storms behind this front. The Aztec was getting buffeted about by the up and down drafts to such an extent, that the wings appeared to be flapping of their own volition like some metallic bird of prey.

John glanced quickly at Ray whose eyes were screwed shut. His huge arms were locked out in front of him against the dashboard.

The Aztec's altitude varied from six-thousand to ten-thousand feet. The down drafts were getting more frequent, and the updrafts were now non-existent. This signified that they were nearing the end of the storm. John was beginning to count his blessings when the planed lurched into a sickening dive.

John cut power and pulled back on the control yoke to no avail. It felt as if a huge anvil was tied to the plane. The Aztec was descending at an alarming rate. Within thirty seconds, they had descended from nine-thousand to five thousand feet, and weren't slowing.

John realized that they were caught in a micro-burst, a powerful down draft of air that has the destructive force of a tornado; 747's were unable to climb against their force.

John then pushed the throttles and propeller pitch to full and had the control yoke pulled back to its stops. The plane began to buffet. The plane was about to stall and go into a spin from which there would be no recovery.

As they descended through three thousand feet, John pushed the nose of the Aztec down in a last desperation move. Instead of fighting against the force of the micro-burst, John was going to try and use it to his advantage and hope to use its force and speed to slingshot him and Ray to safety.

The airspeed was at two-hundred-fifty knots and increasing. They had exceeded the maximum speed rating of the aircraft. John was wondering what was holding the wings in place. At two thousand feet, MacLennan thought it would be now or never and pulled back on the yoke. The features of both John's and Ray's faces were stretched as the G forces increased. John guessed they were pulling four G's. The descent rate slowed. At one-thousand feet John leveled out and eased back on the power settings. As the airspeed decreased to acceptable levels, John began a steady climb back to altitude.

The gamble had worked. They had rode out the micro-burst and were out of the storm. Hard as it was to believe, they were in smooth air and sunshine.

After John contacted air traffic control and advised them of his status, he remembered Ray.
Ray was in a catatonic-like state, with his eyes still shut and his arms still straight in front of him.

"Ray, are you alright?" No answer.

"Ray, say something. Are you ok?"

Very slowly Ray opened his eyes and turned towards John, "There's no place like home."
"There's no place like home."
"There's no place like home."

****

In their hotel room at Boca Raton, John and Ray were getting ready to go out for supper.

John was out of the shower and towel drying his hair, while Ray had just finished talking to his wife and kids while lying on his bed. After the thunderstorm and micro-burst, the rest of the trip was uneventful, and Ray was surprisingly quiet.

"Mac, I don't mind saying, during that thunderstorm, I was never so scared in all my life. And to make matters worse, I felt totally helpless. I don't like either feeling and I don't ever want to be in that position again."

"I know what you're saying. I wasn't too happy myself. I've been through thunderstorms before, but never like that. That micro burst scared me shitless too."

"Mac I'm serious, any hint of a thunderstorm in the area, and I'm not getting anywhere near an airport."

"Ray, I promise, and rest easy. Tomorrow there's no chance of thunderstorms, and we have a clear and easy trip to sunny Jamaica, with emphasis on sunny."

"Please, please tell me you didn't get that information from Flight Service."

"Nope, the weather channel."

"Great."

"Trust me Ray."

"Great."

****

During his travels, John had been to Boca Raton before, and knew of an out of the way restaurant in Deerfield Beach, about eight miles south of the airport.

The restaurant had the innocuous name of Hooters, a national chain, and was located on the beach overlooking a small harbor. After they were seated by the hostess and the waitress had taken their order, there was no doubt in either man's name what the place was named after.

John and Ray had finished dinner and were having desert. Ray was having a hot fudge sundae and John Cappuccino and German chocolate cake.

"No wonder you like this place." Ray said. "Have you searched the continent for places that serve cappuccino and German chocolate cake?"

"As a matter of fact Ray...."

"Please spare me. It's so peaceful now, it almost makes me forget about thunderstorms."

Ray was right there John thought. There was a full moon shimmering over the water and the temperature was a mild seventy-five degrees with a light breeze.

He was beginning to worry about Ray after their conversation in the hotel room. It was not like Ray to take such a serious approach to anything. John had often made light of Ray's fear of flying, something he wouldn't do again.

John was glad Ray was beginning to feel like his old self

"Ya know Ray, it's so nice and romantic out, I could almost kiss ya."

"Eat your heart out Mac." Ray managed to say between mouthfuls of his sundae.

"By the way, how much water do we have to fly over tomorrow?"

John had a wise remark for Ray but decided to go easy.

"It's not going to be that bad Ray. We have about five-hundred-sixty miles to travel. Most of it we'll be within throwing distance of land. The longest stretches of open water will be at the beginning and end of the trip."

"How far?" Ray asked.

"The first leg will be about one-hundred miles. The first large piece of land will be Andros Island. There'll be a few islands in between, but nothing major. After that, we'll be following the Bahamas southeast, around Cuba, by the way, remind me to stay out of Cuban airspace."

"Cuban airspace?" Ray asked.

"Oh yea, minor details. This trip is gonna take us about an extra one-hundred-fifty-miles because we have to fly around Cuba. Jamaica is just south. You ever take geography Ray."

"Yea, but I cut class to go lift weights."

"Anyway, we fly from the Bahamas, over the western tip of Haiti, and then another hundred miles of open ocean to Jamaica."

"How Long?"

"I'm not planning on stopping, the weather and winds won't be a factor, a little under three hours. Piece of cake Ray." John said as he took a bite of his cake.

Ray just sat in his chair and stared out into the harbor for a moment before he spoke.

"Nothing like today?"

"Ray, I never break a promise." John said. "I promise, there won't ever be anything like today."

"There's still no place like home."

****

The next day dawned sunny and clear.

The morning was uneventful and John and Ray were airborne by ten o'clock. After reaching an altitude of five-thousand feet, which was well below the scattered cloud cover at nine-thousand feet, John turned to a heading of one-four-zero degrees and headed towards Bimini, a small island about sixty miles off the coast. Bimini had a VOR that was out of service most of the time, and today was no exception. John didn't think that would be a problem, and within ten minutes of flying, he was able to see the island.

John had always wanted to go to Bimini, but had never been able to find the time. Bimini was known for its great scuba diving and mysterious submerged rock foundations that some scientists theorized were made by extra-terrestrials, but that was for another day.

After passing over Bimini, John turned to a heading of one-three-zero. This would bring them to San Andros.

San Andros, which was about one-hundred-twenty miles off the Florida coast, was the largest island in the Bahamas and was primarily unpopulated except for some resort areas that dotted the eastern side of the island. It was composed of coral and mangrove swamp. Like most everywhere else in the Caribbean, the diving was excellent, with a large number of shipwrecks dating back from the seventeenth and eighteenth century when English privateers would prey on the gold-laden ships of the Spanish Armada.

If John had any one dream in life, it was to find a shipwreck full of gold and silver. The fact that he was flying over waters that held a king's ransom in sunken treasure just whetted his appetite.

While flying over San Andros, John noticed Ray looking out the window more and more. John felt like throwing the plane into a steep turn to have some fun with Ray, but didn't have the heart after the beating they took the previous day.

"Mac, is the water always that green and clear down hear."

"Usually, yea. I've had some days diving down here where I've had over one hundred foot visibility."

Unlike his fear of flying, Ray had no fear of the water, and had learned to dive the previous year.

"It's a hell of a lot different than New Hampshire water where a good day's visibility is thirty feet." Ray said.

"Don't forget the temperature, off Hampton Beach, the water temp's about sixty in the summer, down below and where we're going, it's around eighty. You don't have to wear a wetsuit or the weights, it makes the diving a lot easier and more fun."

"My next vacation's going to be in the Bahama's."

"It's better in the Bahama's man," John said in a pseudo Caribe accent.

Ray nodded his head and continued to look out the window while John looked down at his chart and plotted his position as they approached the southern tip of San Andros. This was where they had to fly in a southeasterly course in order to stay out of Cuban airspace.

John was glad it was a clear day. In this part of the Caribbean, there was very little in the way of navigational aids.

John had to stay at least ten miles from the Cuban coast, and by his estimation, he was a good fifty to sixty miles out. They were over the ocean with the nearest land a scattering of Islands fifteen miles to their left. Whenever John flew, he would always look for places to land in times of an emergency, particularly when he flew planes with only one engine. If he lost an engine with the Aztec, he still had the other engine to find a place to land which made flying over the open ocean a bit safer.

In about another fifty minutes, they flew over the western tip of Haiti about thirty miles off the Cuban coast. John turned to a southerly direction and paralleled the Haitian coast until he was about sixty miles from Cuba. John was able to ascertain his position with a great deal of certainty since he was picking up the VOR and DME from US held Guantanamo air and naval base in Cuba. The GPS equipment allowed MacLennan to pinpoint his position within feet.

Once John reached the southwestern tip of Haiti, he turned in a due west course towards Jamaica.

"Well Ray, we're on our last leg, about another forty minutes and we'll be over Jamaica."

"Don't I remember you saying that this is our longest stretch over open water?"

"Yup"

"Great."

"Just sit tight there Ray, we'll be there before you know it."

About ten miles out from Haiti, John was able to pick up the signal from the Kingston VOR. Their destination of Boscobel was on the northern coast. Once John reached the coast, he was planning on following it northbound until he ran into Boscobel.

The remainder of the trip over water was uneventful. About twenty miles from Jamaica, with land in view, MacLennan throttled back on the Aztec's engines and began a gentle descent to four hundred feet. This would keep them below the capabilities of the radar at Kingston, the capitol, of Jamaica, and allow them to approach the coast undetected.

As the Aztec approached Port Morant, the easternmost point of Jamaica, John was level at four hundred feet and had slowed to a cruise of one-hundred-thirty knots. He turned to the right and began looking for Boscobel. In five minutes, he flew over the Ken Jones airport and climbed to an altitude of fifteen hundred feet. This would put the Aztec on radar, but it would appear to any controller, that they had just taken off from Ken Jones airport.

In twenty-five miles, which the Aztec covered in ten minutes, John sighted Boscobel. Boscobel was an uncontrolled airport with only one runway running east-west. John checked his flight guide and entered a right downwind for runway two-seven.

For the first time since Haiti Ray spoke.

"How cum you're not talking to no one?"

"Anyone Ray, anyone. You used a double negative. Next thing you know, you'll be splitting your infinitives."

"Thanks. You gonna answer me?"

"We're drug smugglers Ray, we're not talking to anyone."

"Isn't that kind of dangerous?"

John began laughing slowly.

"Ray, and what we're doing isn't?"

Ray started to laugh too.

Before Ray could say anything else, John had landed and was taxiing off the runway.

Boscobel was an uncontrolled airport with no buildings, and tie downs for only twelve small planes. All the tie downs were taken and John had to park on the grass adjacent to the parking area.

John shut down the engines and completed his post flight check list. At the end of the runway, Ray noticed three jeeps coming towards the plane at a relatively high speed.

"Say Mac, how was the meet here supposed to go again?"

"We're supposed to wait here and one of Kananga's people is going to pick us up and take us to the Boscobel Beach Hotel outside of Port Maria."

"There was nothing about Jeeps and armed men was there?"

"Ray, what are you talking about?"

At that moment, John noticed the three Jeeps and the three men in each Jeep, wearing Jamaican military uniforms, with guns pointed at them.

"Welcome to Jamaica mon." the man in the Jeep closest to the Aztec said. "You are under arrest."

Chapter 6
Jailhouse Rock

With rifles pointed at them, John and Ray wasted no time climbing down the wing of the Aztec. They were unceremoniously searched and handcuffed.

John and Ray sized up their situation. There were a total of nine men, all with either rifles or pistols. John noticed there was one man in the front jeep who was giving orders, probably an officer, who remained in his seat while the others had surrounded the plane. It was done fairly quickly and efficiently. They had done this before.

"Gentlemen, you are under arrest for entering the country of Jamaica illegally, I suspect for drug smuggling. Have you anything to say?" This was said by a person with sergeant stripes who appeared to be the second in command.

John and Ray looked at each other and said nothing. John was thinking about trying to bluff his way out, but wasn't quite sure how he would bluff.

If these were Katanga's men, and he tried to tell them they were government agents, they were as good as dead. On the other hand, if these were government troops and he said they were friends of Julian Katanga and were here at his bidding, that may not be a popular approach either. John decided to play out the hand and continued to say nothing.

"Nothing to say?" The sergeant said.

"Maybe a few days stay as a guest of the Port Maria prison will loosen your tongue."

John and Ray were placed in the same jeep and each of their ankles were manacled to iron rings in the floor of the jeep.

As they drove off, John noticed there were two men left behind who began searching the plane. John hoped they wouldn't find the ten thousand dollars in cash and guns John had secreted away behind one of the panels in the nose of the Aztec. If worse came to worse, John was hoping to buy his way out of this. Anyway, it seemed that they were in no immediate danger; MacLennan just couldn't figure what was going on.

Under different circumstances, John would have enjoyed the ride to Port Maria. They were travelling along a winding mountain rode that overlooked the northern Jamaican coast. There was lush green forest that contrasted with the emerald green of the Caribbean ocean.

John and Ray remained silent. The one time Ray tried to speak to John, he was rewarded with a rifle butt in the ribs. With the look on Ray's face, John didn't envy the guard if Ray ever got his hands on him.

As they entered the outskirts of Port Maria, the rampant poverty was evident. John had not been to Port Maria when he was in Jamaica, and now he knew why. In some areas there was raw sewage on the side of the road and shoeless children with rags for clothes. It was a sharp contrast from the opulence of the Boscobel Beach hotel where they were to stay.

The downtown area was slightly better. The streets were cleaner, the shops gaudy, and there were vendors in the street. It reminded John somewhat of the straw market section of Nassau.

"Are we going to court?" John asked risking a rifle butt in the side.

The guards looked at each other and laughed.

"Yea mon, you go to court, in maybe a year or two"

The guards continued to laugh sharing a private joke.

On the other side of Port Maria, the small motorcade slowed down and turned off the main road onto a dirt road. As they traveled towards the interior of the island, the jungle and mangrove swamp thickened around them. Another mile and it was solid swamp. John didn't know what was worse, the mosquito's the size of robins or the smell of the swamp gas.

Out of the corner of his eye, John noticed a movement which he first thought was a log falling into the water. But the movement was too coordinated, almost graceful in its execution. Upon closer inspection only did MacLennan notice the cause of the movement, crocodiles. Ray had noticed the crocodiles also. The jeeps slowed down momentarily and two rifle shots rang out. John and Ray could see three crocodiles scurrying from ahead into the swamp on either side of the road.

One of the guards then spoke, "Port Maria prison is very safe, we have not had one prisoner escape mon." The other guards began to laugh and then another spoke, "Oh we have plenty escape, they just don't live." With this they all began to laugh until they were silenced by a warning glance from the sergeant.

Around the next bend in the road, John and Ray could see their destination. A stockade fence surrounded three dilapidated wooden buildings and what appeared to be a newly constructed two story brick building. In turn, there was another stockade fence that separated the wood buildings from the brick building with guards positioned twenty yards apart. There was a small courtyard with a number of prisoners milling about.

John surmised that the brick building was for the guards and the commandant and the wooden buildings for the prisoners.

The jeeps pulled up to the inner stockade fence and ground to a halt. The officer issued some instructions to the sergeant who then walked to the jeep where John and Ray were handcuffed.

"Gentlemen, Commandant Kalem will see you in the morning. I'm sure you will want to talk to him after spending a night with us. Enjoy your accommodations gentlemen."

With that, John and Ray's handcuffs were removed and they were shoved through a door in the fence.

"Well Stanley, this is another find mess you've gotten us into," Ray said mimicking the line from the comedy duo of Laurel and Hardy.

John didn't answer but looked around him in the courtyard into a sea of black faces.

"Looks like we're a definite minority here Ray."

"Seeing we're the only two white guys, I'd say you're powers of observation are still working fine."

Some of the black prisoner's began closing in on John and Ray and yelling taunts at them.

"Hey mon, look at the buttee man. Nice white butte man, Jesus gonna like you real good buttee man."

"Hey Mac, what does he mean by buttee man." Ray asked.

"Ray we're in prison remember, I don't know who this guy Jesus is, but I think he wants you for his main squeeze."

John then spoke up to a crowd of six prisoners that circled him and Ray.

"No buttee man we're straight."

All six men began to laugh, John noticed the guards spaced on catwalks were laughing too. Some were taking bets.

"Oh yea mon," one prisoner said who was nearly as large as Ray and seemed to be a mixture of both Spanish and Caribe descent. "If I say you are buttee man then you are buttee man and Jesus is gonna fuck you good buttee man."

"Are you Jesus?" John asked

"Yea buttee man, I'm Jesus and Jesus run this place. You my buttee man."

John looked at Ray and an understanding passed between the partners. It was show time and John and Ray weren't about to be anybody's date.

"You know Jesus, you really shouldn't refer to yourself in the third person. It does the Queen's English no justice."

For an instant, a quizzical look crossed Jesus' face. This was immediately replaced by one of intense pain as John planted his foot squarely in Jesus' groin.

As he began to crumple John followed up by two swift punches to the nose and a spinning back kick to the temple.

Jesus was down and out for the count. A long time ago, the elder MacLennan taught John that whenever he was outnumbered, go for the toughest and put him down fast, it would take some of the fight out of the rest, the second degree black belt MacLennan had also helped.

As fast as John put Jesus down, Ray was faster. He grabbed the person next to him around the neck with his massive hands and slammed him twice into the fence.

Two down.

The remaining four split up with two going after Ray and two after John.

Ray waded in after his two and took a punch in the jaw. He shook it off as he would a mosquito bite, grabbed each of his assailants by the head and smashed them together. Both crumpled to the ground in a heap.

John's two attackers proceeded warily. MacLennan wanted this over quickly. He remembered that it only took twelve pounds of pressure to shatter a kneecap. After two quick shuffle steps and a quick front snap kick, one of the attackers lay screaming and writhing on the ground clutching his knee. The last attacker stopped dead in his tracks, viewed his five fallen comrades and ran out of the courtyard into the nearest building.

The crowd that had surrounded John and Ray began to disperse. The total time of the fight had been under a minute. John and Ray grinned at each other.

"Getting kind of slow in your old age, aren't you Ray?"

"Hey, I took care of my three, you only had two. The guy running away doesn't count."

"I'll make it up next time." John answered.

Right about now Jesus began to stir and raised himself to his hands and knees.

"We can't keep doing this forever." Ray said.

"Yea, I know. I think it's time for a heart to heart with Jesus."

****

As John and Ray were debating what to do with Jesus, a figure on the porch of the guard building began to speak to the sergeant who had brought John and Ray back from the airport. The figure was smaller than the sergeant, had a much larger girth and was of relatively fair skin for a Latino. However, there were few people who would say anything derogatory to the face of General Manuel Estaben.

"They fight well these Americano's," General Estaben said to no one in particular.

"Sergeant, tell me, these Americano's had nothing to say."

"Nothing General."

Estaben and the sergeant were joined by a third figure, a middle aged Jamaican wearing olive fatigues and smoking a cigarette.

"Commandant Kalem, those were your best, your toughest inmates? I was particularly impressed by the one who had run away," Estaben said.

Ricardo Kalem was the commandant of Port Maria prison and this was his domain. He was one of Julian Katanga's henchmen who was responsible for eliminating any problems Katanga would have with any bothersome people. The Port Maria prison was infamous for people entering its walls and never being heard from afterwards.

Kalem had met Estaben for the first time last week. He knew of Katanga's relationship with the Panamanian but never had the necessity to meet him or work with him. He still didn't know why the General was here, but it had something to do with these two American prisoners.

"Commandant, I want to prove conclusively who these Americano's are."

"General, I have a feeling you know who these Americans might be?"

"Commandant," Estaben said with disdain towards Kalem, "You have your orders from Katanga, follow them. Or have you forgot our recent encounter with the American DEA informants."

Estaben was referring to the two Jamaican informants that Kalem had disposed of in their voodoo ceremony.

"I do not know why Commandant, you Jamaicans go to such elaborate extremes to dispose of such nuisances."

Estaben often made no attempt to conceal the contempt he held for Jamaicans and their customs

"A bullet in the head and a shallow grave would have served the purpose admirably. Your country's flair for the dramatic is a useless waste of time and energy commandant."

There was not anything about General Estaben that Kalem liked. Estaben was an interloper in his Jamaican world and showed no gratefulness for having been shielded from the Americans after the Panama invasion. He consistently looked down upon his Jamaican hosts; and that would soon be his undoing.

There was nothing less Kalem would like to do than feed General Estaben to the crocodiles that surrounded Port Maria prison.

"Ah general, my country's flair for the dramatic, allow me to show you what my country's flair for the dramatic can accomplish. Sergeant bring me the prisoner that ran away from the fight."

"General, I will show you why there has never been an escape from Port Maria prison and why these prisoners will do anything I want of them."

****

John and Ray had just finished having their tete a tete with Jesus. In this particular instance it consisted of Ray picking Jesus up by the neck with one hand while John explained to him how he would break every one of twenty-six bones in his hand if he should even look at either of them crossly. The other prisoners looked on from a distance.

Four guards opened the front gate and motioned to put Jesus down. One of the guards appeared to move as if he was going to prod Ray with rifle stock but wisely had second thoughts.

Two of the guards stayed at the front gate with rifles at the ready position while the other two went into the crowd and grabbed the prisoner that had run away from the fight with John. The prisoner began to struggle and squeal, however a hit to the back of the head from a sap of one the guards had quickly taken all the fight out of him. The guards then half dragged, half carried the prisoner through the stockade gate.

There was a strange silence over the prison courtyard.

"What the hell's goin' on Mac?"

"Don't know Ray, but I think we're going to find out fairly shortly."

Jesus then spoke. "You will soon see mon why nobody escapes from Port Maria prison."

The prisoner was taken before the Commandant and General Estaben.

****

MacLennan heard Jesus mutter something to the effect of poor Simone and then cross himself in prayer.

Simone began to beg and squirm between the guards, however the sight of the guards raised sap soon quieted him. He was then led to the outer gate of the compound while the commandant strode over to the prisoners stockade.

The commandant spoke to the prisoners, but looked directly at John and Ray when he spoke.

"You will now see what happens when someone disobeys me and why no one has any chance of leaving this prison without my permission."

The front doors of the prison were opened and Simone was literally thrown outside by the guards. Once the doors were closed, they could no longer see Simone since he had his back to the gate, but they could still hear his cries for mercy. After a short time, the cries stopped and John and Ray could see Simone running down the road looking nervously from side to side.

"Hey Mac, look to the right of Simone, there in the swamp. Is that what I think it is?"

John looked to where Ray was pointing and saw a swirl in the marshy water that soon climbed onto the side of the road just behind Simone.

"Holy shit Ray, that bastard of a commandant has just made a dinner of Simone to that croc that climbed onto the side of the road."

Simone was about a quarter of a mile from the front gates and had long since stopped running. He was half walking, half stumbling, still looking from side to side.

The croc had climbed out of the water behind Simone and began running towards an unsuspecting Simone. The speed of the crocodile was surprising.

Within seconds, the crocodile had narrowed the gap to one hundred yards, fifty, then twenty, and still Simone had no idea of his faith. Simone seemed to sense the croc before he heard or saw him. He barely had time to turn around before the croc was on him. Simone's scream went through John like a knife.

The croc had bitten Simone in the side just above the waist and violently began to shake Simone from side to side. Simone continued to scream for about five seconds until the croc let go of his side and bit him in the neck, instantly snapping it and putting Simone out of his horror and misery.

The body that was once Simone's, and the croc were completely covered in blood. MacLennan had no idea that the human body could contain so much.

The croc had let go of the corpse and re-bitten Simone in the stomach and began rolling over and over tearing chunks of Simone's body into pieces. What could now be only recognizable as a bloody mass of meat was dragged into the swamp by the croc to be devoured at his leisure.

The silence across the prison yard was deafening and was broken by the cackle of the commandant.

****

"Bon Appetit, gentlemen." The commandant said as he turned heel and strode to his quarters.

"That son-of-a-bitch enjoyed that. He actually enjoyed that," Ray said.

John kept on looking at the bloody smear in the road that had once been a human being. "What goes around comes around Ray, he'll get his, it may take a while, but he'll get his."

"Yea, I get the feeling that this isn't the first time that bastard's done that Mac."

Before John could answer Ray, one of the soldiers rang a bell hanging from one of the four guard towers that surrounded the compound. The prisoner's began to line up single file about thirty yards from the entrance to the prisoners courtyard.

'What gives Ray?"

"Don't know. But I also don't know if I want to be first in line either."

John and Ray started moving towards the line but didn't join it.

"Look over there." Ray said as he pointed to three guards wheeling a cart with a steaming cauldron on top of it.

"Looks like dinner." Ray said.

"I can hardly wait."

"I am kind of hungry. I haven't eaten since we left this morning."

"Might as well get in line."

John and Ray got in line as the guards came through the gate and began dolling out dinner.

As John and Ray got closer so they were able to see what dinner looked like.

"If that tastes anything like it smells I'm going on that diet my wife's been nagging me about."

"What is it?" John asked no one in particular.

"Is good mon." one of the guards said who overheard John's question.

"Is crocodile stew. Sometimes croc eat you, sometimes you eat croc." This brought a wave of laughter from the other guards.

John and Ray noticed that none of the prisoners shared the guard's sense of humor.

John and Ray were served their stew and walked over and sat on a bench in the shade of one of the prisoner's hut.

"Crocodile stew, this is more like grease stew." Ray said as he took one spoonful and threw the rest on the ground.

John followed Ray's lead and both settled back to contemplate their situation.

"Well Mac, what do you think?"

"I don't have the slightest idea. I'm wondering if we've been burnt or is this just Katanga's way of testing us."

Ray leaned back against the hut wall in thought.

"I don't think we've been burnt, if we were, it would've been one of us out there on the road dancing with that croc instead of Simone."

"You got a point there," John answered

"The other possibility, though I doubt it, is that these guys don't' know anything about us and they got shit lucky and saw us coming in for a landing."

"Yea, great welcoming committee." Ray said.

"Well whatever the reason is Ray, the one thing you can count on in Jamaica, money talks and if they think we're really smugglers, someone's expecting us to offer them a bribe. I had a cousin who was once arrested here for trying to smuggle some pot out. It seems that once the Jamaicans arrest an American, their usual MO is to give them a taste of a prison and then most are willing to give up their first born. It cost my cousin $20,000 in bribes, but he got out."

"Mac, considering Simone's plight, I think we'd be lucky if all they wanted was our first born."

"Well whatever they think we are, a bribe's not going to hurt."

John and Ray stopped talking as a couple of prisoner's walked by giving them a wide berth. It appeared that the last thing any of the prisoners wanted to do was invoke the ire of Ray and John.

"Jesus Christ," Ray said as he swatted a bug on his neck.

"I think the mosquito is the national bird of this island. I'm worried about being carried away by one of them to be fed to their young.

"Never was one of their better tourist attractions. Let's go into one of the huts and find a place to sack out."

"Think anyone will try fucking with us tonight?" Ray asked.

"Don't know, but let's not take any chances. What do ya say we sleep in shifts tonight?"

"Good idea."

John and Ray wandered into the hut that was nearest them. The inside of the hut was bare except for straw mats. There were already a few prisoner's lying on them that evidently had the same idea as John and Ray.

"I don't think Holiday Inn has anything to worry about in the way of competition, eh Mac?"

"No argument, but I tell ya, I think I'd rather sleep on the floor than one of those mats, no telling what's living inside that straw."

Both partners walked to an unoccupied corner of the hut, kicked the straw mats out of their way, which sent a number of insect scurrying for alternate cover.

"What are those bugs?" Ray asked.

"Ray, you're not afraid of a little ant are you."

"Ants, spiders, beetles, take your pick, I don't discriminate."

MacLennan never knew of his partner's phobia for insects and he was already thinking of some practical jokes to play when they got back. As an afterthought, he thought if they get back, which he soon put out of his head.

Even though they slept in shifts, the night was relatively sleepless and fitful. No one tried to jump them and Ray killed 24 ants, spiders and assorted creepy crawlers.

As the sun began to rise, activity began to increase in the prison.

"Hey Mac, tell room service I'll have my bacon crisp and eggs over easy. By the way, what's that God awful smell?"

"That's the Jamaican version of bacon and eggs. I think it's called gruel."

"Seriously?"

"Seriously."

As the two partners queued in the breakfast line, three armed guards approached them and prodded them out the gate towards the commandants building.

"That's what I like, the VIP treatment."

John and Ray were escorted up the steps and through the doors where two other soldiers stood guard.

They were marched down a corridor into a spacious dining room and veranda overlooking the jungle. Under different circumstances, the view would have been enjoyable. Seated at the veranda table were the commandant, two other officers, and a Hispanic recognized by both agents as Estaben.

"Mr. MacCloud and Marino." Kalem began in between mouthfuls.

"How nice to have two agents of the Drug Enforcement Agency to join us for breakfast. Please gentleman, have a seat."

Chapter 7
A FISTFUL OF DOLLARS

John and Ray looked at each other. The fact that Kalem used their undercover names and not their real names lent some credence to MacLennan's belief that this was a test by Katanga. If it was, what were they expecting? MacLennan decided to continue the bluff and eventually keep with the bribe of plan A

"DEA agents. Very good." MacLennan said.

"We're also virgins, well he is," Ray said pointing to MacLennan.

This brought some laughter from the Jamaicans that were seated. Estaben remained as stone faced as ever.

"I like a sense of humor. Please be seated and join us for breakfast gentleman. I'm sure you'll find it more appetizing than what the other prisoners are being served."

Both John and Ray sat at the table opposite Kalem and were served a variety of fruits, eggs and sausage. Ray wasted no time eating while John leisurely buttered his toast and arranged his plate.

Both Kalem and Estaben noticed how controlled and calm their prisoners were. Estaben thought to himself that these people were exactly who they said they were, or very cool operators.

"You appear to have us at a disadvantage." John said.

"You know who we are, though neither of us know anyone here. It leads me to believe that we have a mutual friend. Though you are all wet on our line of work," MacLennan said.

Kalem was somewhat impressed. MacCloud had made a possible reference to Katanga without mentioning any names. Playing his cards close to his chest was smart. Kalem's orders from Katanga were to find out who these two were without killing them. All Katanga had given them were their names and the rest was up to him. Kalem strongly suspected that these were new pilots working for Katanga who needed to be tested. It was not the first time Kalem had been asked by Katanga to ferret out possible agents or informers. What Kalem resented was Estaben's presence.

"Well tell me Mr. MacCloud, if you are not agents of the DEA, then you must be smugglers, in which case you will be spending a very long time here at Port Marie prison."

"Well commandant, and I will take the liberty of assuming that we are nothing more than businessmen, we are importers of commodities who enjoy making a profit, and we further realize that the people we deal with should also enjoy making a profit. But we can assure you, we never intended to do anything illegal."

"Then tell me why you fly into my country with no flight plan and land at an airport that has no tower, eh Mr. MacCloud."

"It is very simple commandant, we merely got lost and wanted to land at the first airport we saw."

When no one said anything John continued.

""We are also prepared to pay any landing fees and taxes to you that we missed by not landing at an airport of entry plus administrative fees to atone for our mistakes."

Ray was beginning to wonder when MacLennan was going to get to the bribe, and he liked the way he did it.

"And how will you do this? My men have searched both you and the plane, and all we found were your guns, another crime in Jamaica that will add to your prison time."

Both John and Ray noticed that Kalem seemed to be concentrating on the prisoner aspect as opposed to them being agents, neither felt comfortable enough to let down their guard.

"Commandant, I'm sure you can understand that those weapons are purely for self-defense, and as for the money, if your men had found it in the plane, they would no longer be of this world."

131

When John saw Kalem's quizzical look, he continued. Ray was also curious, but reached for a second helping of eggs and just nodded in agreement.

"You see commandant, our money is hidden in the plane and also booby trapped. Anyone attempting to remove the money without de-activating the safeguards would blow themselves, and the money to kingdom come."

Ray knew the money wasn't booby trapped, at least he thought he knew, but by saying that, MacLennan hopefully eliminated any chance of the money being found.

Kalem ate some of his breakfast pondering what MacCloud had said. By playing this through, he might be able not only to test MacCloud and Marino for their authenticity, but also come out of this with a fistful of dollars.

There was a brief silence in the room as everyone was left to their thoughts and breakfast.

Estaben was becoming increasingly restless with the verbal jousting that was transpiring between Kalem and whomever MacCloud said he was. His methods were more direct, quicker and accurate. Where Kalem felt fairly confident that John and Ray were genuine drug smugglers, Estaben was still doubtful.

Estaben then spoke.

"Commandant, enough of this, let us find out once and for all who they are. As for any money in their plane, I suggest we dispatch some men, and take their plane apart piece by piece. I doubt very much if there is any money, much less a bomb."

"General Estaben", Kalem said. "You are very unconcerned about the lives of my men if there is a bomb, and if there is, I care not to lose either any of my men or the money."

"If there is any money."

It was obvious to both Ray and John that considerable animosity existed between Estaben and Kalem. Something that could be to their advantage at the right time.

"Commandant", Estaben went on as if he didn't hear Kalem.

"I suggest we find out once and for all we find out who these two are."

Kalem finished the last scraps of his breakfast and sighed deeply. As much as he disliked Estaben, Kalem's life would not be worth a ganja leaf if these two were actually agents and he was not able to ascertain that.

"Well Mr. MacCloud, I hoped you and your friend enjoyed your breakfast, because it may be your last," Kalem said ominously.

John and Ray looked at each other, John thought there might be some kind of test, but he had no idea what it may be.

Ray felt that the situation was serious enough that he stopped eating.

"Commandant Kalem," John began, "I don't understand, as I said previously,"

"Yes I know what you said." Kalem cut MacCloud off in mid-sentence.

"But words are cheap, tell me where the money is in your plane and how to de-activate the bomb."

"I will be more than happy to, Commandant, take us to the plane."

Kalem and Estaben looked at each other and Estaben nodded curtly.

"Mr. MacCloud I will take your advice. Your friend, he is as silent as he is big, I wonder if he is as fast?"

Kalem gave some unseen signal and four guards entered the room and pointed their guns at John and Ray.

"Mr. MacCloud, you will be staying with us, as for your silent partner, he will be going back to the plane, maybe."

Upon saying this two of the guards motioned Ray out of the room and closed the door behind them.

"This way Mr. MacCloud." Kalem said as he pointed to the open doors on the veranda, you can monitor your partner's progress.

MacLennan began to walk out on the porch and began to understand what Kalem had in mind.

In a few moments, MacLennan's worst fears were realized as the front gates to the compound were opened and Ray was motioned outside by a wave of the guard's guns.

"As you see Mr. MacCloud, your friend is free to go to your plane. Just as long as he doesn't disturb the crocodiles.

A wave of fury began to sweep over MacLennan. His best friend was about to be killed. If there was one thing MacLennan wasn't going to do was to stand by and watch idly.

"What is it you want Kalem."

"Nothing really, just the truth Mr. MacCloud. What are you doing on my island and where is the money on your plane?"

"Commandant, we are what I said, we are, importers, the cargo may at times be in a gray area, but we are here at the behest of a very important man in your country."

As MacLennan was still trying to talk his way out of the predicament that he and Ray were in, his mind was racing towards an alternative plan of action.

MacLennan had made up his mind a long time ago, that if ever he was in a desperate situation, he wasn't going to go easy, and he wasn't going to go alone.

Ray began a slow trot from the gates while looking around him for any crocodiles. About twenty yards from the gate, Ray stopped momentarily and broke off a ten foot low hanging limb from a tree. It wouldn't do Ray much good against a croc, but it would be some help.

If MacLennan couldn't convince Kalem and Estaben in the next two minutes of their authenticity, he would make his move. Though he wasn't quite sure what that move would be.

"Mr. MacCloud, you can save your friend from a horrible faith, and go free. Where is the money and what are you doing on my island?"

Ray was now about fifty yards from the main gate.

John decided to bend a little.

"The money's in the forward baggage compartment under a false floor, the master switch must be on, if it isn't, the compartment will burst into flames if you force the floor. As for who I am, I can't change what I told you."

Kalem didn't expect that. He was beginning to believe more and more that these two were actually smugglers working for Katanga. Kalem's feelings were that if one had to be killed to ascertain the others reliability, then so be it, it was the cost of doing business.

Before Kalem could respond, one of the guards on the veranda pointed to a movement in the water. A crocodile, and Ray was about eighty yards from the gate.

If MacLennan wanted to do anything for Ray the time for talking was over. Everyone's attention was momentarily occupied by the crocodile sliding through the water towards Ray.

MacLennan lashed out and struck one guard on the side of the neck with the knife edge of his hand. As the first guard crumpled in a heap, MacLennan shattered the knee cap of the second guard with a side thrust kick while grabbing his rifle. A third guard entered the room pointed his rifle, and fired at MacLennan. MacLennan was quicker and shielded his body with the guard whose kneecap he shattered. The bullet slammed into the guard's stomach. Well, he wouldn't have to worry that much about his shattered knee. MacLennan grabbed the fallen guard's pistol and let off a snap shot at the remaining guard. The gun recoiled in MacLennan's hand as the third guard dropped silently to the floor.

MacLennan then pointed the guards 9mm Berretta at Kalem and Estaben who were unarmed.

"Don't even think about it." MacLennan said as Estaben crouched as if to charge him.

"Now Commandant", MacLennan said as he moved inside the building out of sight of the guards, order your men in the tower to shoot the croc and send a jeep to get my partner."

When Kalem hesitated, MacLennan fired a shot about six inches from his head. Kalem needed no more prodding.

As he walked to the Veranda, the gun in MacLennan's hand did not waiver from his mid-section. Estaben was shoved into a chair and MacLennan locked the door to the room. It wouldn't keep anyone out for long, but it might buy him a few needed seconds.

John heard Kalem shout in Caribe to the tower guard. His commands were quickly followed as MacLennan saw splash's in the water around the crocodile. He wasn't sure if the tower guard got the croc or not, but Ray had stopped running and John saw a jeep accelerate through the gates to pick him up.

"Very good commandant, it appears you're as good at taking orders as you are at giving them."

"What are you going to do now Mr. MacCloud," Kalem said as sweat poured down his face.

MacLennan hadn't gotten that far yet in his plan, but he thought that now might be as good a time as any to think of something. After a moment's delay, MacLennan decided to play the bluff through.

"We're going to go for a ride, you Estaben, Ray and me. We're going to our plane, and we'll pay our landing fees to you Commandant; after that, well, we'll see."

Both Kalem and Estaben were taken by surprise. Both had questions to ask, but both could see that MacLennan was in no mood for answering those questions.

"Now commandant," MacLennan said.

"I want you to tell your men to leave the jeep running by the main gate and have your men go to their quarters. I also want you to tell your men in the guard towers to come down and also go their quarters."

""Why? What are you going to do?"

John answered Kalem's question by firing another shot in the vicinity of Kalem's head.

"Commandant, I will not miss you the third time."

Kalem wasted no further time in carrying out MacLennan's instructions.

MacLennan walked over to one of the dead guards and took a pair of handcuffs from his belt. After motioning Estaben to his feet and Kalem to come back into the room, he handcuffed Kalem and Estaben's right hands together. In this fashion, one would be forced to walk backward or with his hand awkwardly in front of him lessening the chance of an escape attempt.

"Gentleman, and I do use the term loosely, we're going for a little ride."

Kalem and Estaben walked out of the headquarters building back to back with MacLennan holding a rifle against Kalem's head.

"Nothing personal commandant, I just don't want you or any of your more enthusiastic guards to get any ideas of rescue."

All three walked towards the main gate where Ray sat in the Jeep along with both guards.

"Tell your guards to drop their weapons and walk away from the jeep."

"Good thing you sent the chauffeur's to get me, that croc was about to meet his maker." Ray said grinning from the passenger's seat of the jeep.

"Yea, probably get terminal indigestion from eating Italian food."

"Not funny."

John then gave Ray the rifle, and shoved Estaben and Kalem in the back seat.

"Commandant, how nice of you to give us an escort and guided tour back to our plane."

"What are you going to do with us?" Kalem said as he was shoved into the back seat of the jeep along with Estaben.

"Don't worry Kalem," Ray said as he pointed the rifle at Kalem, "you won't be dinner for anything."

MacLennan got in the driver's seat, started the jeep and drove out of the compound.

"Nice place to visit but I wouldn't want to stay for long."

"Room service had a lot to be desired," Ray added.

"Looks like the parties over."

"Back to the plane and the states?" Ray asked.

"Yea, and so much for this business trip. I really hope you don't mind seeing us off boys, and please, no tearful goodbyes."

Kalem and Estaben said nothing, but they were relieved that Ray wasn't going to feed them to the crocodiles.

The trip back to the airport was uneventful. People took little notice of two army officers handcuffed and held at gunpoint as if it was an everyday occurrence.

As John and Ray approached the airport they saw the Aztec where they had tied it down.

"Place looks deserted," Ray said to no one in particular.

"If you remember correctly, it did when we landed and look where that got us."

John pulled up to the plane and both he and Ray got out. John then undid Kalem's cuffs and told him to get in the front seat. Once Kalem did, he looped the cuffs through the steering wheel and re-cuffed him. MacLennan then threw the keys to the cuffs and the jeep in the woods.

"Don't think they'll be needing those."

"Yea, they can work on their tan."

John began doing a quick pre-flight of the plane as Ray kept an eye on Kalem and Estaben.

"Hey Mac, do you hear anything?"

"Sounds like a helicopter coming this way."

"Uh-oh."

"Uh-oh?"

"Yea Uh-oh. As in let's get going."

As John and Ray got in the plane, the sound of the helicopter approached the airfield. John switched the master switch on and turned the starter of the left engine.

Nothing.

"Ray?"

"Mac, this is not the time for jokes, I see a jeep coming at us across the field."

"No joke Ray, we're out of business."

"I wanted to go back by boat anyway."

The helicopter was now over the field, apparently landing next to the grounded Aztec. The Jeep, again with a driver and three armed men, pulled up next to the Aztec and leveled their guns at John and Ray.

"Oh well, at least there're consistent." Ray said

"But boring. Any ideas for escape come to mind."

"Not at the moment." Ray answered.

"Besides, you're the brain, I'm the brawn of the team."

The helicopter had since landed and the rotor blades were coming to a halt as a tall, well dressed Jamaican exited surrounded by two armed men and what appeared to be two aides. He did not seem concerned of any potential danger that John and Ray posed.

As he approached the plane, one of the guards motioned John and Ray to get out of the plane.

"Seems like we've done this before Mac."

"Yea, but that was the dress rehearsal."

"Tell that to the croc."

The well-dressed Jamaican met John and Ray as they jumped down from the wing of the Aztec and stared at them in silence for a moment.

"Ah, Messieurs MacCloud and Melena, so you are not DEA agents after all."

MacLennan looked at the man who had spoken to him and Ray.

"Mr. Katanga, I presume, a pleasure."

Chapter 8
The Trouble Blues

"Ah, Mr. MacCloud, the pleasure is mine. You are as deductive as you are resourceful. It is encouraging to have two men such as yourselves in my employ. And as for you Commandant Kalem, well, all in good time."

Katanga was immaculately dressed in a blue silk Armani suit and tie. His white shirt was crisply starched and it was a wonder to MacLennan why Katanga was not sweating in the hot Jamaican sun. His accent was more British than Jamaican and his overall demeanor commanded respect. MacLennan was not surprised that he had achieved his position of power and notoriety in the Jamaican government and drug world.

"I apologize for the inhospitable welcome offered to you by Kalem and Estaben, but your background had to be ascertained. I reasoned that if you were agents of the DEA, you would have told the Commandant, and that gentlemen would have sealed your faith."

"Tell me Mr. Katanga," Ray said.

"If we had said we were in your employ, would that have made a difference?"

Julian Katanga gave both Ray and John what appeared to be a benevolent smile.

"Gentlemen, I'm sure you already know the answer to that question. No one is in my employ who tells their tale at the first sign of distress. You both passed admirably; and Mr. Marino," Katanga said with a smile, "my money was on you if you were to battle the crocodile."

"Thanks, I feel so much better."

Katanga ignored Ray's sarcasm.

"Gentlemen," Katanga said as he made a sweeping gesture, "my helicopter awaits."

140

John noticed that the helicopter was a Hugh's Long Ranger, the larger version of the more popular Jet Ranger model.

John and Ray were in the helicopter with Katanga, the pilot and what appeared to be two bodyguards that were almost Ray's size.

As the pilot applied power and pulled up on the collective, the helicopter lifted off and turned in an easterly direction.

Katanga must have noticed Ray appraising his bodyguards.

"I naturally heard how you swiftly disposed of six prisoners and Kalem's guards, and I assure you gentlemen, you will not have the same success with mine."

"I would think Mr. Katanga", John said, "that we would have no reason to do so; or are we to be tested again?"

"You are always tested by me and my minions, by your actions and performance gentlemen, but tests such as the one you took at the prison are over."

Both Ray and John noticed how smooth and confident Katanga was. Both his actions and manner were precise and clipped as was his speech. MacLennan guessed a classical British education at Oxford.

"If I'm not being too forward, where are we going? I could really use a shower."

"Some room service would be nice too." Ray added

"Hopefully better than our last hotel."

Katanga chuckled and turned towards Ray and John.

"We are going to my personal estate on Blue Mountain. You will enjoy everything. Now I have business."

Katanga then turned his back on Ray and John while talking on his phone.

"Sounds as if that was an order and by the way, I hate helicopters more than planes. Do these glide if they lose an engine?" Ray asked John.

"Yea, they glide about as good as a streamlined anvil."

"I want my mama."

"Sit back and enjoy the ride."

As the helicopter turned south and headed inland from Boscobel, MacLennan once again appreciated what a beautiful country Jamaica is.

He remembered that Blue Mountain was the highest point in Jamaica and overlooked the Port of Kingston the "wickedest city in the world" in the sixteenth and seventeenth century.

The trip took only fifteen minutes but in that time, they passed over coral beaches that gave way to flat lands which merged with a small jungle and swamp land to a small mountain range whose highest peak was Blue Mountain at eight-thousand feet.

About five miles from the mountain, the helicopter circled what appeared to be a deserted valley. Both Ray and John strained their eyes but were unable to see anything of interest and both filed the location away for future reference. MacLennan reasoned that Katanga wasn't a person to waste time viewing the scenery and there was a reason why the helicopter circled the field. As they approached Katanga's home, MacLennan was able to see what appeared to be a small village about two-thirds of the way up the mountain. Upon closer inspection, the buildings, five in all, were much too luxurious, and the grounds to well-manicured to be anything but Katanga's private estate.

The Long Ranger proceeded to the northern end of the compounded where it came to rest on a well-guarded helo-pad. Only after the rotor stopped did a guard come over and open Katanga's door. The first thing that MacLennan noticed was how cool it was compared to the sweltering heat of the lowlands.

Katanga was once again the congenial host.

"Gentlemen, one of my servants will take you to your quarters. My house is yours. Enjoy a swim, shower, whatever you want. If you have no objections, we will be having a late lunch at three-o-clock. Until then." Katanga then made a sweeping gesture with his hand, a slight bow, and turned on his heel followed by two bodyguards before either John or Ray could say or ask anything.

One of the guards who had met the helicopter approached Ray and John.

"Hey mon, follow me."

"He's not even going to get our bags." Ray said in mock surprise.

"Hard to get good help these days."

John and Ray followed the guard to the visitor's quarters which were located behind Katanga's mansion. As they approached their quarters, John noticed the ten foot high fence and security camera's located around the compound. John was willing to bet that he probably had dogs and motion sensors outside the fence. After their bout at the prison, MacLennan felt that Katanga was a man that left little to chance.

"This your place mon. I come get you at three-o'clock."

Without saying anything else, the guard turned and left.

The guest quarters consisted of a large living room with two bedrooms and attached baths.

"Guess we don't rate the guest rooms in the mansion" John said

"Friendly type isn't he." Ray said.

"Think this place is bugged?"

"With everything else Katanga has and how thorough he is, I'd be disappointed in him if it wasn't. Probably a miniature close circuit camera somewhere too," John answered.

I don't know about you, but I'm tired. Ray took off his shoes, threw his bag on the couch and was asleep before his head hit the pillow.

Sleep was a pretty good idea. MacLennan hadn't gotten that much the night before and had no idea what was in store for either him or Ray. After looking around a bit more, MacLennan saw what he wanted to see, went into one of the bedrooms and laid down on the bed. Sleep didn't come as easy to him as it did to Ray. His mind was too busy trying to plan an escape if the shit hit the fan.

The best idea that he could come up with based on what he saw, wasn't that comforting. MacLennan forced the thoughts from his mind and dozed off to a fitful sleep.

****

Katanga looked at Ray asleep on the couch from his hidden camera. He then studied John as he walked around the room and looked out the windows. Katanga's head of security was with him in the security office in the Mansion.

"Those two look like they could be trouble Mr. Katanga"
Unlike the other guards, Katanga's security chief was English.

"Yes, they are trouble Jacob. The question is for whom?

"After their stint at the prison, you still have doubts."

It was more of a statement than a question.

Chap 9
The Last Time

MacLennan inched the throttles to their forward stop increasing the RPM's to the red line and slightly beyond. Ray was in the copilots seat with his eyes screwed shut not believing what they were about to attempt. But before MacLennan released the pressure on the brakes, he thought back briefly to the whirlwind of events of the past twenty-four hours.

After being greeted by an armed welcoming committee at Boscobel for the second time, the Aztec was searched for radio frequency detection gear. No bugs were found and neither were John and Ray's guns or the ten thousand dollars secreted away in the forward compartment of the Aztec.

John and Ray were then ushered aboard Katanga's personal helicopter and flown to his mountaintop residence where they had lunch with Katanga who told them that in addition to their upcoming surveillance duties, they would be making a delivery for him outside the Florida Keys. Naturally, the delivery was a drop of cocaine to a waiting boat at specified GPS coordinates.

The meeting with Katanga was disappointing. After advising John and Ray of how well they had performed in their "test" at the prison, he told them the GPS coordinates of the drop and the location and radio frequencies of the surveillance locations on the East Coast from Miami to Maine; and as an afterthought, Katanga had just one more requirement. The purpose was, as he stated, "to test MacLennan's competency as a pilot". Simply MacLennan was to land the Aztec in a six hundred foot landing strip that had a slight upward grade located on Katanga's compound.

This was not a problem MacLennan remembered telling Katanga, since the Aztec had relatively good short field performance and the uphill grade would help. However, even under the best of conditions, which were certainly not now present, there was no way that the Aztec was going to take off in less than one-thousand feet without having a steam catapult.

Katanga had just smiled and then showed John and Ray his landing strip. Ray looked in bewilderment while MacLennan understood Katanga's meaning immediately. John had read about pilots during what Katanga had in mind, but had never did it, or ever intended too, himself.

Simply, the landing strip began and ended at the edge of a cliff. If a plane did not have sufficient take off speed at the end of the runway, it would pick up speed as it fell off the cliff and would hopefully have enough airspeed to fly before it reached the bottom of the cliff two-thousand feet below.

When John had told Ray what they were going to do, he just looked at him in disbelief.

"Ray don't worry." John said, "It'll be just like a roller coaster ride.

Ray looked at John in further disbelief.

"I hate roller coasters."

****

Within an hour MacLennan had landed the Aztec on the mountainside strip and had gotten some idea of how it was to land on an aircraft carrier. It wasn't his smoothest landing, and he had to stand on the brakes, but as pilots say, "any landing you walk away from is a good landing."

John and Ray spent the night in Katanga's guest room not saying much to each other for fear of the room being bugged.

After a breakfast of juice, coffee and rolls, John and Ray found themselves in the Aztec staring at the cliff's end.

As MacLennan released the pressure on the brakes, the Aztec began its downhill takeoff roll to the edge of the cliff.

With maximum fuel and two hundred pounds of cocaine in the rear passenger compartment, the Aztec was close to gross.

After two hundred feet, the Aztec had accelerated to only 25 MPH. Recommended takeoff speed was 90 MPH and stall speed was about 60 MPH depending on plane weight and weather conditions.

At the end of four hundred feet they were at forty miles per hour. When they were a hundred feet before the end of the runway, John lowered the flaps to thirty degrees to increase the lift and lower the stall speed. As they approached the end of the runway MacLennan quickly pushed the yoke forward and just as quickly pulled back and bounced the plane off the runway over the cliffs edge. The Aztecs speed was at fifty-five, and she was only able to obtain this speed due to the downward slope of the runway, and as soon as she was airborne, the stall buzzer went off.

MacLennan pushed the nose forward into a dive in order to gain airspeed and raised the landing gear which gave them a few more miles per hour. With one thousand feet left to the bottom of the cliff, The Aztec's airspeed was a relatively comfortable 100 MPH. Having a large margin of safety, MacLennan pulled back on the yoke and began to navigate his way to the shore.

As far as roller coaster rides were concerned, this was only marginal. What MacLennan was wondering is how he would enter cliff flying into his logbook; just something else to add to the resume.

Within five minutes they were over the coast and MacLennan leveled out at 500 feet. He was below Kingston radar but high enough to offer a somewhat comfortable margin of safety.

John had a nagging feeling he was forgetting something. He then realized that Ray hadn't said a word since they had gotten in the plane.

John looked over at Ray and saw him in his usual takeoff position. The main difference was Ray's catatonic position never lasted this long after takeoff.

John leaned over and none to gently shook Ray.

"Hello, Helen Keller, you're still alive."

"Never again. This is definitely the last time, ever, ever, ever."

John had a couple of comebacks for Ray but figured he'd leave well enough alone.

DEA had installed a number of disguised instruments prior to his takeoff from the states that they thought might come in handy.

One was a spare Automatic Directional Finder, ADF. However, it was an ADF in appearance only. When turned on and tuned to a certain frequency, it acted as a RF detector and would point to any hidden microphones in the plane that might have been installed by Katanga's lackeys.

After fiddling with the dial, MacLennan was able to ascertain that the Aztec was bug free. The next instrument DEA installed was a backup radio. This was in fact a radio not only in appearance but operation. However, this had a special high frequency that was not one of the approved civilian aircraft frequencies, but a classified military frequency in case Katanga was monitoring the normal in-flight radio channels. In addition, there was a scrambler that would make it virtually impossible to intercept their communications to DEA.

By the time they had cleared Jamaican airspace, Ray was beginning to emerge from his zombie like state.

Fortunately for Ray, it was a letter perfect day for flying. There was little or no turbulence and no forecast of storms until early or late evening.

John then dialed in the frequency for one of DEA's Cessna Citation that should be airborne.

"Mama Bear, Mama Bear this is Goldilocks, over." John said into the mike using the prearranged code names. After two more attempts, the pair of undercover agents were rewarded for their efforts.

"Goldilocks, this is Mama Bear, your transmission is scratchy but readable. Be advised Fat Albert is down."

"Yea Mama Bear, the porridge is warm and Goldie is on her way home."

"Roger that, how you going to get there?" Steve Novel's voice came through clearly.

"We have clearance to go by the most direct route. Repeat by the most direct route. The Big Bad Wolf has more connections than we thought. We also have a bag of goodies to drop off at a rabbit hutch."

In code, MacLennan had relayed to DEA that they were going to be flying to Key West over Cuba, the most direct route, and make a drop prior to landing in Key West.

Ray then took over the radio and rattled off the latitude and longitude coordinates of the drop off. This was in code also.

Within fifteen minutes the Aztec was in Cuban airspace.

"I don't like this Mac. What happens if some Cuban fighters come after us?"

"Simple, we crash and burn."

"Great!"

"I don't think that's going to happen though, remember we got some intelligence that some of Katanga's flights were over Cuba, this just confirms it."

"As far as I'm concerned, it'll be confirmed when we get through this in one piece."

"Can't argue with you there, Ray."

DEA's Citation had to take the long way around Cuba to Key West. But even at 60% power they would get to Key West ahead of MacLennan's Aztec.

The flight across Cuba was uneventful.

"How about that. Not even a Cessna 150 as a welcoming committee." Ray said somewhat relieved.

"It looked like a nice Island."

"Yea, my Dad visited it a few times in the pre-Castro days, he said it was the Las Vegas of the south but only with nice sandy beaches and eighty-two degree crystal clear water."

"Ray hand me that nav-chart of Key West. I want to see where we're going to make the drop in relation to Key West, we only have ninety miles to go."

John plotted the GPS coordinates and whistled softly.

"What's up?" Ray asked.

****

"The drop off is just north of the Marquessa Keys."

"That sounds familiar." Ray said.

"That's the general location of one of the biggest treasure finds ever."

"Now I remember. That's where Mel Fisher found that sunken Spanish ship. What was it called?"

"The Atocha. I remember reading about it. He has a museum in Key West full of gold and silver and Emeralds."

"We're definitely in the wrong business Mac."

"Amen."

Ray began to look at the instructional packet that they had received from Katanga.

"Mac what's this about Fat Albert not being operational for the next week?"

MacLennan had gone over the packet the previous evening before going to bed.

"Fat Albert is a tethered balloon fifteen thousand feet in the air just north of Key West. Attached to the balloon is a downward looking radar that can discern low level planes even flying at wave top level. It's pretty accurate too. It's helped interdiction efforts by about a hundred percent. Only problem, it's down for maintenance just as much as it's up."

"This guy thinks of everything," Ray said. Then as an afterthought;

"Well almost everything."

In a few minutes MacLennan had the Florida Keys in sight. They were still flying at five hundred flight and MacLennan began making a slow descent to two-hundred feet while detouring to the south of Key West.

"What's up Mac.?"

"This is the toughest part of the flight. There's a naval air station on Key West that controls all legitimate airborne flights. In order to look legal, we have to circle Key West well below its radar's capability, turn around, and then start to climb to about one-thousand feet."

"I give up why."

"Elementary my dear Melena, we'll then contact Key West approach and tell them that we're a seaplane that just took off in route to conduct a photo survey north of the Marquessa Keys. Not uncommon since treasure hunters can sometimes find shipwrecks from the air. That'll explain our circling and low altitude. In addition, approach control will vector all flights away from our area."

"Pretty slick. This way Katanga has the US Navy working for him."

"Like you said Ray, this guy Katanga thinks of everything."

Ray then tried to contact DEA's citation and was met with an instant response.

"DEA and the coasties are all set and in place." Ray said after about two minutes of banter with the DEA.

"Novel said that there are three forty-one footer's in the area and they all have the target boat, a sixty-two foot sailing schooner, on radar.

By this time, the Aztec had circled around to the north of Key West and began to make its ascent to one thousand feet.

John then turned the other radio dial to one-one-nine-point two-five, and contacted Key West Approach.

****

"Key West approach this is twin SeaBee five-four-four Papa X-Ray, we've just taken off from Sugar loaf Shores enroute to north of the Marquessa's for a photo survey at or under one-thousand feet."

The commander of the naval air station had already been brought on line with the plan and all had agreed it would be best to continue the charade over the radio frequency in case any of Katanga's men were listening.

"Roger twin Seabee, we have you on radar but just barely, your air space will be clear but be advised there are a number of F-18's ten miles south of you carrying out exercises. They should be no factor. Monitor this channel for any further advisories."

"Roger Key West Approach, we'll advise of our return trip."

****

Aboard the sixty-two foot schooner, Serenity, a man who was monitoring flight frequencies toggled the intercom switch to the main salon.

"They're on their way Bill."

"OK, get Jim and Rico ready with the Zodiac to make the pickup."

Bill Daley controlled the largest cocaine distribution ring in the Florida Keys. Just a few more drops like these and Daley was going to retire to an Island he bought in the Greater Antilles. Life was good he thought.

He then flipped the intercom switch to talk to his radioman.

"Let me know when you've got confirmation with him."

"No problem."

MacLennan and Ray were by now over the coordinates of the drop zone.

"There she is Mac. What a beauty."

Ray pointed to the schooner below as MacLennan tuned in the frequency to talk to the drug runner in the pre-determined code to tell him that there were no law enforcement types in the area.

"I hear you flyboy."

"Hello Serendipity, this is day watch. The fishing is good."

"I still hear you, but my radar shows a couple of boats eighteen miles off my bow at zero-six-zero degrees. Give them a double check for me."

Daley didn't get where he was by not being cautious.

"We copy." John answered. "Be right back."

"Guy doesn't take any chances, does he?" Ray said.

"Mmm. Probably why he hasn't been caught."

Ray informed DEA what they were doing.

"That course and distance should put you right over the cutters, "Novel said from the citation.

"Roger," Ray said. "We'll tell him it's a couple of sport fishermen."

In a few minutes the Aztec was over the schooner.

"Serendipity, your coast is clear, looks like a couple of sports fishermen."

"OK, make your drop, we'll be standing by in the zodiac for the pickup."

John slowed the Aztec to under eighty miles per hour and saw the re-enforced rubber zodiac depart from the schooner.

"All right Ray, just let the packages fall out the door. The slipstream will take them under the rear of the plane."

****

"You sure these won't hit the ass end of the plane?" Ray asked as he started to grab the first of four fifty pound sacks of cocaine.

"Ray."

"Yea, I know, trust me."

Ray opened the door and threw the first bag of coke out and watched it sail under the tail of the Aztec with a sigh of relief.

Just as this was happening, a Coast Guard helicopter took off from Key West Naval Station with a crew of Navy seals and a DEA agent.

The sack hit the water with a splash and then floated to the surface as a result of the foam packed inside along with the coke.

Ray repeated the procedure three more times, each time with a visible sigh of relief as the coke cleared the tail of the Aztec, and each time watched the coke float to the surface and retrieved by the zodiac.

MacLennan kept circling in the Aztec until Serendipity's captain called him.

"We got everything, how's it looking."

"Nice and clear," John said.

"Ok we're outta here. If anyone asks, I didn't see you and you're blind."

"Got it, John answered.

"How about that guy, not so much as a thanks."

"Maybe the coasties will teach him some manners."

Ray then radioed the citation that the drop was complete and they would be heading to Key West airfield, and Steve Novel let Ray know what was in store for the schooner and crew of Serendipity.

"Those guys aren't taking any chances," Ray said to John.

"Why, what's up?"

They've got a helicopter full of Navy seals that's going to board the schooner," Ray said.

"Ok, why? I thought they were going to follow it and take it out at the dock."

Ray then relayed the plan to John that Steve Novel had told him. "Unlike the scheduled pick-ups, they don't know where this one came from. So they got a squad of Navy seals on a coastie helicopter that are going to board the schooner and if anyone's left, interrogate them."

"Why the coastie helicopter and not a Navy one?" John asked.

"The coasties have jurisdiction and the Seals are operating under that authority. There's also a DEA agent on board who will do the interrogating."

"Talk about interagency cooperation."

"Yea, Steve told us to check into the Hyatt at Key West and he'll call us tonight."

"Sounds good Ray. Well, step one done. Hope those Seals will be alright."

"You were never in the service were you Mac. The last people in this world you have to worry about are Navy Seals."

And then as an afterthought, "except for US Marines that is."

John then dialed in the frequency to Key West airport and began his landing procedure.

Chap 10
WE DON"T NEED ANOTHER HERO

Just another day in paradise. The forecast was typical for that time of year in Key West; hazy sunshine, temperature in the eighties with a chance of an afternoon shower. Even though each day's forecast said a chance of showers, it only rained once or twice a week at this time of year.

It was nine AM and John and Ray were having breakfast on the deck by the Hyatt's pool.

"Ya know Mac, I could get very use to this type of life. Now I know why you come down here on vacation so much. Is this where you usually stay?"

"I've stayed here once but the other times we stayed at the Marriott's Casa Marina. The rooms here at the Hyatt are a little nicer, but the grounds at the Casa have everything."

A waitress approached their table wearing only an alluring one-piece bathing suit and tropical wrap around skirt slit up the leg. She also had a nametag which said Sheri and Boston, Ma, written underneath.

After she had taken Ray and John's order, Ray asked what the Boston, Ma on her name tag meant.

"Oh, that's where I'm from. Almost all the waitresses here are displaced from somewhere in the states."

"How'd you come to pick Key West?" Ray said.

"I wanted to get as far away from Boston winters that I possibly could and still be somewhere where they speak English. Key West fit the bill. That was two years ago, and still going strong."

"Can't say I blame you."

As the waitress left to get their coffee Ray turned to MacLennan.

"Let me know when your next vacation is, I think the bride and I will join you."

"Ray I don't think you're gonna want to go with me on my next vacation," MacLennan said with a cryptic smile.

Before Ray could ask anything else about John's next vacation, they were joined by Steve Novel.

"How's it going?" Steve said as he sat down and motioned to the waitress for coffee.

People were starting to settle down by the pool for another day of sunshine.

"Great view." Steve said as he was watching one girl take off her robe to reveal a one piece thong bathing suit.

"I use to have a girlfriend that had a theory about bathing suits," MacLennan said also enjoying the view.

"At one time or another you had a girlfriend with a theory about everything," Ray said.

"What was the theory?" Steve asked.

"If the suit couldn't fit in the palm of your hand when it was balled up, the suit had too much material," John said ignoring Ray.

"I think I'm in love with your old girlfriend," Steve, who was also a bachelor, answered.

"Why is she an old girlfriend and not a current one?"

"She wanted to get married and have babies," John said.

"I see what you mean. What a terrible way to break up a great relationship," Steve said.

"Oh well, all good things."

After the waitress brought Steve his coffee, conversation turned to the day's work at hand.

"How's the flying look?" Steve asked.

"Pretty good. There's just an outside chance of showers and they usually dissipate by the time they reach Bimini."

"The rendezvous is supposed to be ten miles north of the island at the very edge of the shipping lanes well out of US water's," John said and then asked Steve if there was any change in plans.

"No. We'll be up there in the Citation and the coasties will have a couple of forty-one footer's plus one of their new go-fast boats."

"Excuse me," Ray interrupted.

"Go fast boats?"

"Yea, the coasties are getting pretty smart. Most of these offshore pickups are made in cigarette boats that can do about seventy MPH. The Forty-one footer's will provide radar support and we'll shadow the bad guys back to port in a go-fast boat and helicopter."

"More Navy Seals?"

"Not this time. Yesterday the Seals were the only thing we could get in a pinch. Kevin Finn, who's an ex-army ranger now in the Reserves, will lead a force of ten specially trained DEA agents making the arrest. They'll be at Homestead Air Force Base standing by to board a Blackhawk helicopter borrowed from Kevin's unit, and fly to where ever the bad guys dock. We'll also be coordinating with local police and DEA agents on the ground. Hopefully we'll be able to take them down without any gunfire, but we're prepared for the worst."

"Any idea, where the bad guys will be going after the pickup." John asked.

"None. But we have teams from both Dade county and Monroe county sheriff's department on standby. What's your flying time from here to there?"

"It's about a two hour flight if we go non-stop, but I'm planning on landing at an uncontrolled airport just north of Key Largo for a pit stop and to see if there's any change in plans. If we have to wait, I rather be on the ground than circling in the sky."

"Amen to that." Ray said.

"After that it's about a thirty minute flight to the rendezvous point. So we'll leave Key West about noontime. How 'bout you guys?"

"We'll be leaving in about an hour and doing a lot of circling. Last report has the bad guy's boat where it should be and it'll be on time for the rendezvous. The citation's been specially equipped and we're going to be re-fueled in the air."

"Sounds like fun." Ray said sarcastically.

"I heard about your trip down." Steve said more to Ray.

"It's not everyone who can experience a thunderstorm the way you did Ray," Novel said with a hint of a smile which brought a scowl to Ray's face.

"Not funny."

"Some people have no sense of humor."

****

At Key West airport John began the ritual pre-inspection of the Aztec. The fuel had been topped off the previous night and he was checking it for any water content when Ray grabbed his arm.

"Hey Mac, what's that plane over there?"

Ray was pointing to a twin engine plane tail dragger that could seat about 20.

"It looks like a modern version of a DC-3."

"That's exactly what it is. Someone came up with a new design that put turbo-props on the plane and some modifications to the nose and tail. Instead of just flying at 140 knots, she'll do about 220. It also improved its takeoff roll and overall handling ability."

"I've never seen one like it."

"There aren't many. You figure you're looking at close to half-million dollars in improvements including the paint job.

Not many people have, or are going to spend that kind of money on a plane that's about sixty years old."

After a moment's thought, Ray said, "I think I like it better the old way."

"Yea, I agree. It takes away a lot of its character. Hell, my grandfather flew in one of those crates during the Normandy invasion. He was in the 101st airborne."

"That explains it."

"Explains what?"

"Where all your crazy genes come from. It's hereditary. It's also catchy too, because I'm doing these crazy things right along with you. And don't say trust me."

John just smiled, and as an afterthought:

"Hey Ray, no need to hide the guns any longer in the nose of the plane. Might as well take them with us, just in case."

"Yea, just in case."

After he was done the pre-flight, both partners got in the plane, and for the umpteenth time in as many days and started the takeoff procedure.

****

The flight north along the Keys was relatively uneventful. It was smooth going with the same emerald green and blue water they had seen during their recent flying.

As they approached Key Largo, MacLennan took a look at the stats for Ocean Club airport where they were going to land. It was a privately owned airport, but John had met the owner's son on a previous trip to Florida who told him that as long as he calls ahead, he's welcome to land for fuel and a bite to eat at the private resort's lounge.

The runway was thirty-five hundred feet, and generally well taken care of, but then again, anything was better than Katanga's airstrip.

When the Aztec was 10 miles out, MacLennan broadcast his intention to land to anyone who may be in the general area.

"Ocean Reef traffic, this is Aztec five-four-four-papa x-ray, ten miles to the southeast inbound for landing."

As the Aztec approached the airport they heard no other radio traffic.

"Isn't that odd Mac, no other traffic?"

"Not really, the airport was built as part of a condominium complex. There's a pool and little lounge next to the runway for the residents only and the only people who can land here without permission are residents."

"Gotcha."

MacLennan entered the airport pattern announcing his intentions to land. Crossed the midfield point of the runway at twelve hundred feet to scan for traffic and see which way the wind was blowing.

As expected, it was an easterly wind and there were no planes on the runway waiting to takeoff.

MacLennan then descended to one-thousand feet and entered the downwind leg of the eastern runway.

As he turned the base leg of the landing pattern, MacLennan noticed what appeared to be a newly constructed dock and warehouse. The only boat tied up to the dock was about a fifty foot Bertram that probably cost the owner close to one and half million dollars.

Upon landing, MacLennan had to back taxi off the runway and pulled up next to the restaurant/lounge/terminal building that had only three or four couples.

"Not much of a Mecca, is it?" Ray said seeing the sparse crowd.

"No, I guess not. When I called, I spoke to a bartender. He said my buddy wasn't here but we could land anyway."

After parking and securing the plane, John and Ray sauntered into the lounge.

"How ya'll doin'. You the young fella I spoke to?" The bartender greeted them as they approached the bar.

"Yes sir. Thanks for letting us land."

"No problem. But I hope you don't need any fuel. The tank developed a leak about a year ago, and with all the new environmental regulations, it just wasn't worth the expense."

"No problem, we got gas in Key West and after the trip up here we have over four hours of fuel left and only two more hours of flying."

"Great, can I get you anything to eat or drink?"

"That dock over there new?" MacLennan asked the bartender pointing to the dock he saw from the air, now over a mile away.

"Yea, one of the residents here, guy from Miami, built it especially for his boat and his use. The warehouse is supposed to be for some fish processing. Kind of a recluse, he won't let anyone else use it, and, funny, he never uses the boat that much anyway let alone fish for the warehouse, and God knows why he erected that fence. I guess when you have all that money you can afford to do strange things.

""Nice to have money," MacLennan answered. He thought it was kind of strange too, but he had other things on his mind.

After John and Ray had ordered, John asked if there was a phone he could use since he had left his cell phone on the plane.

"Yup, over in the corner."

"Be right back Ray."

John walked over to the pay phone in the corner. As he dialed DEA's office in Miami he enjoyed the view of the ocean off of Key Largo. He could see himself moving down here very easily and he felt that he could do beach bum with the best of them.

His daydream was shattered by the ringing of the phone on the other end of the connection. The number he was given was a private number and the conversation was to be short unless there was a change in plans, in which case he would be given another number and instructions.

The phone was answered on the third ring with a simple hello by a female voice.

"Hello mom, this is Goldie. How you feeling?" John said into the phone feeling a little foolish with the semi-cloak and dagger talk.

"Everything is fine dear. Hope to see you soon," followed by an immediate click.

Well that was good. The voice at the other end was very sultry, and if John wasn't so involved with Darcy, he would've looked forward to meeting "mom". Oh well, he wasn't complaining.

"How's everything going?" Ray asked on his return to the bar.

"On schedule. It's one-thirty now, we can leave at two-thirty and still have plenty of time."

"Oh goody, more flying."

"Ray, will you ever get over your fear of flying?"

"Mac, I've been in a killer thunderstorm, and a free fall off a cliff, not to mention all the flying over water. This whole case has been the plane ride from hell. NO."

John could only laugh.

"Yea, we have had easier flights."

Just then lunch came and both partners concentrated on their food. The way these operations went, it could be their last meal for a while.

By the time they finished eating, and naturally having dessert, it was getting close to two-thirty.

"Time to get going."

Ray paid the bill, making sure to get a receipt for his expense account, and both partners headed to the plane.

The takeoff was as uneventful as the landing and MacLennan climbed to thirty-five hundred feet for the hop to Bimini.

About twenty miles south of the rendezvous, John passed over an ocean going tug.

"That tug looks out of place in the Caribbean without anything to tow, "John said.

"It's pretty big too, over a hundred feet I'd guess. Wonder if that's our rendezvous boat?" Ray answered.

"Could be. Anyway, we'll know soon enough. Time to call mama bear."

"Mama bear, mama bear, this is Goldie over." Ray said into the mike, and then as an afterthought;

"I refuse to call myself Goldilocks."

"But Ray, it's you."

Before Ray could answer, Steve Novel answered his call.

"Hello Goldie, everything's a go and your dinner will be on time."

"Roger mama bear, we'll advise you of contact."

"No need, we're monitoring already."

"You see the citation at all Mac?"

"I think so. Looks like it's above us at around ten thousand feet. Well, since our friends are going to be on time, we have about one-half hour of circling to do. Might as well check around."

MacLennan flew a circle in the sky that was roughly ten miles in diameter, and slowed the Aztec to about one-hundred-twenty knots.

"At this speed we'll be able to make a couple of large circles Ray. I think that's one of the Coast guard boats over there just behind that coral reef."

"Looks like it."

MacLennan had pointed to a boat that was about ten miles northeast of the rendezvous point adjacent to a shallow reef system that ran north and south of the Bimini Island chain.

As they reached the southern portion of the circle in the sky they saw the ocean going tug steaming towards the rendezvous point.

"Looks like that tug's our baby." Ray said looking out the window appearing to have momentarily lost his fear of planes as the rendezvous approached.

"There's something else we missed before, Mac, I see another wake about ten miles behind the tug, looks like that's the second Coast Guard boat with the cigarette boat behind it."

"Aren't they kind of close to the target boat?"

"Not really Ray, before we took off, I not only got a weather briefing from flight service, but I also listened to the marine report. It's real hazy, and visibility on the surface is only limited to five miles. So with their radar down, they won't be able to see the good guys until it's too late."

"But they won't be expecting that will they, since they have us," Ray said.

"Nice when a plan comes together."

"Knock on wood."

"Any sign of the pickup boat?"

"Don't know? There're a lot of sport fishermen's we passed over. It could be any of them."

Towards the end of their second circle, the Aztec was hailed on the pre-arranged channel. By then, the Cessna Citation was nowhere in sight.

"Four-Papa-X-Ray, this is the RV Sea Slug. Do you copy? Over."

"Hello Sea Slug, this is your eye in the sky. We'll wiggle our wings." Ray answered as John gently rocked the Aztec from side to side.

"The coast is clear thirty miles to the north and at least ten south."

After a brief silence the same voice answered on the radio.

"We copy. Check further south and east and let us know anything suspicious. You do know what a Coast Guard cutter looks like, correct."

"That's what you pay us for," Ray answered sarcastically.

"What's he take us for?" Ray said.

"At least we're not Goldilocks," John said as he pointed the Aztec east.

"Ray, one of the Sport fishermen seems to be heading towards the Sea Slug."

"Yea. I see it Mac. Probably the pickup boat. Let's call it in."

"Sea Slug, Sea Slug, no apparent heat, but it looks like there's about a forty foot blue and white fishing boat heading your way."

"We copy. That's our contact. Continue surveillance."

"Roger."

"Looking good. I'll contact the Citation Mac. Mama Bear. You copy that."

"We got it and we're on it. Goldie. Good work."

"Mac, we gotta get a new code."

MacLennan then turned the plane south. After flying over the two Coast guard boats, they continued a little further, and then radioed the drug boat.

"Sea Slug, Sea Slug, You're six o'clock is clear."

"Understand four-papa-x-ray, keep circling and we'll advise."

John and Ray continued to circle for the next hour while the Sea Slug met and unloaded a dozen bales of marijuana and one hundred keys of cocaine aboard the sport fisherman.

During that time they saw the Coasties position their boats for an interception and coastline surveillance.

"Still haven't seen the Citation Mac."

"Neither have I. But they're around somewhere. After we finish with the Sea Slug, let's see what they want us to do."

Another half-hour passed before the loading was complete while John and Ray kept circling.

"How's everything look up there papa-x-ray? We're about ready to wrap it up." The voice from the Sea-Slug crackled.

"Everything's clear," Ray answered.

"OK, we'll see you in a couple of days in Charleston."

"Understood, good luck fishing."

"Yea right."

While Ray was talking to the Sea Slug, the sport fisherman pulled away from the mother ship and headed west towards Miami as its bow rose and then settled down as it accelerated and planed out.

"Mama bear, targets on its way. What would you like us to do?"

"At the target's current speed, they'll be in sight of land in about two hours. You can either circle over the Biscayne VOR, or land and rejoin us."

"What do you think Mac?"

"I think I've had enough of circling for one day. Let's land, top off our tanks and then meet them over the Biscayne nav aid just southeast of Miami."

As Ray relayed the info to Steve Novel in the citation, MacLennan turned the Aztec towards South Bimini airport ten miles away.

"It'll take us about fifteen minutes to get there and land, another thirty to make a pit stop, fuel, and take off, and twenty minutes of flying time to get to Biscayne Key. Plenty of time to make the party.

"Mac, we gonna need a passport or anything? I've never been to the Bahamas."

"No, just the driver's license. DEA already cleared us."

"Famous last words."

True to form, the flight in and out of Bimini occurred without incident. The Bahamian custom agent barely looked at Ray and John's licenses to the point that Ray commented he could have shown his son's Mickey Mouse card and still have passed. Tourism, especially American tourism, was the Bahamas biggest industry, and far be it for any official of the Bahamas to offend one of those tourists who would spend vast sums of money in their country, and if they were to engage in some illegal activity, well it was no concern of the custom agents what went from their country to America.

After taking off, MacLennan climbed to forty-five hundred feet while Ray contacted Steve Novel in the Citation.

"Ray," Steve was also getting tired of calling Ray goldilocks. "They made a course change and it looks like they're heading for someplace in Key Largo. It simplifies things somewhat since we'll be out of Miami airport's traffic space and closer to where Kevin's team of agents are at Homestead."

"How far out are they?" Ray asked.

"They're about ten miles from the northern tip, and it looks like they'll be going inside the key. Kevin's team has already taken off from Homestead and they're going to be standing by just south of the airport. They're only two minutes flying time from the water."

"Roger that." Ray answered

"Where to Mac?"

Something was bothering MacLennan, but he couldn't quite place it. There was something familiar about this. He then reached for the sectional map and looked at the area where the target boat was heading when it suddenly came to him.

"Ray I know where they're going."

"Say what?"

"I know where they're going."

"And how is that Obie Wan," Ray said with mock reverence not quite believing his partner.

"Ray remember that new dock and warehouse that was built at the Ocean Reef Club?"

"Yea vaguely. I had my eyes closed when you were landing but I remember you talking to the bartender."

"I can't be one-hundred percent, but I'm ninety-nine percent sure that's the boat that was docked there, and remember the warehouse that was never used, he'll dock around dusk, and once it's dark, he'll unload the stuff. From the bar, the warehouse obscures the boat, so you or any patron won't be able to see what's being unloaded, even with binoculars.

"Mac, I'm semi-impressed." Ray said after digesting what MacLennan had told him.

"Only semi-impressed?"

"Yea, if you're right, then I'll advance to fully impressed."

Ray then got on the radio and relayed MacLennan's theory to Steve in the Citation.

"That makes sense," Steve replied after talking to one of the coasties in the Citation who was familiar with the area and at one time also wondered about the warehouse.

"I'm going to direct Kevin's team to head over that way. Even if you're wrong, they'll still be in position to go elsewhere." Steve said.

"One thing we didn't consider is that they would go back to the Keys. We don't have any local cops in position over there. It'll take a good hour for them to get a team there and if you're right, the boat's only half-hour out. I don't think Kevin's team is going to need any back up, but it's nice to let the good guys know what's going on."

"Alright, we're going to fly over there and see if we can help," MacLennan said into his headset."

"Ok, I'll let Kevin know. They'll be there before you, but stay out of there way if it gets hairy, they're armed for bear and all you guys have are pistols. We don't need any hero's," Steve said after a moment's hesitation.

"Don't worry." Ray answered.

"I left my hero's cap at home. Out."

MacLennan had already turned towards the Ocean Reef Club and was already beginning his descent.

"Any idea what we're gonna do once we get there Mac."

"I think we'll have to play that by ear. Chances are, this is gonna be a cake walk."

****

Kevin Finn checked for the third time that his M-16 was locked and loaded. He looked around at his assault team as the Blackhawk helicopter was taking off. Of the ten DEA agents in his team, eight, including himself, had prior military training, and five of them had either Special Forces or Ranger training. All had seen action in one form or the other, whether it was in the Persian Gulf, Somalia or one or two classified actions that were known to only a select few.

Since the Waco Texas fiasco with ATF, the mode of thinking within law enforcement had changed drastically in regards to operations of this nature. Gone were the days of entering a situation with only handguns and thinking the bad guys would surrender in fear once you yelled police. Too often were they only not surrendering, but shooting it out with the various law enforcement agencies, usually outgunning and sometimes out manning the good guys.

DEA operations were now being carried out in military fashion in full combat gear. Not only did the agents have their Sig Sauer automatic handguns with sixteen shot clips, but military issued M-16's with full automatic settings; and if that wasn't enough, it would be difficult to outgun a Blackhawk helicopter with its two machine guns, not to mention its array of missiles.

The Black hawk was skimming over the brief stretch of water that separates the Florida mainland from Key Largo at fifty feet while doing one hundred twenty miles per hour. The pilot was making a circuitous route, first circling to the south, and then heading north in order to keep out of view of the drug boat now five miles to the north.

"Captain." The pilot of the helicopter addressed Kevin using his military title.

"What's the plan once we get there? We're about a minute out."

"There should be a fence surrounding a warehouse and a dock. Set us down outside the fence, we'll pick a spot once we see it, and then we'll get the go or no go within five minutes. If this is the spot, take off and go to the south of the runway. If we need you for fire support we'll call."

"Roger Captain," and then as an afterthought,

"Don't hesitate to call if these are druggies, we'd love to rock n' roll. A friend's son nearly died of an overdose a while back."

"Nothing like payback," Kevin answered.

"We've got the airfield in sight captain," The pilot said to Kevin.

"And I see the warehouse."

Kevin then went to the front of the helicopter next to the pilot.

"See that blind spot in the southwest corner?" Kevin pointed as he talked.

"That's a good as place as any. There aren't any windows on the south side, and I only see one small window high up on the west side."

"Confirm," was all the pilot said as he throttled back and began to flare the Blackhawk for its landing.

****

Lt Commander Pasquale DiFruscia, Pat to his friends, was a third generation Italian whose grandfather had fought under Patton in WW II and whose father was a marine stationed at Khe San during the TET offensive. He was proud of the fact

171

that he was commanding a Coast Guard cutter in the war against drugs. Though he was constantly ribbed by the two older Difruscia as being a member of the shallow water Navy, they were equally proud of him. He was fighting a war that they both considered just as dangerous as the ones they had fought.

Difruscia was commanding, the TAMWORTH, one of the Coast Guards one-hundred-ten footer's that was shadowing the drug boat now heading towards the Ocean Reef Club. Both Coast Guard ships were tracking the Bertram, the make of the Sports Fisherman that they had just recently identified after closing to within three miles. Visibility had deteriorated as the day progressed and Difruscia wasn't worried about the druggies identifying either of the Coast Guard ships since they were just at the limit of visibility. The Bertram was only one-half mile from the dock and Difruscia was getting tired of this cat and mouse game and hoped that he and his crew would take part on the actual apprehension as opposed to just being an ornament while DEA had all the fun.

"Skipper, I have the Blackhawk on radar now and it's approaching the warehouse from the southwest. Should be on them at any second and you should just be able to see it."

"Good work Frenchie." Difruscia said to his radar operator. He knew that it was difficult if not impossible to identify a low flying helicopter with his onboard radar. Frenchie had done a good job of distinguishing it from the background clutter on the screen.

Difruscia knew what he was looking for and was able to see the Blackhawk's approach. What he didn't count on seeing was the puffs of smoke emanating from the warehouse. Sound travels at six hundred miles and it would have taken a full fifteen seconds for any sounds to reach the TAMWORTH. However Difruscia didn't need fifteen seconds to realize what was happening.

"Helm, full speed ahead, all hands, Battle Stations."

****

"What the hell..." was all the bartender at the Ocean Reef
Club was able to say as the Blackhawk roared past the lounge
decelerating from one-hundredsixty miles per hour.

His draw dropped more when he caught a brief glimpse of
the machine guns and rockets slung low on the side.

He began to walk outside the lounge to get a better look
when all hell broke loose.

****

Barry Brenner lived in the Keys all his life and was brought
up on the water. He had been running drugs for fifteen years
and at thirty-five his wealth was more than people could
imagine, but he still wanted more. He was planning to buy
the entire Ocean Reef Club and establish his own empire. His
friend in the Monroe County detective division kept him
informed of any drug investigations that may come his way,
and he assured Brenner that he was free and clear.

The operation he had going with Dennis Green was
virtually fool proof. The plane overhead acting as a spotter
during a pickup was genius. As soon as he found a pilot he
could trust, he was going to buy a plane and start his own
surveillance operation. There was never such a thing as being
too careful.

"Hey Barry, you got the radar on?" One of the deck hands
asked him.

"No. Why?"

"Boat! Just on the horizon behind us. Can't make them
out." The deck hand had only spotted one of the Coast Guard
surveillance ships

173

Brenner knew the waters off the Keys like he knew the way around his house. With that knowledge and the combination of the spotter plane, he felt pretty secure and hadn't bothered to switch on the radar since it was usually nothing but a distraction in clear weather. Besides, he prided himself in the knowledge that he didn't need any instruments to get from point A to point B.

Brenner switched on the radar and not only saw the boat that his deckhand was referring too, but a second blip that was a mirror image of the first.

Brenner could make out that they were boats as large as his fifty two foot Bertram and they were on an identical course to his. He knew that they couldn't be the Coast Guard, and he had the biggest boat on Ocean Reef, so what could this be. His worst fears were soon confirmed as his thoughts were interrupted by the gunfire from his warehouse.

****

Brenner had five guards who were on duty at the warehouse playing cards on the second floor in air-conditioned comfort. Brenner could afford such luxuries as an air-conditioned warehouse that could also bunk ten men. It was only by pure chance that one of the guards got up from the poker table to stretch and looked out the window. At first he was partially blinded by the sun that was beginning to set in the west. He was then stunned for a moment by a sight that he couldn't believe, there was a helicopter landing thirty feet outside the perimeter fence with black clad men disembarking with M-16's.

"Cops, get your guns, they're coming out of a helicopter."

David Gale, like the other four guards were either ex-cons on parole or wanted for one felony or another. They all had a lot to lose by being arrested and one had a death penalty hanging over his head. They were all motivated to evade arrest, and if it meant killing a cop, well, for some of them it wouldn't be the first time.

Two of the guards began to fire from the second story with semiautomatic pistols while the other three ran downstairs to get the automatic rifles. From the second story the DEA agents were fifty yards from the warehouse. At that range, handguns would begin to lose their accuracy. Both guards emptied their clips of fifteen bullets each with only two agents being hit.

One was hit square in the chest and knocked on his back. The vest he was wearing stopped the bullet, but with a velocity of eleven hundred sixty feet per second, the impact from the nine millimeter slug cracked a rib over below his heart, but saved his life.

The second agent was hit in the shoulder.

The remaining agents didn't need an order to return fire. They dropped to the ground and began to spray the warehouse. Corrugated tin was no match and offered little resistance to a .223 bullet fired from an M-16 on full automatic or three round bursts.

When the agents first returned fire, only three of them knew that the shots were coming from the second floor window. The other agents sprayed the entire west side of the warehouse in what they hoped would be suppressing fire.

The first barrage killed one of the guards on the second floor and wounded another. The bullet entered David Gale's side over his left kidney and exited through his back. A clean non-fatal wound that could easily be healed. It was the first time that he was shot and he was surprised that the pain wasn't that bad. There was a burning sensation but nothing he couldn't handle. After he emptied his clip, he ran downstairs to get a rifle and something to put over his wounds.

Of the three guards that were running downstairs, none were hit, and by the time they made it to the windows, they were greeted by a fully loaded Blackhawk helicopter.

As one of the guards grabbed a mac 10, the entire side of the building disintegrated by a rocket fired from the Blackhawk. The disintegrating wall acted as shrapnel killing all the remaining guards except for Gale who was momentarily knocked senseless. Before he blacked out totally, his thoughts were that this was going to be a very bad day.

After the Blackhawk leveled most of the building with its rocket volley, the pilot began to spray what was remaining of the warehouse with his machine guns when Gale began to regain consciousness. Though his vision was blurred, and he was groggy, he was still able to see Kevin Finn and his men cutting through the fence that surrounded the building, and he wasn't sure what the noise was that sounded like basketball size hail pounding the building. He looked around and saw one of the hand-held LAW (Light Anti-tank Weapon) that Brenner had in case of an emergency.

At this particular time, Gale considered this an emergency and having been in the army briefly, he was familiar with its operation.

He grabbed it, extended the tubes at either end, aimed it at Finn and his men who were almost through the fence and fired.

The round from the rocket sliced through the fence two feet over Finns' head. Fortunately for Finn and his men, the round contained in a Law's rocket is armor piercing and not high explosive. The high explosive round would have detonated on contact with the fence, while the armor piercing round went through the fence and exploded harmlessly one-thousand feet away.

When the rocket passed over Finn's head, he knew he had just had a close call, but not from what.

The Blackhawk's pilot, a warrant officer who was a Persian Gulf veteran, didn't have to look twice to know a rocket when he saw it. He immediately began tracing an eight hundred round per minute line of fire along the path left by the LAW's smoke trail. When Warrant Officer Lynn Williams reached what he thought was the origin of the rocket with his machine guns, he decided to take no chances and fired another round of rockets. What little was left of the building vanished under the Blackhawk's volley and salvo.

As Finn and his men began to search the ruins of the warehouse, Williams knew that his work was done here and saw no reason why he shouldn't lend the Coasties a hand.

He ascended to 100 feet, pointed his nose towards Brenner's boat and began to accelerate.

David Gale no longer had to worry about having a bad day.

****

Brenner, who was by now, only one-half mile off the coast saw his business that had taken him years to build, destroyed within minutes, but Brenner was one who planned for the unforeseen and didn't give up easily. He rammed the throttles forward and turned south. He was hoping to lose the coasties in the reefs that would be too shallow for them to navigate, scuttle the boat and make his way to the safe house he thought he would never have to use. He was beginning to wonder what went wrong but had the more pressing problem of the Blackhawk.

Brenner was better prepared on his boat than the guards at the warehouse. While he had one of the deck hands take the controls, he went below into the aft cabin. Within seconds, he emerged with a hand held Stinger surface-to-air missile.

By this time Williams and his Blackhawk were two hundred yards off the bow of Brenner's boat and the Coast Guard boats were still a good two miles away, and since Brenner went to full speed, the only Coast Guard boat that was gaining was their cigarette boat.

Williams then got on his intercom, "Ok, everyone strap in. We're going after the bad guy's boat wide open and I'm going

177

to put some rounds off his bow. If that doesn't work, a few rounds in his bow should do it."

"Rock 'n roll skipper."

The Blackhawk came in low and fast with guns blazing.

By the time Williams was abreast of the bow, Brenner was on the stern with the stinger shouldered. By the time he took aim, and locked on, the Blackhawk was only two hundred yards away, and then he fired.

****

As the brief firefight proceeded at the warehouse, MacLennan descended to three thousand feet to get a better look.

"Mac, in case you've forgotten, this isn't an F-18."

"I haven't forgotten Ray, and unless they have a fifty caliber, we're safe at three thousand feet."

At that moment the LAW's fired from the warehouse exploded.

"Mac, that wasn't a fifty caliber, but it did make a good boom. LAW's rocket I'd guess." Ray momentarily forgot his fear of planes and the marine in him took over. But any worries they had about the crew of the Blackhawk and the assault team's safety was soon put to rest with the destruction of the warehouse.

As the Blackhawk closed on Brenner's Bertram, MacLennan further decreased his altitude to two-thousand feet.

Both MacLennan and Melena were clawing at the bit not being able to get into the fray. Neither partner was used to being a spectator when it came to a good fight.

"Mac, you're going lower."

"Yup."

"There's nothing we can do ya know."

"Yup."

As the Aztec began to circle the Bertram, Ray was the first to notice Brenner on the stern of the boat shouldering the Stinger.

"Holy shit Mac, that's no LAW's he's got, it's a God Dam Stinger."

Ray grabbed for the radio to inform DEA's citation just as Brenner pulled the trigger.

****

The army's warrant officers are amongst the best helicopter pilot's in the world, not only in flying, but reaction time, and Williams was one of the best. When he heard the tell-tale tone of the Stinger missile attempting to get a lock on his Blackhawk, he immediately began evasive maneuvers while activating his electronic counter measure techniques. The range was too close to completely avoid the missile, but it was only the speed of Williams's reactions that saved him and his crew.

As the stinger headed for the main turbine under the Blackhawks rotors, Williams stomped the right rudder to the floor while pulling up on the collective and yanking the cyclic to the right stop and then down.

The Blackhawk already at maximum speed for its altitude jumped up to the right and surged ahead.

The stinger missed the main intake but exploded near the tail rotor putting the Blackhawk partially damaging it and making control difficult.

****

The extra speed and the height that Williams gained in the Blackhawk allowed him to partially recover and head towards shore presenting the smallest target towards the possibility of another stinger, and at that moment, Brenner was motioning to one of the crew for another stinger. He had three on board and was happy to see that his investment in the stingers was about to pay off. If there was one thing that Brenner hated, it was an investment that yielded no return.

In the Aztec, both Ray and MacLennan saw Brenner getting the second stinger from one of Brenner's deck hands.

MacLennan pushed the throttles of the Aztec to its stops and laid it over on its side as the plane hurtled towards the ocean.

The maneuver caught Ray by surprise as his head bounced off the roof of the Aztec.

"Mac, what the Christ are you doing? That's the ocean down there, your boats in New Hampshire, and remember, you're not a fighter pilot."

"Yup," MacLennan said as he pitched the Aztec in a forty-five degree dive heading towards Brenner's boat and gaining speed as the dive steepened.

"Mac, you're red lining both engines," Ray yelled over the scream of the props.

"Yup".

The Aztec was just below one-thousand feet and one-half mile from Brenner's boat.

"Mac, you've passed the max speed for the Aztec"

"Yup".

"I know this may be a bad time to bring this up, but have you any idea what you're going to do?"

"Yup".

"Oh shit."

At five-hundred feet, MacLennan flattened out his dive and was approaching Brenner's boat from the port side, Brenner was on the stern of the boat shouldering the Stinger in order to finish off the Blackhawk.

When MacLennan was one-hundred feet from Brenner's boat he began to level the Aztec and began to skim the waves. Brenner's back was towards him. Ray had long since given up talking and had the sides of his chair in a death grip.

MacLennan had made up his mind long before on what he was going to do.

At a range of fifty feet from Brenner's boat, the Aztec was traveling at two-hundred-sixty MPH, twenty MPH more than the never exceed speed. It was here that Brenner heard the screaming engines of the Aztec and turned to see his new threat, too late.

MacLennan made a final flick at the controls milliseconds before cutting Brenner in two with the starboard propeller.

Blood sprayed across the windshield of the Aztec and was quickly dissipated by the slipstream. The right engine began to shake violently as MacLennan throttled back and feathered the propeller, while gaining altitude and banking away from Brenner's boat. The Aztec had plenty of airspeed and more than enough power to fly on one engine, though at a considerably reduced level of performance. If one of Brenner's crew decided to take a shot at the Aztec, they were finished.

By this time, DiFruscia had closed the gap between The Tamworth and Brenner's boat to two miles and had seen everything from the firing on the Blackhawk to MacLennan's dive from hell. He felt it was about time the Coast Guard got in on the act and gave orders for the Tamworth's .57 mm bow gun to open fire.

The first short fell twenty yards short of the stern.

"Skipper, they're surrendering, they should be cutting their engines," Frenchie yelled to DiFruscia from the radio room located next to radar.

"Looks like they've had enough."

"Cease fire. Keep the fifties manned and prepare a boarding party."

Brenner's crew had it. Between seeing their boss cut into shark chum and the Tamworth opening fire, any fight they had left in them was gone.

MacLennan had climbed to five-hundred feet and was heading towards the airport when they received the message that the smuggler's had surrendered and were being boarded by the coasties.

While beginning his approach to Ocean Reef, MacLennan turned to Ray.

"You okay partner, I guess I just got a little crazy."

Ray, who was as white as a ghost began to shake his head in disbelief.

"Mac, you just gave close air support new meaning."

****

That night in the lounge of the Quay, one of the better Key West restaurants located at the end of Duvall Street, Steve Novel, John and Ray caught up on the day's events.

"Will you guys be able to fly tomorrow?" Steve asked John.

"Yea. We lucked out," John answered and then continued. The FBO at the airport overnighted a prop, and it'll take less than an hour to put it on."

"Great," Steve answered. "And DEA will pick up the cost."

"Thanks. I kind of figured that. We told the mechanic that we flew into a flock of birds and that explained the blood all over the plane."

"By the way," Steve said, "What's an FBO?"

"That stands for fixed base operator. They're on airports and they usually have anything from mechanics to flight schools with instructors and pilot shops," John answered

"Gotcha," Steve continued. "That was quite the move. Williams, the pilot of the Blackhawk, wanted me to thank you and he owes you one."

"On another note, what had happened after their final drop off?" Ray asked.

"The boats started moving in and were about two miles off when the coasties sent zodiacs over and boarded the boat"

"How'd the boarding go, the bad guys resist." John asked.

"Briefly. As the first coastie dropped onto the deck, one of the deck hands went for a gun. He was taken out by one of the guardsman with an M16. That ended any further resistance."

"How'd the interrogations go?" Ray asked.

"Pretty good. What we were worried the most about was word getting back to Katanga and jeopardizing the rest of the operation. As it turned out, our man Katanga has quite a reputation and the money is already wired to him prior to the drop. By not hearing anything after the drop, that tells him everything has gone alright, and if it doesn't go right, he still has the money."

The head of this operation, Barry Brenner is, was, one of the biggest operators in the Keys and southern Florida. He's obviously not talking, but one of the boys on his boat is. I should say the US government's boat, since we now seized it. Incidentally your organization will be getting a piece of the action, and from what we're able to gather, a lot more is on the way."

"Good. By the way, what are you doing with Apley?" Ray asked.

"Well we squeezed him a little more and he was going to testify at Dennis Green's trial."

"What do you mean was going?"

"Seems like Green's girlfriend saved us the trouble. Shot him dead two nights ago after she got the crap beat out of her."

"Thank God for little favors," MacLennan said.

"Yea, that's one guy I have no sympathy for. He gives asshole new meaning. Make that gave asshole new meaning," Ray said.

183

"What's going to happen to her?"

"It looks like she's going to get off on the murder charge. She was beaten pretty well. Her jaws wired shut, and as far as Green's drug business and background are concerned, she's cooperating with us. We'll get all of Green's assets and she'll probably get probation."

"Not bad. Probation huh, she should get citizen of the year for killing that scumbag," Ray said.

"No argument here. So what's next on Katanga's itinerary?" Steve asked.

"No surprises really," John said.

"We have eight stops on the coast starting at Miami and ending in Portsmouth NH, until now that is."

"What's Green's death going to do with the NH drop?" Ray asked.

"It makes life easier." Steve answered.

"We took out an insurance policy. We were able to get an undercover on the boat. He's the radio operator, so we pretty much control all of the communication. Not only that, he was able to permanently disable their radar. In addition, he put a homing receiver on the boat that's state of the art and can be tracked at distances up to forty miles. Right now the boat's thirty miles south of Miami and should make the rendezvous point tomorrow at fifteen hundred with time to spare."

"Who is that guy, James Bond?" Ray asked impressed with the DEA agent's accomplishments.

"No, more like Dirk Pitt."

"Who?"

"He's the hero of author Clive Cussler," MacLennan answered.

"Excuse me," Ray replied.

"Anyway, as far as Portsmouth's concerned, we're going to meet the boat and take them down on the high seas. It simplifies matters somewhat, and that hopefully will be that."

"Sounds good. What are you going to do with Katanga," Ray asked.

"Good question. He's entrenched solidly in Jamaica, and we don't have enough proof that will shake him loose."

"Proof?" Ray answered incredulously.

"What do you call getting chased by an alligator?"

"Whoa, back up."

Ray then relayed to Steve their sojourn in a Jamaican jail.

"Good story for the grandchildren, "Steve said.

"But all they'll do is deny it. Face it. We're just going to have to leave Katanga for another day.

Ray and John said nothing and both kept their thoughts to themselves.

John was thinking how to get Katanga, and Ray was thinking on how he would dismember Katanga.

It would be for another day, but that day would come.

****

To everyone's pleasant surprise, the rest of the operation went without a hitch, but the two partners still had their thoughts of Katanga and Estaban; for another time.

Six Months Later

Chap 11
Danger Zone

"You're kidding me," Ray said in between bites of his roast beef sub at the task force office.

"It's now official, you are definitely denying some poor village of an idiot."

"People die over there, and you're taking vacation time to go. It's all the flying you've been doing at high altitudes, the lack of oxygen has finally affected your brain."

"Ray relax, it'll be like a walk in the park. Ferris tells me that finding cocaine labs in Bolivia is like going out on a Friday night and finding someone who's driving under the influence. The bad guys see you coming, fire a few shots in the air and run away. It'll be a learning experience."

"That's not what I hear John," this from Kathy Morse with more than a hint of concern in her voice.

"What I hear is that the shining path guerrillas have expanded from Peru and are now making headway into Bolivia and northern Chile, those guys shoot first and don't even bother to ask questions later. We won't even begin to talk about the Tupac Amaru. Your so called walk in the park is going to consist of dodging bullets, humping up mountains in dense jungles, crossing streams infested with piranha's and fighting off ants and spiders big enough to carry you off to their young for an afternoon snack."

"Sounds like fun," MacLennan said with a smile, "want to come?"

"I give up," Kathy said while throwing her hands in the air, she did, however, have a second thought about taking him up on his offer.

****

Tom Ferris had worked with MacLennan for five years in Salem PD, where they had become close friends before he applied and was accepted by the Drug Enforcement Agency. He was all of six-foot-three, and had a four hundred bench. While he was in DEA, he applied and was accepted to their air wing, where he not only got his commercial pilots license, but also his rotary wing license and was checked out in turbo props and turbines.

Shortly thereafter, he had gone to the Army's Jungle training school at Spider Island where he soon found out how the island got its name, then the Navy's language school in Monterey California, where he became versed in Spanish, and jump school at Fort Bragg where he learned how to jump out of a perfectly good airplane with only a piece of silk on your back.

All of this was in preparation for his volunteering for operation Snow Cap.

DEA's Operation Snow Cap was a combined effort of specially trained DEA agents and Army Green Berets. With the permission of the Bolivian government, they set up "fire bases" with the Bolivian National Police, known as Umopar. There function was simple, find a cocaine lab, intercept a shipment and the people, and neutralize it. Depending on the type of resistance encountered, neutralize could take on different meanings.

Contrary to popular opinion, most of the world's cocaine is not harvested and processed in Columbia, but further south in Bolivia. Columbia received most of its notoriety as a result of that country being the primary staging area for smuggling into the United States.

The operation had been in effect for two years when Ferris, a bachelor, had volunteered. The assignment consisted of living in a base camp for three months on the jungle fringes, and participating in search and destroys missions. The assignment doubled the pay of the agents since it was considered hazardous duty in addition to giving them a very elite status in the agency. This was a boon to anyone who was particularly career oriented or wanted to work in a particular geographic location after his return. However, the agents didn't do it for fortune and glory, but out of dedication to putting bad guys where they belonged. In this case, in the ground was just as good as behind bars.

Ferris had just finished a briefing in the first week of his second tour, and the rules of engagement had changed significantly since the last time he was in South America, and it had to do with a new kid on the block, the Shining Path. He laid back on his cot and reviewed the briefing.

The shining path guerrillas first appeared in Peru after the turn of the century as an insurgent movement under the leadership of Sendero Luminoso, which is Spanish for Shining Path, a Maoist revolutionary group. The group's aim was to overthrow the government and establish a communist regime.

No one was safe with the Shining Path, who operated from the Andes mountains and surrounding jungles. Tourists traveling mountain roads were robbed and often killed, especially if they were American. Missionaries were put to death, and even army convoys were attacked.

The Path believed anything that remotely assisted the government was their enemy. As a result, everything was fair game. They were ruthless and had no conscience.

By 2003, the Maoist revolt caused the government to declare a state emergency. Government troops and gun battles with the Path were virtually everywhere.

With the election of Garcia Perez, the government made a concentrated effort, on not only eradicating the Shining Path, but cocaine trafficking. This war on drugs saved the government since it was able to receive large amounts of aid from the United States as well.

The aid came in the form of money and DEA agents.

When Abimael Guzman Reyhosa, a University professor, became the leader of the Shining Path. He reorganized the Shining Path and formed an allegiance with the local drug lords.

He continued the guerilla tactics from the mountains and his continued success allowed him to expand into Bolivia with help from the drug cartels.

The drug lords felt that the Shining Path would eventually be a threat, but the United States and DEA were the more immediate problem. With the expansion of the Path, the druggies felt that this would be another factor the DEA and the Green Berets would have to deal with, and hopefully, take some of the heat off of them.

The assignment was dangerous enough without the Shining Path, but their presence added a very unknown and lethal element. When jungle labs were found, there would be a very brief firefight that always ended with the druggies running off into the jungle. There was no organized resistance until the Sing Path became a factor.

Unlike the druggies, the guerilla's got into pitched fights with the joint task force on two occasions. There were no casualties, but Apache gun ships were needed during the last fight to drive back the guerillas.

From the dead bodies the DEA recovered, the Path was getting better equipped, and the threat to personal safety increased tenfold.

In the middle of all this, Ferris' friend John MacLennan was coming down. Ferris always knew MacLennan was a few french fries short of a happy meal, but on further reflection, no more than he.

Tomorrow, Ferris would travel a little over one hundred miles by armored Hummer to the Bolivian Capital of La Paz to pick up MacLennan.

Fortunately the main Bolivian highway to La Paz, which is comparable to an American two lane back road full of frost heaves, was well patrolled by the military and the threat of an ambush by the Path was minimal, though knowing MacLennan, he'd be looking forward to an ambush.

Before he dozed off, Ferris' last thoughts were not of the Shining Path or MacLennan, but dreams of the most recent Playboy centerfold molesting his body beyond his wildest imaginations.

****

As MacLennan settled in on the Bolivian Airways DC-10, he was pleasantly surprised at his surroundings. He was half expecting the plane to be crowded with livestock and the flight attendants to be wearing parachutes since all of the major American airlines had long since retired the DC-10.

However, the plane, from what he could see, was well maintained, the interior spotless, and the flight attendants were wearing uniforms that showed whoever was doing the hiring had an affinity for buxom women with size fives or sevens. There was something to be said for Latin American, macho, chauvinistic countries after all.

The takeoff and trip were uneventful until the plane began its approach to La Paz airport, which involved a circuitous route between mountains.

La Paz was eleven thousand feet above sea level, which was just about the maximum operating ceiling of a number of small planes MacLennan used to fly.

What pleasant surprises MacLennan experienced on the trip to Bolivia were soon replaced by the reality check at La Paz airport.

On short final, MacLennan was able to see, not a modern day tarmac with numerous runways bristling with modern hangers and terminals, but a one runway airport overgrown in some areas with grass, in addition to five or six pigs using what appeared to be a crashed DC-3 as a barn, and what he thought were sandbagged emplacements with machine guns. He was beginning to wonder if the pilot had taken a wrong turn somewhere and he was really in Russia during the winter.

As the plane taxied to what appeared to be the main terminal, MacLennan grabbed his knapsack and gym bag, which was all the baggage he carried. When it came to packing, he always felt that if you couldn't run with the luggage you had, you were over packed, and from the looks of it, he may be doing some running.

As MacLennan debarked the plane, he was surprised at how cool it was, about fifty degrees with a westerly wind, which was common for that altitude and latitude of Bolivia.

As he entered the terminal building he felt a vice-like grip on his left arm and a slap on the back that nearly knocked him over.

"Getting kinda skinny you little shit," Ferris said good-naturedly.

"Yea, well I can at least get out of my own way. How the hell you doing?"

"Pretty good when I'm not ducking bullets. It's starting to get pretty hot down here."

"You're shitting me. I thought this was a walk in the park. Just like getting drunks on a weekend night if I remember correctly."

"I shit you not, and that's the way it used to be.

Ferris then brought MacLennan up to date on the recent developments with the Shining Path as they walked through Bolivian Customs and out to the Hummer.

MacLennan threw his bags in the back and jumped in the passenger's seat as Ferris went to the driver's side.

Before Ferris opened the door he bent down to look under the Humvee.

"What are you doin', checking the engine's rubber band," MacLennan said kiddingly.

"No, just checking for bombs," Ferris said seriously.

MacLennan looked over to his friend and didn't know whether to take him seriously as he got in and started up the Hummer.

"Seriously?"

"Yea seriously. The Shining Path has upped the stakes and they've been known to attach bombs to either the starter or the muffler."

MacLennan knew a little about bombs from a seminar he had attended over the years and was familiar with the typical car bomb that used the electrical current from a four hundred-amp starter to ignite it, but had never heard of the bomb on the muffler.

"Why and how the muffler?"

"Gives the bad guy time to get away," Ferris answered.

"He puts the bomb on the muffler, the muffler eventually gets hot enough to ignite the fuse after five or ten minutes, and then boom."

"Boom?"

"Yea, usually a big boom. A couple of Bolivian police guys got blown up and we figured it wouldn't hurt to start checking."

"Good idea. Feel free to keep checking."

Ferris put the Hummer in gear and pulled into traffic.

La Paz airport was built on a plateau outside of the city, which made for light traffic. The only thing, MacLennan thought, that was good about this airport.

As Ferris skirted the city proper and wound his way down the mountain, the two friends brought each other up to date on their personal lives. MacLennan told Ferris about Darcy and Ferris told MacLennan not to do anything stupid.

By the time they reached the bottom of the plateau an hour later, the temperature had risen to eighty-five degrees and MacLennan felt like the humidity was about one hundred.

"I don't believe how fast the climate changed," MacLennan said.

"Yea, it's like this up and down the west coast of South America."

"You freeze your ass off in the mountain, descend five or ten thousand feet which may represent only a five mile travel distance, and you're in a sauna."

"No shit!"

"The best is yet to come, wait till we get into the triple canopy layer of the jungle. The camp at Chimera isn't too bad, but the humidity in the jungle is something else."

As they drove through the country the poverty reminded John of what he saw in Jamaica, but more rampant.

He was particularly surprised when he noticed a pretty girl walking on the side of the road and was taking a second look when she just squatted to defecate on the side of the road.

"Ahh, you got to be shitting me. No pun intended." MacLennan exclaimed to Ferris.

Ferris just laughed.

"Yea it's typical down here. Hygiene isn't on the top of their priority list"

"Don't say it Tom"

"How'd you like her sitting on your face?"

"I asked you not to say it."

About seventy miles out of La Paz, the two lane paved road they were on turned to dirt.

"Are you taking the back way to avoid ambushes," MacLennan asked.

"Back way? This is the main east west highway, the back ways are through the jungles."

"Nice"

"Oh by the way, we're going to be crossing some streams further up, make sure you keep your hands in the car."

"Dare I ask why?"

"Only if you want me to tell you about the piranha and crocodiles."

"That's one way to take a bite out of crime," MacLennan answered.

Three hours later, they pulled in to the base camp at Chimera.

Chimera was one of five base camps that had been established in Bolivia by operation Snow Cap.

The base camp had a trapezoid like design. The smaller length was the front gate, which was delineated by barbed wire and two sandbagged gun emplacements at either corner with M-60 machine guns. In addition, there were two larger emplacements well inside the front gate that could cover both the front and sides. Each side of the camp went out at an angle and ended at the base, which was a three thousand foot grass and dirt runway where there were also sandbagged gun emplacements at the corners. Just inside the camp and adjacent to the runway was a helicopter-landing pad where there were three Huey's bristling with M-60's and rockets.

Each side was also marked by barbed wire. Surprisingly enough, the north side of the camp, which was facing the runway, had no barbed wire perimeter fence. To MacLennan, all one had to do was just walk around the barbed wire fence and into the camp from the runway.

The camp had an area of fifteen acres with four barracks in a V shape in the middle of the camp just behind the interior gun emplacements. All the barracks had sandbagged roofs and sandbags piled six feet high around the outside walls In the middle of the barracks complex was an M113 armored personnel vehicle.

The area outside the camp had been cleared for one hundred yards in a circular fashion except for the side by landing strip, which was cleared for one-half mile.

"OK I give up," MacLennan said. "Why is the side facing the landing strip as bare as a newborn's ass? Anyone can just stroll in."

"Not really," Ferris answered as he drove through the front gate. There's only about sixty of us at the camp. About two dozen DEA and Special Forces type of equal number, and about fifty Umopar and support personnel. It depends on what's happening elsewhere. We can't defend all sides of the camp, so we hedged our bets by mining the other side of the landing field and letting everyone in the world know about it. So if we ever get attacked, we figure it's not gonna be from there."

"How 'bout the APV, that doesn't go with you in the jungle," MacLennan asked.

"Nope, that's when we have to go into town to buy eggs."

Once again MacLennan didn't know if Ferris was joking, but he wasn't going to give him the satisfaction.

As they drove through the front gate, Ferris waved to the Umopar police who were manning the machine guns.

"You trust those guys."

"About as much as everyone else. They're pretty dedicated little fucks and they've taken their share of lumps, but the only ones I really trust are the green beanies and us drug guy types."

Ferris pulled the Hummer around the huts and parked next to the APV.

"C'mon, you'll be bunking with me, the rest of the guys are out on a search and destroy mission in the other two choppers and they should be back by dinner time."

MacLennan followed Ferris into the hut. Ferris had explained to MacLennan that three huts were used as barracks to house the troops and the fourth was a combined kitchen, mess and activities hut.

When asked who does the cooking Ferris had told him not to asked but gave him the usual admonishment not to drink the water and make sure the meat was well done.

As MacLennan entered the barracks he noticed that there were no cots as in a traditional army barrack, but hammocks.

"Why hammocks, they cooler?" MacLennan asked.

"Nothing's cool down here. Ferris answered"

"Our hammocks are there," said Ferris pointing to the far corner of the room.

"I already set a hammock up for you next to mine, figure I'd keep an eye on ya."

"You're much too good to me," MacLennan said with mock thankfulness.

"Think nothing of it, you're in much better hands than you should be."

MacLennan just shook his head.

As he laid his gear by his hammock, MacLennan began to sniff the air.

"You smell something?" he asked Ferris.

"Smells like gasoline," he added.

"Oh yea, I forgot to tell ya, that is gas you smell, we spray it on the ropes of the hammocks."

"I give up, why"

"Keeps the snakes from crawling down the ropes and into bed with you, and by the way, hang your boots upside down from the hammock ropes, keeps the snakes from crawling in."

"Thanks. Anything else you forgot to tell me."

"Yea, no smoking in bed"

****

That night while he was lying in his hammock, MacLennan went over the events of the day.

About an hour after he got settled and Ferris finished the tour of the camp, the Snow Cap team flew back in with twenty Umopar police. MacLennan was then introduced to the Americans and the Captain of the Bolivian Police.

They hadn't found a lab that day, but had found chemical residue on a tributary stream and would try again tomorrow. Both MacLennan and Ferris would be on this patrol. They didn't expect much resistance and the Umopar would be on standby if needed.

Dinner that night was an education. None of the Americans would eat any of the local food, especially the meat. The meal consisted of canned ham and cooked fruit, not bad for the middle of nowhere. When MacLennan had asked what the Umopar officers were eating since it looked and smelled pretty good, he soon lost interest when he was told that it was grilled donkey.

MacLennan was questioned at length by the leader of the Snow Cap contingent, Dick Kasteele, on his knowledge and use of the M16, and after he was satisfied that MacLennan knew the difference between the business end of the rifle and the stock, he was issued one to carry on patrol.

Ferris introduced him to his jungle web gear and jungle fatigues.
The web gear consisted of four, one-quart canteens, twenty clips of twenty round ammunition, first aid kit which included chlorine tablets and the army's current version of food, MRE's, meals ready to eat.

When MacLennan asked how they tasted, Ferris told him that MRE really stood for Meals Rejected by Everyone. The only good thing about them was they provided about three thousand calories and if you were lucky, you would only have to eat one per day, unless they were doing some serious humping, then you could have the luxury of a second MRE.

The main concern in the jungle was dehydration, and in order to prevent that, the average soldier could drink up to two gallons per day.

MacLennan knew that water weighed about eight pounds per gallon and carrying more than a one days supply was usually prohibitive due to the excess weight.

Ferris explained that if they were out any longer, they would get their water from vines which were abundant. The only catch was there were four types of water bearing vines, and only one had drinkable water, of the other three, two were poisonous and the other vine would react with the mouth's saliva to form a type of glue that would shut your mouth permanently. Ferris had always wanted to see if it worked by trying it on his ex-wife.

The briefing after dinner outlined tomorrow's mission, which was a search and destroy for the cocaine lab where the chemical residue they spotted today originated. The team would be a dozen Americans, and a squad of Umopar's on three Huey's that would drop them in a small river clearing about two miles south of the tributary. The other Umopar would stay and hold down the fort. They would then follow the river to just a mile below the lab and approach it from the jungle side. From the amount of residue it looked to be a small lab and not too much resistance was expected, but they were taking no chances.

MacLennan was still mulling over the briefing when he drifted off to sleep.

****

MacLennan was up before daybreak. He was sure that he had a worse night's sleep sometime, but he couldn't remember when.

"What the hell was all that screaming last night?" he asked Ferris.

"Oh that, just the Howler monkeys. The jungle is never quiet. You'll get used to it."

"They are loud."

"Yea they are somewhat vocal."

"Reminds me of an old girlfriend," MacLennan quipped.

"If I remember correctly, almost anything could remind you of an old girlfriend."

"Glory days," MacLennan said with a shrug.

It was before five when the monkeys stopped and the birds took over.

After a quick cup of coffee and toast in the mess, they gathered around the helicopters for the final briefing and gear check.

They would be two Huey's with men from snow cap in each one, and a full squad of eight Umopar in the other. Both Huey's had Umopar pilots.

After dropping off the raiding party, the choppers would return to the base camp and wait for their pickup call and position from one of the handheld Global Positioning Systems that could now fit in the palm of your hand. With any luck, there wouldn't be too much humping through the jungle.

The Huey's took off and flew slightly above treetop level for thirty miles until they reached the Pojo River where they dipped below the tree line and followed the river north.

"I take it these guys are pretty good pilots."

"Yea, for beanies, they're not bad. Pretty fair set of balls too." Ferris answered.

Then as an afterthought, "I'll still take an army warrant officer in a Blackhawk any day."

This was the first time MacLennan had experienced any type of combat flying, and he found it exhilarating.

The Huey was flying about thirty feet off the water at about sixty miles-per-hour around the bends and faster on the few straight area's they encountered. It was impossible to see beyond the banks of the river due to the thickness of the jungle. By flying that low and at that speed, it would make it very difficult for anyone to get an effective shot at them.

After following the river for another fifteen minutes, they came to a bend in the river where a rock-strewn riverbank was slightly exposed. The Huey's slowed to a hover about five feet over the bank in order to allow the snowcap task force and Umopars to jump to the ground.

The Umopars separated into two groups, one on each side of the river, while Americans split into two groups, one point group of three, and the other with the Umopars on the left bank of the river.

The group of Umopars on the far bank of the river was called the cut off group if any of the bad guys decided to beat feet.

The Huey's didn't waste any time heading back to the base camp.

The patrol headed south along the riverbank. By now the sun had come up and the rocks along the river began to warm and radiate heat. MacLennan had a couple of questions for Ferris, but since no one else was talking, he decided to follow suit.

After about forty-five minutes, Kasteele called for a break.

"Ok, last chance to light 'em up if you have 'em and lock n'load."

MacLennan, like everyone else on the patrol, was soaked to the bone.

"Sweating a little bit?" Ferris chided him.

"Walk in the park." MacLennan responded.

"It might not be from here on in." Ferris said in an atypical serious matter as he pointed to a gasoline like slick on the partially dried riverbed, a sure sign that a cocaine lab was nearby. The labs were built by rivers for convenience. They supplied water for the men who ran and worked the labs, and it eased supply problems since it was much quicker traveling by river than through the jungle.

Once they start to get close to a lab, they spread out more and the going got slow. Every fifty yards or so, one of the point men went in the jungle to check for ambushes, and until recently, once the look outs saw the patrol advancing towards the lab, they would take off running into the jungle. It was just a matter of time before they were going to be engaged in a pitched battle.

Another twenty minutes of walking up the river, and the slick on the river was always noticeable. There was also a heavy gas smell in the air that the slick on the river alone couldn't account for.

Another ten minutes, and they were able to spot whiffs of smoke emanating from about one-quarter-mile up the river and one hundred yards in the jungle.

"Won't be long now," Ferris said.

"Try to make an effort and not get hurt".

"Thanks, but I was thinking a little flesh wound would be very dashing."

Before Ferris could respond, an explosion followed by the rapid statacco of machine gunfire pierced the air.

Of the three point men, one was being dragged into the jungle while the other was laying down covering fire.

The patrol on the other side of the river was nowhere to be seen and MacLennan and Ferris were running into the jungle for cover.

Kasteele began barking orders for the group to spread out and advance to where the point team had taken cover.

"Get on the radio and call for a med-evac in addition to helicopter air support."

The team began to advance through the jungle.

MacLennan heard the men on the left flank laying down sporadic covering fire. The purpose being to keep the heads of the bad guys down.

The machine gun fire had stopped and the team advanced towards the point men.

In two minutes they were there. The patrol medic began to bandage a bullet hole in the side of the green beret's neck. He took two others in the chest but they were stopped by his bullet proof vest.

MacLennan's feelings were the same as the other men. Their comrade's life lay in the hands of the medic and God and there wasn't much they could do except extract vengeance. With Snow Caps first casualty, the game had taken on new meaning and it was payback time.

Kasteele once again began barking orders. He left two men with the wounded soldier and medic and had the rest of the team spread out.

"Alright, we're going to advance up the jungles edge until we're at our best estimate of being even with the lab, and then we'll wait for the other team.

Ferris quickly explained to MacLennan that the job of the men who were on the other side of the river was to quickly advance upriver above the lab, cross the river and cut off any escape.

The rest of the patrol was to wait for them to open fire so they could determine their location from the sound of the M16's which was very different then the harsh sounds of the AK-47's used by the druggies and Shining Path.

The underbrush was thick by the river, which made the going slow. All members of the team made sure to find cover and stay low. The machine gun crew hadn't fired again but no one was taking chances.

Before the team was in position, the quiet was shattered by the explosion of hand grenades followed by small arms fire from the jungle. The small arms were both AK's and M16's and neither were pausing for refreshments.

Kasteele gave hand signals to advance towards the fire fight when the machine gun opened up again.

MacLennan heard bullets whistle by as he dove to the ground and tried to do his best imitation of a mole.

The machine gun crew hadn't used the intervening time to move positions, and as a result, the point team that had taken the initial fire had a good idea where they were and opened fire.

At the same time Kasteele and two other's lobbed grenades. As they exploded, the team moved towards the machine gun emplacement.

Ferris had glanced at MacLennan to see how he was doing, but he needn't worry. MacLennan was advancing with the rest of the patrol firing short three round bursts. This didn't go unnoticed by the other team members. MacLennan was holding his own.

The machine gun crew now found themselves in a crossfire. Their previous bravado gone, they left their post and started to run towards the lab. They didn't get ten steps before they were cut down by the combined fire of the two teams.

The point team now began the process of rigging a stretcher to carry the wounded green beret to the riverbed where they would secure a landing zone for the Huey.

The fire team once again began advancing toward the gunfire. They reached the edge of the clearing and were able to see the cocaine lab. There were three buildings that were constructed from the wood that was cut in the clearing. The roofs were thatched from palm leaves with open sides.

There were two bleeding bodies of guerillas in the open and eight men were returning fire from various places in the buildings. All had their backs to the main Snow Cap force that just advanced from the river. The guerillas were the proverbial sitting ducks.

Once Kasteele gave the order to open up, it was over in seconds. Surprisingly, none tried to surrender. When they found out their position was hopeless, they made a break for the jungle, not an orderly retreat, but a headlong flight. Again, no one made it more than ten feet before they were cut down.

After Kasteele gave the ceasefire, the jungle was strangely quiet. Both Snow Cap groups entered the camp from opposite directions. All of the guerillas were dead, and once the camp was secured, sentries were placed at four different positions and a perimeter was formed while stock of the camp was taken.

This was a camp of the temporary variety as most were becoming.

Snow Cap was getting so good at its job at destroying labs, that the druggies were setting up labs for only a month or two and then moving on to another location. If they didn't do this, it would only be a matter of time before they were detected by either the telltale gas slick, as this one was, or by the more pervasive aerial surveillance. The adage of jungle fighters on the move being harder targets, was in fact, very true.

Of the three buildings, one was a storage area for the finished product, another, a storage area for the chemicals and the third was the sleeping and eating quarters for the druggies.

The cocaine was initially processed in an open area where there was a make shift pool of wood and waterproof canvas that was about twenty feet by twenty feet and two feet high.

In this vat, the cocoa leaves were mixed with gasoline. Local natives were then hired to go in the tubs and stomp on the leaves for ten to twelve hours until a paste was formed. The lucky ones had boots. The others left the tubs with raw and bleeding feet.

The paste was further processed with acetone and hydrochloric acid, and the end product, cocaine hydrochloride made its way to the streets.

The ranking officer of the cutoff group explained to Kasteele that the workers had fled once they started firing, and they let them go. The Shining Path guerillas were the ones who stayed and put up the fight. Outside of the one point man who was wounded, no one else was hit in the fifteen-minute fight.

A quick survey showed a little over one hundred kilos of finished cocaine and another two hundred of paste. It took about ten pounds of paste for every pound of refined cocaine.

Kasteele was on the radio talking to the Huey pilot. The distinctive woppa woppa sound of the Huey could be heard in the distance. MacLennan heard the medic say that Sullivan, the wounded Green Beret, appeared stabilized and miraculously, the wound was clean and no major arteries were hit. He thought he was going to make it. This immediately lifted the spirits of everyone on the patrol. Everyone kept working, piling the cocoa leaves in the outdoor vat and throwing gas on the three buildings, but the banter amongst them had returned.

"Shouldn't we be worried about lighting the jungle on fire", MacLennan asked Ferris as they were dousing the huts with gas.

"That's what I thought first time I did this, but everything around here is so dense and wet that nothing will ignite without the gas."

"This'll go up like a funeral pyre, but once it burns itself out, that's it.

The last part of the operation was the most grisly. After searching the dead bodies for any forms of identification and intelligence, which there were none, they were thrown in the huts to be burnt. In essence, it became a funeral pyre.

Kasteele did the honors of setting the blaze.

"Up in smoke. After it was cut and split, a street value of about one-hundred million," MacLennan said.

"And the said part," Ferris added, "It's just a drop in the bucket.

"One drop at a time"

The Snow Cap team watched the fire long enough to insure that everything in the camp would be destroyed and then started back to the river after radioing the base camp for evacuation.

Kasteele was taking no chances. In addition to point, he established a rear guard. As Kasteele entered the Huey and settled in for the ride back to Chimera, he knew that things were going to get worse than better. The war on drugs had just escalated.

****

The ride back to the camp passed in silence. MacLennan was experiencing the post-adrenaline rush experienced after combat. Back at camp, everyone stripped down their gear, cleaned their guns, and only then, stripped to shower. It seemed as if every bone in MacLennan's body ached.

Kasteele was busy with his Umopar counterparts in addition to spending a considerable amount of time on the radio. The post-op briefing would be after dinner that night.

Before dinner that night, Kasteele had announced that Sullivan, the wounded Green Beret, was at the hospital at Cochabamba and was recovering after the operation. He was still in serious condition, but stabilized and improving.

Dinner saw everyone back to normal. The pall of Sullivan's possible death had passed and everyone was up after a dangerous and successful operation.

The briefing that night was going to be held in the mess, so after dinner everyone lounged around drinking, talking and playing cards until Kasteele came in.

"OK, everyone grab a seat. As of this moment, the camp is on twenty-four alert and E&E protocols are in effect", he said without preamble.

Anyone who wasn't paying attention immediately was. The camp had never been on twenty four hour alert and E&E stood for evade and escape.

"Recent intelligence from the consulate at Santa Cruz indicates an attack on the camp is imminent"

"Whoa, wait a minute, what did we miss," someone behind MacLennan said.

"Let me get back to it, but I wanted to get your attention and to let you know we are in a potentially serious situation."

Before Kasteele continued, he looked around the room. All the twelve DEA agents were there in addition to the remaining eleven Green Berets and five Umopar officers. To say that he had a captured audience was an understatement.

"Until today we've been on the offensive. The resistance we encountered today at the lab was a first. According to intelligence officers at the embassy, the Shining Path has declared war and is going on the offensive. The other Snow Cap base camp at Sabaya came under mortar attack last night and they are expecting an attack any day. They've been reinforced and their normal complement of forty is now up over one hundred. Their reinforcements are Umopar, not army and they've temporarily suspended search and destroy missions until the situation can be better assessed"

"Can we expect any reinforcements", someone asked?

"Not right away, we're on our own. We've been offered Bolivian army reinforcements, but I'd just as soon wait for Umopar."

"That's because we don't know whose payroll the army officers are own," Ferris whispered to MacLennan answering his unasked question.

"What's our battle plan?" from another.

"Right now we going to reinforce the camp's defenses and cut down more of the woods by the front gate. We have one hundred yards to the woods and we're going to try and extend that another twenty-five to fifty yards. This will give us a clearer line of fire and extend the enemy's danger zone in case they decide to attack."

"Get a good's night sleep, because if you think humping through the woods is work..."

The rest of the sentence was drowned out by groans and good-natured catcalls, but everyone knew what they had to do and would do so without complaint.

The guards were doubled that night and everyone went to bed early as Kasteele suggested.

At breakfast the next morning, everyone got their assignments. MacLennan and Ferris were assigned to the tree cutting detail.

MacLennan soon learned that the army had a unique way of cutting down trees.

Instead of using chain saws to cut down the trees, a one to two inch thick strip of C-4 explosive was wrapped around the base of a tree, a blasting cap affixed to it, and then, boom. The tree was usually blown two to three feet side-ways and fell in that direction. The chain saw detail that Ferris and MacLennan were assigned to then cut the branches, and after that tied a rope from the trunk to one of the Humvees which was then dragged to the camp's perimeter as additional fortification.

That night, the branches were gathered in a pile doused with gasoline and burnt.

By the end of the first day, the jungle had been pushed back another ten yards and most of the perimeter had two layers of tree trunks.

During the day MacLennan had watched a detail of Green Berets along the perimeter of the camp and inside some of the sandbagged emplacements. Ferris told him they were probably rigging booby traps ranging from claymore antipersonnel mines to any number of traps they learned from Viet Nam and God knows where else. Whatever it was, it wouldn't be pleasant.

"Hope you're enjoying your vacation", Ferris joked as he and MacLennan dragged their sorry asses to the mess that night after showering.

"What're you going to do next year, diamond mines of South Africa?"

"Actually, I hear the Falkland Islands are nice this time of year."

After dinner that night, and while Ferris and MacLennan were having coffee, Kasteele came over to them and spoke to MacLennan.

"I've got some bad news for you, you're going to have to leave early, it's getting much to hot here for noncombatants."

MacLennan had half expected this. He and Ferris had talked about it the day before and Ferris was surprised that MacLennan wasn't already gone.

"We just got some more info, courtesy of communication intercepts from the National Security Agency, an attack on the camp is imminent".

"I've never left a fight before and just for the record, I'd like to stay," MacLennan said.

"And we'd like to have you, we can use another fighter but the decision's not mine to make," Kasteele answered.

"Instead of the limo ride back, you'll be getting the VIP treatment," Kasteele joked.

"A Casa will be flying in tomorrow with supplies and you can hitch a ride back with them to La Paz. We've made some special arrangements for you. From there you'll be jumping onto a C-130 that'll take you to Miami, and from there you're own your own."

"A C-130 cargo plane, yikes new highs in luxury," MacLennan joked."

"And all for you," Kasteele said with a smile as he extended his hand to MacLennan.

"Good to know you, and in case I don't see you tomorrow, happy trails."

"You too," MacLennan said.

Kasteele then left the mess and headed to a newly constructed command bunker made of sandbags and recently cut logs that was in the middle of the camp. It was hastily constructed that day, but would be able to withstand a couple of direct eighty mm mortar hits, which was the mortar of choice, used by the Shining Path.

"Oh well, all good things..." MacLennan said.

"You watch your ass, I'm obviously not going to be here to watch over you any longer," MacLennan said to Ferris.

"Thanks. What are you going to do with the rest of your vacation?"

"Well, since I'm being flown in style to Miami, I might as well spend some time there. I'll probably give the new girlfriend a call and see if she wants to come down."

"God, are you getting whipped."

Before MacLennan could reply, he was interrupted by the increasing whine of a mortar shell.

"Incoming," someone shouted and everyone in the mess buried their faces in the dirt floor.

As the first mortar shell crashed into the compound, the machine gunners opened up at the front gate. The first shell fell in between the compound huts and the parked Huey's. Two other shells fell in quick succession each one closer to the Huey's.

By this time, everyone was rushing to their barracks to get their guns and gear and then towards their assigned positions to defend the camp.

The Huey pilots started running towards their choppers to get them in the air but too late.

One of the mortar shells found its target and hit one of the Huey's square in its fuel tank. The explosion not only destroyed it, but the one next to it.

"Now I know why they're called mortar magnets," MacLennan quipped.

By this time, three green berets and six Umopars had piled into the M113 personnel carrier and started out the gate and towards where they thought the mortar position was. By the time they hit the jungle edge and disembarked, the rounds had stopped. In a period of five minutes twelve rounds had entered the camp. It was enough to completely destroy two of the four Huey's and damage the other two.

The Huey's were essential to the camps defense and Kasteele put a repair team on them right away.

Of the eight men who hit the jungle Kasteele recalled them back to camp. The chance of an ambush at night was too great.

The M113 was positioned behind a sandbagged fortification and the camp was on full alert that night.

Ferris and MacLennan were positioned inside one of the barracks that was sandbagged facing the east side of the camp.

There was a squad on the far side of the runway providing cover for the team of mechanics working on the Huey.

One Huey was too far-gone to repair with mortar fragments that penetrated the turbine compartment and two completely destroyed. However, with any amount of luck Chuck Massahos, the mechanic, thought he could save the other from the parts he had on hand, in addition to stripping parts from the one that was beyond repair.

The next two hours passed without incident. At midnight Kasteele gave the order to get some sleep. Sleep, while on camp alert, consisted of remaining at your post and sleeping for two hours on and two hours off while your partner stayed awake.

At one o'clock everyone was instantly awakened by an incoming mortar shell that exploded ten feet away from one of the interior gun emplacements wounding one of the UMOPAR with shrapnel. For the next hour, at fifteen-minute intervals, a solitary shell was fired into the camp.

The purpose was obvious. It prevented anyone from getting sleep in addition to sending the mechanics scampering every time they heard an incoming shell.

By the second hour of this, Kasteele was getting fed up and sent three men into the jungle to reconnoiter.

Reconnoiter evidently has different meanings to different people. Only one more shell entered the camp after the three Green Berets entered the jungle. A short firefight signaled the demise of the crew.

Twenty minutes later the team was back in camp reporting to Kasteele with a captured prisoner, mortar and ammunition.

There were two guards and a spotter in addition to the mortar team of two. The guards were taken out silently with knives while the crew was shot and the spotter wounded.

The mortar, to no one's surprise, was a Russian made 80 mm. They were also able to salvage 15 rounds of high explosive rounds.

The wounded prisoner quickly broke under one of the Special Forces interrogators. The primary reason seemed to be that he would be turned over to the UMOPAR interrogator if he didn't answer his questions.

The Umopars method of interrogation was much more physical than cerebral. While Shawn Pattern, the American interrogator explained this to the prisoner who said his name was Juan, an UMOPAR officer stood next to him with a knife in one hand and a caged poisonous snake in the other. The snake, Bothrops Sanctaecrucis, or the Bolivian Lance Head, was a 25 inch viper that insured a painful and excruciating death by coagulating the victim's blood and insuring death within 45 minutes.

According to the prisoner, there would be an attack on the camp at dawn, when the defenders would be the most tired, by over three hundred guerillas. They were currently three miles from the camp sleeping.

Kasteele radioed this information to his bosses in the embassy and then called for a meeting of all the Americans and UMOPAR officers.

Kasteele briefed the assembly on the information they extracted from the prisoner.

"Here are our options. We can stay. There's a possibility the prisoner is lying and this is a ploy to take over the camp without a shot. I don't buy that. I don't think they're that sophisticated and I don't like leaving a fight." Kasteele looked at MacLennan and smiled as he said that.

"If we stay and there's a fight against three hundred guerillas, well, a lot of them are going die, but I don't put our chances of survival very high without air support."

"Can't we get any from the Bolivian Air Force," one of the agents asked.

"We can have them on standby, but I'm told not to depend on them, and if we can, their scramble time to get here is a minimum of thirty minutes. That could be way too late."

"We can't even rely on the one Huey we have. Massahos tells me it'll be ready by morning, but as soon as it's ready, we've been ordered to take the prisoner back to Cochabamba. MacLennan will be on that flight also.

Before MacLennan could say anything, Ferris clamped a massive hand across his mouth.

"How about US air support?" Ferris asked.

"That we can get, the problem is they can't fly into Bolivian airspace without permission which we can get, but it'll take time and their response is about 45 minutes. Still way too long."

"That brings us back to square one. If no one has any serious objections, we're going to stay. If we feel the camp is going to be overrun, we've added some surprises that hopefully will give us the time to E&E."

As Kasteele looked around the room everyone nodded their heads in agreement. MacLennan and Kasteele weren't the only ones who disliked missing a fight.

"OK men take your posts and good luck. MacLennan, the chopper leaves at 0500, two hours from now. Be ready."

The first shots were fired by the Shining Path at 0430.

****

Massahos had just finished work on the Huey and was having a cup of coffee in the mess when the RPG slammed into the Huey from the other side of the landing strip just before the minefield.
This was the direction where the main attack came from. As the Huey started to burn, Massahos just shook his head.

The first guerilla's that entered the minefield didn't have to travel far before they and anyone near them were blown to bits. The mines were a variation of the bouncing Betty's of Viet Nam.

As they were activated by foot pressure, they were spring propelled ten to fifteen feet in the air where they sprayed razor like shrapnel a diameter of thirty feet.

The results were devastating. The attack from that side was broken up within the first twenty feet of entering the two hundred foot minefield. Between the mines and fire from the camp defenders the guerilla's retreated with at least thirty dead and wounded.

MacLennan and Ferris were with Kasteele in the command bunker once again saying goodbye.

"Looks like you got your wish MacLennan." Ferris said.

"In the future, I really gotta watch what I wish for."

The second wave came from the opposite end of the camp and charged the front gate.

At first it seemed that both machine gun emplacements were laying down withering fire decimating the front ranks of the guerillas.

After fifteen seconds of fire, MacLennan saw the gunner on the right emplacement slumped over his gun with a bullet through his head. What MacLennan didn't know was the gun shot came from the UMOPAR who was feeding the machine gun. He then pushed the gunner out of the way and trained his gun on the other machine gun emplacement killing both Umopars. With both machine guns out of commission, the guerrilla's surged forward. To make matters worse, the turncoat UMOPAR began firing the machine gun at the camp's defenders.

None of this went unnoticed by Kasteele in the command bunker. He grabbed a control panel and pushed four buttons. The first button activated the mines that were located inside the traitor's gun emplacement. The machine gun stopped as the traitor UMOPAR was blown clear of the gun emplacement.

The other three buttons triggered napalm mines approximately seventy-five yards outside the front gate catching the front line of the guerillas and temporarily halting their advance.

The fire from the defenders was once again renewed as both machine guns were once again manned and trained on the attackers.

The guerillas still surged forward with decimated ranks. MacLennan and Ferris were outside the command bunker firing full clips at a time into the advancing mass of flesh. The entire front perimeter of the camp was unmanned as a result of the renegade Umopar. There wasn't an American who wasn't wondering how many other traitors there were amongst the other Umopars.

The interior gun emplacements were now coming under heavy fire.

Three more Umopar were dead in addition to five wounded. Two Americans were also wounded. The tree trunks that had been laid down the previous day were now affording protection to the advancing Guerillas as they reached the perimeter.

Once the guerillas reached the perimeter, Kasteele pushed another series of buttons on his control panel.

Over twenty guerillas died as the claymores set at the base of the perimeters exploded. They also had the effect of destroying the perimeter once formed by the fallen trees. This broke the back of the charge. As the guerillas began to retreat back to the safety of the jungle, three Umopars who wanted to make up for their counterpart's treachery entered the M113 and started towards the front fence with the .50 caliber blazing.

Kasteele yelled to his radioman in the bunker to get them on the radio and get them behind the safety of the sandbags. It was too late.

While the fifty caliber was wrecking havoc amongst the retreating guerillas, it was what the men manning the RPG's in the jungle were waiting for.

Once the APV reached the front gate, they opened up. The first one hit the upper portion, knocking out the machine gun and killing the gunner. The second and third rockets hit dead center causing it to erupt into flames and killing all inside.

There was a momentary lull in the firing as the guerilla's reached the safety of the jungle.

Kasteele called the Americans together in the mess and quickly took stock. The wounds on both the Americans were superficial from RPG shrapnel. Both were mobile. The Umopars were down to about forty men.

After sharing a few words with the commander of the Umopars, they shook hands and the commander left the mess to direct his troops.

Kasteele then addressed the Americans.

"The situation has gone from bad to worse. The consulate in Santa Cruz was attacked, but the marines stationed there were able to hold them off. The Umopars are going to hold the camp while we initiate E&E."

"You mean we're bugging out?" asked one of the Green Berets, clearly not happy with that option.

"I know how you feel." Kasteele answered him.

"But our orders our specific. In the event that the camp is going to be overrun, we're to try and make it back to the consulate. The army has been put on alert, and the Umopars, with any luck, will get reinforced. But as we just saw, we don't know who to trust, and we're on our own," making reference to the turncoat Umopar on the machine gun.

"Where're we off to?" one of the DEA's asked.

"I think we'll take a little stroll in the jungle, and head towards Santa Cruz. While in route we'll attempt to contact the Consulate there for instructions."

"I'm going to guess we'll be evac'd somewhere outside Santa Cruz."

"Santa Cruz?" groaned one of the DEA's.

"That's over 150 miles from here. If that's what you call a stroll, I can't wait for a hike."

Just then, the Umopar started firing the mortar that was taken from the dead rebels in the tree line.

"Ok, that's our cue," said Kasteele

"Once they go through about 10 rounds, they're going to lob some smoke grenades outside the perimeter. That's when we make our break through the minefield to the jungle. Make sure everyone follows the guy in front of you single file, and don't bunch up."

With that Kasteele led the way out of the hut followed by the twenty-three remaining Americans.

The mortar shells were temporarily keeping the guerillas from attacking; adding to the confusion of their retreat and disrupting the leader's attempts to organize them.

MacLennan and Ferris were in the middle of the pack as they started through the minefield with Kasteele in the lead.

"Think he remembers the way" MacLennan asked jokingly.

"Don't worry, we made it KISS simple," answered Ferris referring to the Keep it Simple Stupid method.

"It's a straight line beginning at the 500 foot marker on the runway and running for two hundred feet on a course of 090 degrees. After that we start picking them up and putting them down."

By the time they cleared the minefield, the Umopars were lobbing smoke. The Americans double timed it to the edge of the jungle and made it to the edge without any shots being fired. Kasteele sent two guys on point and two more for a rear guard. They were still far from clear sailing since this was the area of the guerilla's initial attack. By the time they were ½ mile into the woods, the Americans were able to hear the renewed attack on the base. One of the Green Berets that was the rear guard stayed on the jungles edge to view the attack on the base camp. What he saw was not encouraging.

****

Major Estaben was also at the jungles edge; but he was at the front of the camp directing what he hoped would be the final assault. He had already lost over ¼ of his force but he had achieved significant results. He had forced the Americans to flee, which had significantly reduced the opposition, and he still had one remaining agent in the camp that had informed him that there were no more claymores or booby traps awaiting the guerillas. He felt that once he had eliminated the two .50 caliber machine guns, the outcome would be without doubt. The attack began by his remaining mortar reigning smoke grenades into the camp. His second in command wanted to try to take out the machine guns with HE rounds; however, Estaben felt that they couldn't find their asses with both hands let alone pinpoint accuracy. His plan was to advance on the wall and take out the thirties with the easier fired RPG rounds. In addition, he hoped to capture the machine guns intact. The smoke rounds were doing their job. There was little wind around the camp and once the rounds exploded, the smoke just hung in and around the camp. This allowed the guerillas to advance to within 20 yards of the camps perimeter before some sharped eyed Umopars began shooting. By then it was too late. The RPG's found there mark and hit the sand bags surrounding both machine guns and multiple hits on the sandbags killed the men manning those guns by concussion, but kept the guns intact. As the guerillas breeched the perimeter, the fighting went hand to hand and while the Umopars were superior fighters, they were overwhelmed by sheer numbers. Not all were killed outright and there were 8 survivors, all wounded, who were taken prisoner. Major Estaben had plans for them.

Once the camp was secured by the guerillas, Major Estaben called for the prisoners. One was wounded in the leg and couldn't walk and Estaben put a bullet in his head. To the remaining Umopars credit, none begged for their lives and just glared at Estaben.

"That was just a preview of things to come unless I have your full cooperation," Estaben said to the prisoners.

He continued, "All you have to do is tell me the way through the minefield".

The Umopars looked at each other and a sergeant spoke up, "Senor, we don't know the way, the Americanos never told us."

"We'll see."

With that, one of the guerillas grabbed the sergeant and marched him over to the minefield with the other prisoners, Estaben and guards following.

"Walk," said Estaben.

The Sergeant hesitated, but he started walking after one of the guards raised his rifle.

Surprisingly, he got 20 yards before stepping on a mine. Estaben continued sending the prisoners down one by one and they set off the mines one by one. The holes in the ground and body parts clearly marked the way. The second to last prisoner started and was able to make it to the end of the mine field and started to run towards the jungle beyond. Estaben gave the signal to 3 guerillas and for a moment, it looked as if he would make it before he was cut down by a concentrated burst from one of the guerillas. Estaben looked at the remaining prisoner who was Estaben's other Umopar informer.

"Gracias major," he said as he began to walk towards Estaben.

"One second Juan," Estaben said while once again drawing his gun and pointed it at his informer.

Juan stopped in his tracks and stammered, "But major, I have done everything you asked."

"Yes you have," Estaben replied. "But you have betrayed your people, where is your loyalty?"

"It is to you major," the former Umopar replied while looking furtively around him, possibly for an avenue of escape.

"My point exactly Juan. The best judge of future behavior is past behavior. How do I know you won't betray me?"

"But ..." the informer was not able to finish his sentence as Estaben shot his second prisoner of the day in the head.

****

Kasteele and the other Americans were making progress through the jungle. They were able to find an animal trail and were making reasonably good progress as they travelled east towards Santa Cruz. The sound of the attack on the camp followed them for about 40 minutes before the shooting stopped, and it was another 50 minutes before he called for a break. Kastelle got on the radio to his rear guard.

"Rakes, send Cavanaugh up here and do what you do best." After telling the point men to take 10, Kasteele addressed the snow cap berets and DEA agents. "I suspect the guerillas are going to follow us. We'll be humping through the jungle for at least 20 miles where we hit the Chimore River. If we can find a clearing, we'll call for air support to come get our sorry asses." Hopefully we'll stay ahead of the guerillas and this may be a stroll in the park. Any questions?"

MacLennan looked at Ferris and mouthed, "A walk in the park?"

Ferris just shrugged.

"No questions? Ok, let's move."

And with that, the snow cap crew began moving east.

****

Sergeant Rakes Lynch was a 15 year veteran of the Army, joining after high school, and was a Green Beret for 13 of those years. He was wiry, tough and built for speed and endurance. He advanced relatively quickly to an E7 and was liked and respected by everyone in his A-Team. No one knew his first name, only that it started with A. His specialty, what he does best, is to make life miserable for an opposing trailing force. He was an expert at demolitions and booby traps. The fleeing American force was leaving a trail thru the jungle, that had a minimum footprint, but given the jungle thickness, even on a game path, it could still be followed. His job was to slow the guerillas done while inflicting damage. He would have liked to have dug punji pits, camouflaged holes with sharpened stakes at the bottom but he didn't have the time; so he resorted to quick hit and run traps. His first one was a grenade with monofilament wire across the path. The pin would be pulled but the lever was kept down by the weight of a stone. As someone tripped over the wire, it would pull the grenade onto the path releasing the lever and boom. Next were toe poppers. These were bullets planted in the ground within a tube and over a nail. The tip of the bullet would protrude from the ground (camouflaged, of course). An enemy would come by, step on the shell which would strike the nail in the same way a gun's firing pin did and boom. This was especially lethal when done with shotgun shells. As he left the traps he doubled timed it through the jungle and realized he had time for some punji pits after all. As he finished the last pit, he augmented it with grenade traps on either side of the trail. There was a bend in the trail that made for a good ambush site. He took up position at the bend and set his last trap, a claymore, making sure the business end was pointed down the trail. His plan was to open up on the guerillas after the trap was sprung. The guerillas would then dive to the side of the trail triggering the grenades and if they charged him, the two claymores he set would take care of that.

****

"So why do they call him Rakes?" MacLennan asked Ferris as they moved through the thick brush.

Just then, the jungle sounds were punctuated by a far off explosion. "No one knows, I suspect that it's because Lynch rakes the bad guys over the coals. Kinda like what's happening now," Ferris answered.

"Makes sense."

****

Estaben was not one to lead from the front, or the rear for that matter. He was securely ensconced in the middle of his 150 man force having left a handful back at the camp to loot then burn it. The middle was safest place in case of attack or what they were experiencing now, booby traps. Estaben was a mercenary and a survivor. He survived, Panama and Jamaica and as a soldier of fortune, his bank account was increasing significantly in Bolivia. There was always money to be made in drugs. The Shining Path were offering him a bonus if he could wipe out the American Force. His plans were to do just that and buy and retire to an island off Andros Cay in the Bahama's. He had already figured out that the Americans were heading to Santa Cruz and he had a surprise for them. There were 50 guerillas waiting for them at the

Chimore River, it would be a classic hammer and anvil pincer movement. He would lose men, but that was irrelevant compared to the money he would receive. Just then, his thoughts were disturbed by a scream as the seventh point man met an ignoble faith. But it didn't stop there. It was followed by the chatter of a fully automatic M16 and two more explosions. Estaben thought that maybe the Americans were making a stand, but then he realized it was a rear guard ambush.

****

Rakes took a position to the right of a bend in a trail. Once the point guerilla stepped into the punji pit, Rakes opened up on 4 guerillas as they came to his aid. There were additional screams as his bullets found the mark. These were then overshadowed by two grenade explosions, one on each side of the trail as other guerillas went to take cover on each side. It was at this time that Rakes took off at a run down the trail. What saved him was he tripped as bullets from three AK 47's went over his head. Unbeknown to Rakes, Estaben, in addition to point men, had sent 3 men out on his flanks. Rakes was now caught in a crossfire. All of a sudden, there was another grenade explosion and the 3 men on Rakes right flank were either dead or dying.

"I figured I'd have to save your ass," Mark Cavanaugh said. "I convinced Kasteele to let me come back and reinforce you, and not a moment too soon."

"Thanks but I had it covered," Rakes replied.

Just then one of the claymores went off and the firing from the guerillas in front slacked.

"Let's go Mark, time to get out of Dodge, there's one more claymore still out there that'll give us some more breathing space."

"Gotcha, we have a rendezvous place with the rest of the guys at the Chimore River. Kasteele is calling in for air evac, seems like these sneaky bastards have another force of about 40-50 guys trying to cut us off."

"Marvelous! This just keeps getting better and better."

"Hey, it's not just a job, it's an adventure."

With that, Cavanaugh radioed an update to Kasteele and both started back to rendezvous with their main force.

On their way back Cavanaugh grabbed Lynch's arm. "Rakes, over there, do you see something shiny?"

"Yea, what do you think that is?"

"I'm thinking a plane, let's go do a quick recce. Those last traps will slow them down some."

"OK, but quick in and out,"

"Huh, oh yea, kinda like you fucking."

"Funny."

Fifty yards into the jungle, they were able to see that it was a crashed DC 3 with the words Knight Moves written below the pilot's window. To add to the macabre sight, was a skeleton of the pilot, with the head and left arm out the window, still wearing a leather flying jacket. All the other clothes, were rotted away, and any flesh that may have been remaining after the crash was long ago eaten by creatures of the jungle. Lynch and Cavanaugh entered the plane through the plane's cargo door that had been ripped off.

"Holy shit," Cavanaugh exclaimed. "There's enough pot here to get all of New York high."

"Cav, come on up front. Shit, look at this," as Rakes held up an M-203 launcher. "Not only this, we've got 4 bags of shells to go along with it. If we make a stand, this will definitely help, and lordy, lordy, a bottle of Jack Daniels. I love these fly boys."

"I hear ya," Cavanaugh answered. "And just in case, let's leave a bag of grenades with a surprise in case the bad guys find this."

"Yea, and I'm thinking we make sure they find it," Lynch said.

"You're an evil genius Rakes. I like that in a man."

And with that, Rakes left one of his patented booby traps while Cavanaugh started a fire using some of the marijuana in the plane that wouldn't last long, but would create lots of smoke.

****

After the guerillas recovered from the last booby trap, Estaben had blood in his eyes.

"We will kill every last one. Leave two men with the wounded, gather the men and forward.

"Jefe look smoke."

"Another trap, send 10 men to investigate"

****

As Lynch and Cavanaugh approached the river, there was a huge explosion from behind them.

"I just love it when a plan comes together."

"Like I said, you're an evil genius Rakes," and as an afterthought, "Oh shit. I forgot to bring the Jack Daniels."

"Fear not little buckaroo," Lynch said as he held up the bottle of whiskey. "I got ya covered. I also found a logbook, and I'm bringing that too."

****

Kasteele had called for a second break and called the consulate in Santa Cruz on his satellite phone. He then addressed the men.

"Ok guys, we're going to double time it to the Chimore River, when we're about 30 minutes out, which should be in two hours, we'll call the consulate and they'll be sending three Blackhawks and two Apache gunships as escorts. They'll be flying from La Paz and they're leaving in about 30 minutes with about two-half-hours flight time. So once we get there, we'll need to make or find an LZ and secure it. It's going to be tight. The spooks at the consulate are showing that there's an intercepting force, about platoon strength, heading to the Chimore River looking to cut us off and ambush us. They think they have the element of surprise but they don't know we know and we'll either be evac'd before they get there or we'll be the ones doing the ambushing. It looks like Rakes and Cavanaugh are giving are friends behind us a headache and they're about 30 minutes behind us according to the last radio call from them. If there aren't any questions, let's move out"

No one had any questions, and once the two point men got into position, the rest of the men moved off.

"Here's another fine mess you've gotten me into Ollie," MacLennan joked to Ferris.

"Yea, but look at all the fun you're having."

"How will I ever pay you back?"

"Somehow, I think you'll find a way."

****

Juan Riveria just got off the radio from Major Estaben.

"That Estaben is a pompous ass," he said to his second in command.

"What is wrong jefe?"

Riveria was in charge or the 50 man force that was attempting to cut off the Americans at the Chimore River.

"He wants us to attack the Americans and engage them before his forces get here. What he wants is to sacrifice us so we can kill some of the Americans and increase his odds. He is a coward too."

"But we outnumber them. It should be no problem."

"No problem? Don't be a fool. They are professional soldiers. Look at these men. They may be ruthless, but they are thugs."

"Still jefe".

"We'll see. When we get there we will set up an ambush, which should give us an edge."

****

The snow cap crew reached the Chimore River in good time and as they crossed the river with chest high water they were met by a raucous chorus of screams form a troop of monkeys.

"What the fuck is that?" asked MacLenann.

"Those are fucking Bolivian red howler monkeys I was telling you about at the camp. They live near rivers and they'll calm down in a minute," answered Ferris. "But if you think they're bad now, you should hear them during mating season."

"I can hardly wait."

"What may be good about them is they're quiet once they get used to you, but if anyone else is coming down the path, they'll let you know."

"Nice early warning system," but before they went on, they were interrupted by Kasteele.

"Massahos."

"Yea boss."

"I just got off the horn with the consulate, they show the intercepting force about a mile north of us coming down the west riverbank and the main guerilla force about a mile west of us. Get down the river and see if you can set up some surprises as a welcoming committee. We're going to be blowing some trees for a landing zone so they'll know our position very shortly, so slow them down while we set up a perimeter on that ridge."

"Gotcha, on my way."

With that they Massahos headed the up the river.

Kasteele then set about establishing a perimeter and sent 5 men to take some trees down for a landing zone.

"Get into the jungle about 20-30 yards and clear enough trees so the three Blackhawks can come in and hover. With all the branches, they won't be able to land."

"Pretty smart what he's doing, by going in the jungle, the trees will screen us if we're under fire," MacLennan said to Ferris.

"Yea it would've been nice if they could've hovered over the river we could just jump on. Now we'll have to shimmy up ropes." Ferris replied.

"Glad I didn't have a sheltered childhood and I learned how to shimmy."

Before Ferris could respond, Kasteele started giving instructions to the rest of the group.

"There's a slight ridge on this side of the river. We'll set up a perimeter and the high ground will help, and when we head down to be evac'd, we'll be partially protected. It looks like the choppers are less than an hour out."

With that, Kasteele sent two men east to set some traps for the guerilla force on the other side of the river they just came from and everyone else started digging and getting fallen logs to make a perimeter just as Lynch and Cavanaugh started coming across the river.

"Rear guard coming in," they yelled. "And we come bearing gifts.

"Whadda ya got?" Kasteele asked as Lynch and Cavanaugh came out of the river.

With that, they held up the grenade launches and grenades.

"We came across a downed druggie plane that besides pot, was also running some guns. And we also left the bad guys a going away present," said Lynch.

"Was that the explosion I heard awhile back? Thought it was too loud for a claymore."

"I cannot tell a lie," Lynch said smiling and then held up the bottle of Jack Daniels. "A little something for the celebration party too.

"OK," Kasteele said, "get settled, spread those launches out so we have some covering the northern perimeter and then where you guys just came from, and guard that fucking whiskey with your life."

****

Lynn Williams was in the lead Blackhawk with two more behind him and two Apache gunships as escorts. The Blackhawks were well armed with a crew of three: a pilot, co-pilot and crew chief. For armament, it had two 7.62 machine guns that were controlled by eye pieces worn by the pilot and co-pilot and could be swiveled independent of each other. In addition, Williams's helicopter had two pods of 8 modified

229

hellfire missiles with high explosive shells. The Blackhawk, could also take a lickin' and keep on ticken' as its fuselage was armored and could withstand hits up to a .23 mm shell. As impressive as the firepower on the Blackhawk was, the Apache's had them beat hands down. To say that the AH-64 Longbow Apache was hell on wheels is an understatement. It has a 30 mm chain gun that could destroy a tank in miliseconds in addition to 70 mm air to ground hellfire missiles and air to air stinger missiles. The hellfire missiles could either be high-explosive for personnel, or armor piercing to ruin any tank commander's day. Its armor was impressive and could withstand hits up to .30 mm, it had a range of over 300 miles, a top speed of 230 MPH and could stop on a dime. It could also turn on a dime and was capable of doing barrel rolls and loops. It had a crew of two with extra armor in the cockpits.

Lynn was seeing a lot of action this year. Three months after the shootout in the Keys, he volunteered for Snow Cap and was rotated to Bolivia. He had lots of missions but no shooting, but this looked like it would be a hot LZ. He had also heard that there were some guys down in the jungle that were also in the Keys operation. He never did get to meet MacLennan, who had probably saved his ass that day in the Keys, but he still owed him more than just a few beers. "Blackhawk one to other units, we're about 45 minutes out and there's a good chance that we could be going in under fire. Stay tight and we'll give them hell."

****

The snow cap force knew where the intercepting guerilla force was by the explosions and chattering M16 and AK-47's.

Massahos had set booby traps similar to what Rakes had previously done as a rear guard. A claymore, and then grenades on trip wires off the path. After he emptied two clips into the force, he high tailed it back to the perimeter.

"Massahos coming in on my way back, let the guys know I'm the good guy and coming in."

"Roger that, watch your ass."

****

"Those bastards, give the order to return fire, move forward." Riveria shouted

Unlike Esteban, Riveria didn't lead from the back, however he made a mistake by not having any point men. Between the claymore and the grenades, he had lost 8 men killed and wounded. He then went from a column to a straight line and had his men advance.

"Riveria to Estaben, where are you? The Americanos were waiting for us on the east end of the river. They set a trap and I have men down."

"We're about 15 minutes from the river. Attack and when we get there we'll have them in a crossfire."

"Why don't I wait for you and we'll attack together?"

Estaben was not use to having his orders questioned, especially when it increased the danger to him. "You will attack now Riveria or face consequences."
"Understood."

"That Estaben is a cowardly cabron," Riveria said to his second in command,

"Have the men spread out and advance and put 3 men up front. If they see anything take cover and fire."

****

"Here they come, they're not far behind me,"
Massahos said as he jumped over a barricade and spoke to
Kasteele.

Before Kasteele could ask how far they were, gunfire
erupted from the jungle.

"Hold your fire," Kasteele yelled. "That's nowhere
near us and they're trying to reconnoiter by fire. When you
see them, sound off."

It didn't take long for the three point men's position to
be heralded by the screaming monkeys, and very shortly after
that, they came into view.

Within a minute the guerillas and Snow Cap team were
exchanging fire. The guerillas were getting the worse of it as
the green berets lobbed in grenades from their newly acquired
launchers, in addition their fire was much more accurate.
Within minutes, Riveria's force was down to under 30 men
with no losses to the Snow Cap contingent.

"How come we don't have some of those grenade
launches?" MacLennan asked.

"They wanted to have all the fun," Ferris answered.
"They're killing a lot of monkeys too."

"Fuck it, put them on the endangered species list,"
answered Mac.

"Are you guys ever serious," Rakes said as he fired
another grenade.

"Once, back in high school I think," said Ferris.

Cavanaugh, who was next to Rakes, just shook his
head.

****

232

"Estaben, get over here we are taking heavy casualties and they have us pinned."

"Calm yourself Riveria," answered Estaben

"We will be there within minutes." And he was.

****

The arrival of Estaben's force was heralded by the howler monkeys and the explosion of the last claymore.

"Hit them with the launches Kateele yelled."

The grenades were doing their job, and between that and the chest high water, it was keeping Estaben's force on their side of the river.

"Jorge," Estaben said to one of his sergeants, take twenty men and go down river and cross. Get behind them."

"Yes major."

Estaben then spread his force out which now just numbered about 120, and directed fire towards the American's position.

"Keep firing and don't stop."

The firing was beginning to have the desired effect as an extra 100 guns threw as much lead towards the snow caps position.

"Kasteele to lead Blackhawk, we're taking fire from the east and north and we have casualties, what's your ETA."

We're two minutes out, pop green smoke on the LZ and can you fire red smoke on the enemy's positions," Williams answered.

"That's affirmative"

"OK, I'm cutting the Apaches loose to go on ahead of us."

"Roger that, be advised it's a hot LZ".

"No problem," answered Mike Duggan, one of the lead Apache pilots, "And be advised, we are going to give hot new meaning, we are mobile, agile and hostile, with the emphasis on hostile."

"Roger that," answered Kasteele as he directed men to fire smoke into the guerilla's position and green smoke in the landing zone.

****

"Hey Rakes," yelled Cavanaugh, "You're bleeding."

"I ain't got time to bleed," answered Rakes.

"Huh?"

"I've always wanted to use that line. It's from the Arnold movie Predator, and Jesse Ventura said it."

"And you guys ask if we're ever serious," MacLennan said as he bandaged Rakes arm. Just as he finished, MacLennan felt like a sledgehammer hit him in the stomach and knocked him on his back.

Ferris went over to him and after a brief examination said, "You're ok. The bullet was stopped by the vest. Lucky thing we're all wearing them."

"Hurts like a motherfucker."

"Yea, it'll be black and blue for a while, suck it up princess."

Just then, Ferris was knocked on his ass as a bullet ricocheted off his helmet.

"Son-of-a-bitch, that hurts," as he picked himself up off the ground."

"Don't worry Tom," Mac said. "They hit you in your least vulnerable spot, your thick Polish head, and oh yea, suck it up princess."

The sheer volume of fire was taking its toll on the snow cap team when the jungle to the north and west erupted in explosions as the Apache helicopters fired their rockets into the guerilla's position.

"You're right on," Kasteele radioed, keep hammering them.

"Roger that," answered Duggan and with that, both Apaches started weaving back and forth alternating between rockets and their 30 mm chain guns.

"Apache one to Blackhawk one, Lynn, there's a force of about 20 guerilla's crossing the river south of us looking to flank our ground forces."

"I got 'em," answered Williams. "Blackhawks two and three, proceed to the LZ, I'll take care of these guys.

Williams couldn't have asked for a better scenario, the guerillas were in the middle of the river with no cover and nowhere to go.

"Time to rock and roll," and with that, Williams opened up with both machine guns and a volley of rockets for good measure. Some of the guerillas fired their AK47's with no effect as most missed and the few that hit bounced harmlessly of the armored fuselage. When he was done, the river turned red and bits and pieces of bodies floated down the river.

"Why's the river bubbling?" Williams asked his co-pilot, George Winchell.

"Fish have to eat too. Those, I believe, are piranha." Winchell answered.

"Rampart, wreckage and ruin, I'd say our work here is done George."

"Excellent!"

****

At the Snow Caps perimeter, the Apache's did their work, and both guerilla forces were decimated. The lucky few who were not hit, ran back into the jungle. It was over in minutes of their arrival, and after the havoc wrecked by the Apaches, there were two new clearings in the jungle.

"Ferris, take 3 men with you and see what intelligence you can get from the guerillas across the river from us," Kasteele said. "We'll be loading the wounded aboard the first Blackhawk.

"Alright Mac, stop with the puppy dog look." Ferris said. "You're coming."

Once they crossed the river, they were able to see that there was carnage everywhere. Surprisingly, there were no moans but plenty of body parts. Not one body was intact and there was no intelligence to be collected when Ferris heard MacLennan yell out.

"I don't fucking believe it, I know this guy."

"How the hell do you know someone here?" asked Ferris.

"Remember the case I told you about that Ray and I had about one-half year ago when Ray and I got to see the inside of a Jamaican prison?"

"Yup, and didn't you end up cutting someone in half with your props."

"Yea, and it was just one prop. Well this piece of shit was the warden of the prison we were guests."

"What the fucks he doing here?"

"That's the sixty-four dollar question. Let me see what's in his pockets.

As MacLennan went through his pockets, Ferris and 2 other agents took in the rest of the scene.

"Unbelievable, no one's alive or just wounded." Ferris said. "If they're any wounded," he continued, "they're out of here."

"Either that, or whoever was alive killed all the wounded," Mac answered.

"That's cold."

"Yup. Hey Tom I got something here on Estaben in his pack. A bank book from the Cayman's and a letter from a Vicente Niebla. Isn't he the head of the Sinaloa Cartel in Mexico?"

"Yea he is. Ok take it with you and let's get out of here."

By the time they crossed the river, Kasteele and Lynch were the only ones waiting for them.

"OK, everyone's loaded but us, time to beat feet outta here. Get anything?" Kasteele said.

"Maybe," Ferris answered we'll look at it back at wherever we're going."

"Where are we going?" Ferris asked.

"Cochabama, and we'll see after that."

As the Blackhawk took off, the pilot circled the area to see if anyone was alive.

"Ya know Tom," MacLennan said." For a vacation, this is going to be a hard act to follow. You sure know how to show a girl a good time."

Epilogue
Renegades, Rebels & Rogues

The sign read Renegades Rebels & Rogues and was a typical country western bar in Texas. It had a dirt parking lot and the first thing MacLennan noticed when he walked in was the chicken wire that surrounded the stage where the band played.

"Yo Mac, over here," Ferris yelled.

At a table sat Ferris, Lynch, Cavanaugh, Kasteele, Duggan, Williams, Massahos, Winchell and someone else that MacLennan didn't know was there. In addition there was an unopened bottle of Jack Daniels, an urn, and a picture of a DC-3 named Knight Moves with a pilot in a leather jacket waving from the pilot's window.

Ferris made the introductions. "This is Paul Marchand, he's our newest addition to DEA. He came to us from Ipswich, Ma, PD. He has previous Special Forces experience and he's off to Bolivia on our next rotation."

"Not just a job, an adventure," MacLennan said while shaking his hand and continued.

"Hey that name's familiar, weren't you the cop that Dennis Green crashed into the night he killed some hit man."

"Yea that's me. The midnight shift, more fun than I deserve."

"Well, I see the gang's all hear, what's in the urn?" Mac said.

"Not what, who." Rakes answered. "This," he paused for emphasis while holding the urn, "is Tim Campbell. He was the pilot of the DC-3 that crashed in the Bolivian jungle.

From what we've been able to gather, outside of his drug running, he was a pretty good guy."

"Get the Fuck out." Mac answered.

"Yea, that's what I said," Cavanaugh added.

Rakes went on, "He was an orphan and believe it or not, a lot of what he made running guns and drugs went to charity, including the orphanage where he was brought up."

After orders were taken by the waitress, Mac asked, "Why is he here?"

Kasteele answered, "Once we got back to the states, we did an after action report, and what really saved our asses before the Apache's arrived, was the grenade launches. They kept the guerilla's heads down and suppressed their fire. As it was, we had 10 wounded. If not for Campbell's grenade launches, we would probably have suffered a lot more casualties with a few of us tits up."

"Well in that case," MacLennan said holding up his beer, "here's to Tim Campbell," and with that everyone held up their glasses and took a drink.

"So how'd you find out about him and how did he get back here?"

"After Rakes found the logbook," Kasteele continued, "we got back to the states, ran the serial numbers and found out who he was and where he's from. We contacted the US embassy and they arranged for the Umopar to get him. They then flew him back to the states and the owner of this place took a collection to have him transported and cremated, and here we are. He had mentioned this place in his logbook, and see that bartender over there?"

"You mean the one with long blonde hair, cleavage and long legs that go all the way up to her ass under those short shorts? No, I haven't noticed." MacLennan said."

"That's Melissa, Campbell's girlfriend, well, ex-girlfriend. One thing led to another and here we are. We're going to spread his ashes outside in the parking lot, while having a shot of Jack Daniels from the bottle that was on the plane."

"Speaking of Bolivia," Mac said, "What about Estaben and that Cayman bank book?"

"Estaben was quite the asshole, with the emphasis on was," answered Kasteele. "He had a reputation for being ruthless and efficient and went wherever the money was. After Jamaica, he was hired by the Shining Path and within a couple of weeks, he was given an offer to join the Sinaloa cartel. He had over $20 million in the Caymans which now belongs to Uncle Sam."

Dinner came and went as did another round of drinks when Melissa came over to Kasteele.

"Hi Dick," she said. "Everyone's here who wants to be, are you guys ready?"

Kasteele looked around the table when Lynch said, "Let's do it."

In addition to the Snow Cap contingent, about ten patrons from the bar walked out, all with shot glasses in their hands. The bottle of JD was passed around and there were two other people who spoke besides Melissa, the owner of the club and the director of the orphanage where Campbell was raised. As Melissa spread the ashes around the parking lot, everyone did a final toast to Tim Campbell as the club owner said, "To a true Renegade, Rebel and Rogue."

They started walking back into the club when MacLennan fell in step with Lynch.

"Hey Rakes, back in the jungle, Ferris and I were wondering, where did you get the nickname from. We figured because you "rake people over the coals."

Rakes, started laughing, "That's not it, before I joined up, I owned a small landscaping business and always had rakes falling off the back of the truck, and since I didn't like my first name, it stuck."

"That's funny. I seem to remember your first name starts with an A, what is it?"

"Yea and I heard your first name starts with an L. I'll show you mine if you show me yours."

It was now MacLennan's turn to laugh. "Deal, like you I didn't like my first name either, and Mac stuck. I was named after my grandfather on my mom's side, the actor Leslie Neilson, he starred in some classics like the Forbidden Planet and the Walt Disney series Swamp Fox. Your turn."

After Rakes stopped laughing he said, "The A stands for Aloysious and I have no fucking idea where it came from.

With that, everyone ordered another round.

Made in the USA
Middletown, DE
08 May 2021

38422235R00144